W9-BEX-339

A FOOL AND HIS MONET

Center Point
Large Print

Also by Sandra Orchard and available from
Center Point Large Print:

The Port Aster Secrets
  Deadly Devotion
  Blind Trust
  Desperate Measures

A SERENA JONES MYSTERY

A FOOL
AND HIS
MONET

Sandra Orchard

CENTER POINT LARGE PRINT
THORNDIKE, MAINE

The text of this Large Print edition is unabridged.
In other aspects, this book may vary from the original edition.
Printed in the United States of America on permanent paper.
Set in 16-point Times New Roman type.

ISBN: 978-1-62899-934-1

Library of Congress Cataloging-in-Publication Data
Names: Orchard, Sandra, author.
Title: A fool and his Monet : a Serena Jones mystery / Sandra Orchard.
Description: Center Point Large Print edition. | Thorndike, Maine :
Center Point Large Print, 2016. | ©2015
Identifiers: LCCN 2015050955 | ISBN 9781628999341
  (hardcover : alk. paper)
Subjects: LCSH: Women detectives—Fiction. | Art thefts—
Investigation—Fiction. | United States. Federal Bureau of
Investigation—Fiction. | Government investigators—Fiction. | Large
type books. | GSAFD: Mystery fiction. | Christian fiction.
Classification: LCC PR9199.4.O73 F66 2016b | DDC 813/.6—dc23
LC record available at http://lccn.loc.gov/2015050955

To Laurie Benner—Serena's alter ego

ACKNOWLEDGMENTS

I am so grateful for the many people who helped me with my research for this new series and who made the creative process so much fun. For Angela Bell in the FBI's Public Relations Office (and the other experts she tapped), and for the wonderful agents in the St. Louis FBI Headquarters for showing me where Serena works and patiently answering so many questions.

For Vicki McCollum, Lindsey McCollum, and JoAnne Brands for taking me on a grand tour of St. Louis, for sharing their countless insider insights, for answering all my city-related questions, and for scouting specific locations on my behalf, long after I returned home, and sending me pictures and details.

For retired police and SWAT officer Stan Lawhorne, for his timely and often humorous responses to my police-related questions.

For newsletter subscribers—especially Janet, Jen, and Amatha—who helped me brainstorm names and backstories for my secondary characters.

For Laurie and Stacey for their help with edits.

For the wonderful team at Revell who have brought this book to you.

And for you—with so many books to choose from, I am truly honored that you would spend a few hours reading *A Fool and His Monet*.

A FOOL AND HIS MONET

1

I should have listened to my mother.

Stomping down the panic surging up my throat, I gripped the priceless painting. "Yes, we've definitely got a deal," I said, repeating the code phrase that should have brought the SWAT team charging into my hotel room.

The door's electronic lock clicked.

Relieved, I gulped a breath, then quickly turned it into a cough to divert the bad guys' attention, maybe give my FBI cohorts the element of surprise when they barged in . . . any second now . . . any second . . . any—

A gun swung in my face. "You a cop?" the art dealer I'd just paid snarled.

Seriously? This was happening on my very first undercover assignment? "Do I look like a cop?" I barked. Let alone look stupid enough to fess up to it?

The flat-nosed, bald-headed crook scrutinized me with an unnerving twitch in his right eye as his six-foot-six sidekick flipped through the stacks of bills in the Gucci bag on the bed.

Resisting the urge to back-step toward the door, I moistened my lips and tasted the salty tang of sweat beading my skin. Where was my backup?

Baldy edged toward the still-closed door, his

gun leveled at me, as I mentally eeny-meeny-miny-moed the best cover to dive behind. After a quick gander out the peephole, he shoved his gun back into his waistband.

Okay, okay. *Okay!* Deep breath. I was still in the game and I couldn't mess this up. Not when the undercover agent who'd reeled in this guy and passed me off as his art authenticator had balked at my suggestion that SWAT take me down with the crooks. I could do this. I had to. I'd finally made the FBI Art Crime Team. But if I hadn't been the only available agent who could reliably distinguish a real Kandinsky from a fake, they never would've brought me in.

And they'd never use me again if I freaked out over a little setback.

To buy time to shift my racing heart back into the nonlethal zone, I propped the painting on the desk and admired it from a couple more angles, imagining how thrilled the owner would be . . . if I got it—and me—out of here in one piece.

"It's all here," Sidekick declared, zipping closed the bag of money I'd delivered.

I casually slanted a glance past the partially drawn drapes. Not so much as a shadow darkened the window ledge.

The guys in St. Louis wouldn't have left me hanging this long. I glanced at the digital clock on the bedside table. Okay, it'd been less than a minute, but this wasn't a two-bit drug buy. These guys were about to stroll out of here with half a million taxpayer dollars. In a Gucci bag, no less!

Baldy eyeballed the peephole one more time, then pressed his ear to the door.

My mother's hysterical "You should be giving me grandbabies, not buying paintings from bad guys in some flea-bitten motel room where it'll be days before a maid finds your cold, dead body" babbled through my brain. I hadn't even told her why I was going to Buffalo. She'd guessed.

Well, the hotel was a notch or two above flea-bitten. I had an image to project, after all. Although, considering these guys' mob connections, the rest of Mom's predictions were a little too accurate for comfort. And guys like this wouldn't stop at killing an undercover agent.

They'd go after my family too.

I gulped down another deep breath and started bargaining with God. A minute and thirty seconds, maybe forty, had passed since I'd voiced the code phrase the second time. Another attempt would be too obvious.

I'll be a better person. I promise I will. I'll even listen to my mother. Okay, maybe not all the time, because then I'd have to give up the job altogether. But I'll try harder.

Sidekick sized up my reflection in the mirror over the bureau. Thankfully it bore little resemblance to my usual image: bare-bones makeup job, scarcely styled long blonde hair, pale hazel eyes. I hardly recognized myself with the colored contacts, the tightly bound gray-streaked hair, and the caked-on makeup meant to make me look twenty years older. Seemingly satisfied with what he saw, Sidekick grabbed the Gucci bag. It was a crime for those disgusting nicotined fingers to be touching Gucci. But better contaminating the bag's handles than crushing my throat.

Reflexively, I splayed my hand over my neck. After the dozens of what-if scenarios we'd run through, I should know exactly what to do. "If something goes wrong, keep them talking," the undercover agent who'd prepared me for the assignment had said. "If they're talking, at least they're not shooting."

An involuntary shiver rippled down my limbs. I could do *talking*. Maybe . . . *maybe* I could even get a lead on Granddad's stolen painting.

My chest squeezed, but I tamped down thepang of grief and casually swept a gray-chalked lock of hair from my face. "One more thing"—I fixed my contacts-enhanced baby blues on my target— "if you happen to come across a Blacklock landscape, I have another client who'd—"

The door burst open, spewing Buffalo's finest into the room.

I jerked the desk forward and the Kandinsky slid down the wall behind it as shouts of "FBI! Drop your weapons!" met with gunfire. I dove underneath the desk.

Baldy face-planted the carpet in front of me, his gun bouncing out of his hand.

An agent kicked the gun out of reach and cuffed Baldy's hands behind his back as a second agent took a bead on me. "Come out from under there, lady. Slow and easy. Hands in the air."

Baldy narrowed his eyes at me, clearly suspicious of my role in the takedown.

To the agent's credit, he ordered me around, roughly frisked me for weapons, then yanked my arms behind my back and ratcheted on the cuffs. His muscular build, shaved head, and scarcely contained grin, reflected in the wall mirror, reminded me of actor Vin Diesel and spurred me into top form.

"I don't understand," I whined in my best imitation of a confused, helpless female. "What are you arresting us for?"

Another agent scooped the Kandinsky from behind the newly aerated desk.

My breath stalled with fear, but—*Thank you, Lord*—the priceless painting emerged unharmed.

The agent propped it on the desk. "We'll start with possession of stolen property."

I gasped. "It was stolen?" I pivoted toward Baldy, my eyes wide. "You sold me a hot painting?"

His shoulder rose and fell in a noncommittal half shrug.

His sidekick was too busy howling in pain to comment. By the looks of it, he hadn't gotten off more than one shot toward the door before someone took him down, which must've been when he emptied the rest of his gun in my direction.

Agent "Vin" tightened his grip on my arm and shoved me out the door ahead of Baldy. "I'll take this one down on the elevator."

Over my dead body! I gulped air, regretting the word choice that came to mind at the unbidden image of Granddad's body.

"She'll never make eight flights in those heels," he went on, as if he was doing me a favor.

Forget it. I'd climbed the eight flights. I'd go down that way, handcuffed, leg-shackled, however they wanted.

I stumbled and glared and tried to jerk out of his hold and hoped against hope I looked as if I was resisting arrest. Yes, we'd recovered the Kandinsky, but if these guys didn't convince Baldy and Sidekick to turn informant, sooner or later— and more likely sooner—the pair would be back on the street. And criminals had a code of justice all their own. Not to mention, long memories.

They'd come looking for the person who double-crossed them, and I needed to make sure they didn't think that person was me. Stifling a shiver, I glanced at the hall window.

It was plastered in snow—typical February weather for upstate New York—cold and blizzardy. The chance of scoring a flight home to St. Louis tonight didn't look good. And the frigid Buffalo temps would be nothing compared to the cold shoulder my cat would give me if he had to spend a second night with only Zoe to look in on him.

"The stairs are fine," I ground out under my breath as the agent steered me around the corner. "What was the holdup?"

"Sorry, our key card didn't work on the lock."

Sorry? He sure wouldn't sound so cavalier if he'd been the one with a gun in his face.

"I had to run down for a new one," he went on, as if I didn't nearly get killed while he was traipsing up and down the stairs.

Well, okay, he must've run like the wind to do it in under three minutes. "Impressive," I whispered grudgingly.

He shrugged. "Good job holding it together in there. We'd take you on our team any day."

If he only knew. My stride wobbled, and he glanced down at my high-heeled T-straps. "Nice shoes."

"I borrowed them for the job," I admitted, even though my shaky steps were more likely from my fading adrenaline running amok.

He tightened his hold on my arm and propelled me forward. "They look good on you," he said, then, leaning close to my ear, added, "After we get this lot squared away, do you want to come with us for a bit of a celebration?"

"Uh . . . I don't think it's a good idea for me to

be seen around town with a bunch of FBI agents. Do you?" I glanced over my shoulder and lowered my voice. "The wrong people might catch sight of me."

"You're probably right."

His voice dipped as if he was disappointed, or I might've imagined it, because my attention veered to the closing doors. *Elevator doors!*

"Wait!" I lurched out through the shrinking gap a second before the doors made a SWAT sandwich out of Vin.

He let go of my arm and slapped the doors as they bounced off his chest. "What are you doing?"

"I'm sorry," I squeaked. "I, I—" I wasn't about to admit I was claustrophobic. Not when I'd managed to conceal it through twenty weeks of training at Quantico and ten months on the job. I mean, if I really had to go into a confined space, I could do it. Fisting my hands, I lifted my chin. *I could.*

But no one was going to die if I didn't get on that elevator.

Down the hall, Baldy and his escorts stepped into view.

Oh, great. Here I was just chatting with the guy who was supposed to have arrested me.

Vin grabbed my arm once more as Baldy threw me a glare frostier than Buffalo's nastiest wind chill.

My mom was looking smarter by the minute.

• • •

In the lingo of the art world, if a young artist's work was significantly influenced by another more experienced artist, we say his work was "of the school of that artist." In FBI terms, you could say my work is of the school of my former field-training agent, Tanner Calhoun—the dark-haired, muscular guy standing at Arrivals. Irrationally, the sight of him made me want to give in to the tears I'd been dodging all night while waiting for the plane that had ended up permanently grounded.

But Tanner was a face-your-fears kind of guy. He'd probably disown me if I went all girly-girl on him.

As I weaved around passengers toward him, I decided that I favored the ignore-your-fears school. I hitched my overnight bag higher up my shoulder. Yes, ignoring my fears was definitely the way to go.

After all, it was working for me so far. I still had a lot to learn, but at twenty-eight, I was the youngest agent on the FBI Art Crime Team, and last night I'd cemented my reputation for being fearless.

Whether or not it was true was best kept on a need-to-know basis. And nobody needed to know.

"You didn't have to pick me up," I said, secretly glad he had. "I could've caught a cab." Thanks to being bumped to a 6:00 a.m. flight, it was already practically midday.

He grinned. "Cute hair."

I shot him a don't-make-me-hurt-you scowl and tugged my knit hat over my temporary dye job as we stepped outside. Compared to Buffalo, St. Louis was blissfully brown and almost balmy.

Tanner relieved me of my bag and nudged my arm. "C'mon, spill. How'd it go?"

I plunged my hand into my coat pocket and crossed my fingers like a six-year-old. "Not much to tell."

"Uh-huh." His eyes raked over me far too perceptively. "Sure. I can tell by the sweat stains under your arms."

Reflexively, I lifted an arm to check before I remembered I was wearing a winter coat.

"Gotcha." Tanner grinned. *"Serene . . . uh."*

"Men are so gross," I muttered, ignoring the running jibe about my name. How did he always know when I was lying? Well, not lying exactly. Just being economical with the truth.

"Fine." I gave him a basic rundown of the operation as he drove me home. For fun, I embellished the key card issue and shootout a tad.

No need to go into my uneasiness over the way Baldy had glared at me after the takedown.

Tanner shook his head as I concluded my slightly edited recap. A SWAT guy himself, he'd no doubt seen his share of foul-ups. "I'm glad to hear the operation was a success. I know how much you wanted to join the Art Crime Team."

"Hmm." Yes, I'd been single-minded in my pursuit of that goal.

My insides churned. Too bad I'd been in fairy-land when I'd imagined what it would actually be like.

Yup, definitely going the ignore-your-fears route.

Tanner pulled to the curb in front of my apartment building, oblivious—I hoped—to the fact that his protégé was a quaking mass of nerves. "Get some rest. You deserve it."

"Thanks. I'll see you Monday." *If I live that long.*

Mr. Sutton, my seventy-eight-year-old neighbor, greeted me in the hallway as I dropped my overnight bag in front of my door and dug my key from my purse.

"Discombobulated."

I fumbled the key. "Pardon me?"

Every morning he ambled to the corner to buy a newspaper. He tucked today's edition under his arm and squinted at me through his Coke-bottle glasses. "Our word for the day. It's *discombobulated*. Means disconcerted, unsettled, out of sorts."

"Right. Thank you." Sutton was a retired English professor who'd made it his mission to help everyone in the neighborhood expand their vocabulary. He couldn't have known that I'd spent half the night eyeballing passengers in the

Buffalo airport or that the being-watched feeling hadn't gone away when I climbed off the plane seven hundred miles later.

"Don't forget to use it in a sentence."

"I won't." His theory was that using the new word in a sentence helped cement it into our brains. But my brain was too discombobulated to form a coherent sentence.

"You going to answer that?" Mr. Sutton pointed to my purse.

I stared at it dumbly a second before registering the ringing. "Oh, yes, thanks." I waved good-bye and then pulled out my cell phone and glanced at the screen. My parents' number.

I hesitated. I didn't have the energy to parry Mom's questions right now. Only . . . I did make that foxhole promise about listening to her. Not to mention, Mom never called my cell phone number. She was too afraid she'd distract me from my work and get me shot.

Possible reasons why she'd break her own code suddenly paraded through my mind. None of them good.

I clicked on the phone. "Mum, is everything okay?" My parents are British, and when we were kids, there'd been a few words, like *Mum,* that they'd been adamant about our not Americanizing, which was all fine and good until my first-grade teacher told me I'd spelled it wrong and docked a mark off my paper. After that, I'd doggedly insisted on using *Mom,* but somehow, at the moment, using *Mum* felt right.

"Everything is now that I know you're okay," she said. "Are you still in New York? Did you see your brother?"

"I'm fine." Or I would be after a hot shower, a power nap, and a lobotomy to help me forget the icy glint in Baldy's eyes. "I just got home. And no, I didn't see Shawn. I was in New York State, not New York City." My brother flies all over the world, leading excursions for a big travel company, and was currently in his fourth week in the City, arranging for a spring tour. I secretly think it's his way of avoiding Mom's "You need to settle down and give me grandchildren" pleas. I mean, how long does it take to plan a tour? Not that I blamed him for staying away. Except that it doubled the pressure on me.

"You sound tired. Your uncle Harry said there's an opening at the Tums factory. The hours are good. Weekends and evenings off. You'd have time to date."

"Mum, I . . ." I blanked on a good excuse. I didn't need to get to work. I'd already put in over fifty hours this week and had no urgent cases I needed to get back to.

"I know. I know. You need to go. Come for dinner. We'll talk then."

"Okay," I heard myself say as I clicked off. Agreeing was just easier.

A third-floor neighbor stepped off the elevator. Assuming she'd pushed the wrong elevator button, I called out, "This is the second floor," then picked up my overnight bag and reached for the doorknob.

She lifted a plastic bread bag stuffed with tufts of fur. "I'm bringing my cat's shed fur to Theresa. She spins it into yarn and knits scarves with it."

"Cool." In a crazy kind of way. But who was I to judge? I mean, she could at least ride the elevator.

I loved my eccentric neighbors. Along with the three-story brownstone's historic character and its proximity to Forest Park—almost twice the size of New York's Central Park—they had reeled me in when Aunt Martha begged me to sublease the two bedroom from her so that her beloved cat could stay in his home when her hip surgery forced her out of it. I pushed open the door. *Home.*

One step into the apartment, I glanced at the key in my hand—the key I hadn't used—and my heart missed a beat or three.

I soundlessly set down my luggage and palmed my gun. I knew I shouldn't have asked Baldy about the Blacklock stolen from my grandfather. He might've been smart enough to look up who it was stolen from and discovered there was an FBI agent in the family. A female agent.

The fridge's motor kicked out, plunging the apartment into an eerie quietness.

Okay, maybe I was overreacting. Thinking too much about Baldy and the vengeful glint in his eyes. Zoe could have forgotten to lock up after she stopped in to feed the cat. Except . . . the slightest of scents—a masculine mixture of spice and soap—teased my nostrils.

And it didn't belong to my cat.

Pressing my back to the wall, I peered around the arched opening into my kitchen. Nothing appeared disturbed. I edged forward and peered around the corner of the living room. Again nothing.

By now, Harold should've been twining about my legs. Even when he was mad at me, he'd at least show his face and let out a disgruntled huff.

An odd scruffling sound came from the other end of the apartment.

My gun grew slick in my hands. Using the end of the living room wall for cover, I aimed my gun down the hall. "Come out with your hands up."

A shadow darkened the bathroom's doorway and my breath lodged in my throat.

A second later, a man stepped out, his hands in the air, one palm flat, the other clutching a litter scoop.

I blinked. "Nate?"

His gaze skittered from my Glock to my face, his lips curving into a grin. "Is today's word of the day *paranoid?*"

"Cute." Ignoring my hammering heart, I slipped

my gun into my pocket as nonchalantly as I could manage. Nate, Nathan Butler, was the building superintendent. Although with his tousled brown hair and the scarcely grown-in beard that made him look as if he'd carelessly decided to stop shaving for a week, he could easily be mistaken for a movie star—and definitely a leading man, not the bad guy. "What are you doing in my apartment?"

He lowered his hands. "Your friend couldn't make it and called your aunt, who called me and asked if I could take care of Harold until you got back."

"Is she okay?" It wasn't like Zoe to bail. She worked at the Forest Park Art Museum, which made stopping by my place to feed Harold the minorest of detours.

"Yeah, your aunt said she had a work emergency."

Relieved to hear she was okay, I dragged my knit hat from my head. "She must've been swamped with getting ready for the special Valentine's Day show next weekend. It—"

A dimple peeked through Nate's whiskers and made me forget what I'd been about to say.

"What?"

"I'm afraid I frightened you more than I realized." His gaze flicked to my hair—my chalked gray hair.

I pulled out my hair clips and shook free the

locks in a model-worthy flourish. "Haven't you heard? Gray is the new blonde." Resisting the impulse to explain the disguise, I added, "I really appreciate you stepping in while I was gone."

Harold ambled out of my bedroom and twined around Nate's legs, as if it was perfectly natural for me to have a man in my apartment. If the litter scoop in Nate's hands was anything to go by, he'd taken his cat-watching duties very seriously.

Suddenly my heartfelt thanks didn't feel like nearly enough compensation.

Nate slanted a troubled glance at my bulging jacket pocket. "You okay?"

"Yes." Releasing the gun still bunched in my hand, I jerked my hand from my pocket and flattened it against my side, then brandished a self-deprecating grin. Who was I kidding? I'd been on *one* undercover assignment and was already so freaked out that scoring a job at the antacid factory sounded like a good move. At least I'd get a product discount. And I could use some antacids about now. I'd been fooling myself to think I could handle being an FBI agent. I should just quit like Mom wanted.

"You sure you're okay?" Nate pressed.

I fluttered my hand to dismiss his concern. "I'm fine. Mr. Sutton caught me before I came in. Our word of the day is *discombobulated*." I grinned. "I was just practicing."

My quip didn't earn the chuckle I'd hoped for.

In fact, Nate's smile disappeared altogether. "I imagine all that FBI training keys you up to always anticipate the worst."

"Nah. That's my mother's job. She's petrified I'll get shot by a bad guy before I can give her grand-kids." My cheeks flamed, and I whirled toward the kitchen, mentally blaming my lack of filter on my tiredness. "Uh, did you want some lunch before you go?" I pulled a pound of bacon and carton of eggs from the fridge. "I mean, you cleaned the cat's litter box. The least I can do is feed you."

Nate leaned against the kitchen doorway, looking amused once more. "That's okay. My arteries have already had their quota of choles-terol for the week."

"I'll have you know my granddad ate bacon and eggs every morning of his life and he lived to be seventy-two."

"That's not that old," Nate teased.

"He was *shot*."

Nate's grin dropped, along with my heart.

Ugh, why'd I have to shoot my mouth off?

Nate looked at me as if I was a minefield and one wrong move might set me off. "I'm sorry. I didn't know."

Of course he didn't, and I didn't want to explain. Didn't want to tell him my grandfather was killed trying to stop a burglar from taking a painting. That his murder was the reason I'd become an FBI agent.

I stuffed the uncooked lunch fixings back into the fridge. "It's okay." Except it wasn't. How could I have almost considered quitting at the first hint of trouble? What kind of dedication was that?

A knock rattled the window, and I all but pounced on the kitchen's exterior door to end the awkward exchange. The door opened onto a metal staircase, and my friend Zoe Davids stood on the landing, her hands stuffed in the pockets of her winter coat, her shoulders hunched up to her ears, looking as desperate as she had the time we were ten and got caught skipping school. "I need your help."

The work emergency. "Of course." I motioned her inside. Due to her boss's sudden death last summer, Zoe had been appointed the temporary head of the art museum's security, and I had a bad feeling her midday appearance on my doorstep didn't bode well for her hopes the appointment would soon be made permanent.

She stepped inside and did a double take. "Your hair's gray."

"It's a long story."

Zoe's problem looked far more important at the moment. Her chestnut-colored hair was feathered around her face in a blunt cut that did nothing to soften the worry lines pinching her lips. Her gaze slammed into Nate's and her face went white. "Oh." She backed out the door. "I . . . He . . ."

"Zoe, what's wrong?" I glanced at Nate for his take on her odd reaction.

Back-stepping toward the hall door, he hitched his thumb over his shoulder. "I, um, need to go. I'll see you later."

As the door closed behind him, my attention jerked back to Zoe clattering down the stairs. "What's going on?"

2

I grabbed my coat and raced down the outside stairs after Zoe. "What was that about? Why did you react that way to Nate?"

Zoe had already yanked open her car door but stopped short of climbing in. "That was your apartment superintendent?"

"Yes."

Zoe groaned. "Your whole building could've found out inside half an hour. This is why they didn't want me to come."

"Why *who* didn't want you to come?"

Her gaze darted about the parking lot. "Get in."

I quickly rounded the hood and joined her in the front seat of her twelve-year-old sedan.

Without a word, she turned the key in the ignition, and the instant the car sputtered to life, she sped out of the lot. "The art museum's board didn't want me to come," she said, turning onto Skinker Boulevard. "They're afraid if word gets out, our benefactors will think twice about loaning their personal pieces for future shows."

"Word about what?"

"We've been robbed!"

"Are you serious? When? How?" I was sure I would've heard if someone had stormed into the museum wielding firearms and ripping priceless art off the walls, so I suspected the museum had actually been burglarized, not robbed—a distinction Tanner had drilled into me my first week on the job. Not that the distinction made a hill of beans of difference to Zoe. All that mattered was it had happened on her watch.

I almost felt guilty for my unexpected surge of eagerness to investigate.

"That's the problem. We're not sure when it happened or how. It's a nightmare. If not for the FBI's press conference this morning touting that Kandinsky recovery in Buffalo, I'd probably still be trying to convince the board to let me talk to you."

Unfortunately, a reluctance to report thefts wasn't uncommon for museums and art galleries, precisely for the reason she'd stated. Between that and a desire for the art to appear accessible to patrons, security tended to have a few unplugged holes. But those were what Zoe had spent the past six months addressing with surveillance and determent systems updates. "Do you think it could've happened before you started the security updates?"

She swerved into Forest Park and the engine sputtered out. "Not now!" She cranked the key once, then again. The third time the engine turned over, and she raced toward the museum as if she was on borrowed time, which she probably was.

"Don't you think it's time you replace this thing?"

"Sure, but first I have to make sure I still have a job to pay for it."

"You're not going to lose your job."

"Don't be so sure. Especially if it turns out the paintings went missing after all the updates I pestered the board to allow me to make!"

"Is that what you think?"

Zoe shook her head. "All we know for sure is that the paintings were there last May, and now they're gone."

May? That meant we were looking at a nine-month window! This case was already colder than Buffalo. "Okay, why don't you start by telling me what's missing?"

"Two paintings—a small Monet and a Rijckaert. Except . . ." She wrung her fingers around the steering wheel. "There's a slight chance they could have been misplaced."

"Misplaced? You misplace a remote control, your car keys, maybe even a tagalong little brother in the mall. You *don't* misplace a six-figure Monet."

"I know. I know. It's wishful thinking. But you know how it is with museums. Budgets are tight and we barely have the resources to deal with the pieces on display, never mind taking regular inventories of the pieces in storage."

"So the Monet and Rijckaert went missing from storage?"

"Yes, from vault B-11." She turned her sputtering car into the parking lot and gave it an extra kick of gas to propel it into a parking spot. "C'mon, I'll show you." She led me inside through a back entrance.

A young man in dark slacks and a blue, museum-logoed polo shirt, which flagged him as security to those who knew the color codes, appeared in the hall ahead of us and gave me a once-over.

"It's okay, Malcolm," Zoe said. "She's with me."

He nodded, then disappeared around the corner.

Zoe led me down a back staircase and used a key card to get through the door at the bottom.

"Who else has access to the vault area?"

"My security team. Cleaning staff have access to the floor, not inside the vaults. We occasionally get requests from students to study some of the stored pieces. I can ask records to pull up those requests. But we always bring the pieces up to a study room." Zoe stopped in front of a door labeled B-11 and thumbed through the keys on her key ring. "We stumbled onto the theft by accident when we were searching for a painting for the Valentine's show."

"Why didn't you change these out for electronic locks during the upgrades?"

"The board was worried that an electricity outage would make them more vulnerable than mechanical locks."

"Too bad. If they'd been electronic, we could've checked the records to see when the door had been opened and by whom. Could've helped us narrow down the window of opportunity and suspects considerably."

"We have records for the locked doors at either end of the wing, but unfortunately, they only go back thirty days." Zoe unlocked B-11's door.

It opened into a windowless room that thankfully was large enough to not make me break into a claustrophobic panic. Like the rest of the institution, the room was a comfortable 70 degrees with a relative humidity of about 50 percent—the stable temperatures and humidity essential to prevent a breakdown in organic materials.

Zoe flicked on a light and walked over to one of the many specially designed storage racks that held framed paintings. "The two missing paintings were supposed to be on this rack."

"Were they the most valuable pieces down here?"

"The Monet would've been up there for sure. I was surprised to hear we had one squirreled away. But there are a lot of other pieces here more valuable than the Rijckaert, so the thief either didn't know his artists too well or—"

"Knew it'd be easier to fence a lesser-known work," I finished for her.

"Yeah, but then why take the Monet?"

"Filling a shopping list, maybe." I walked from one rack to the next, hoping to see something that would give me a clue why those two paintings in particular were snatched and who did the snatching. Was it a random crime of opportunity? Or had the thief come with a shopping list? "Those were the only two paintings missing?"

"Yes, I've had my team working around the clock taking inventory ever since the discovery."

"But they don't know why you're taking inventory?"

"Right. Although if it was an inside job, the thief will have figured it out."

My foot hit something metallic, and it rolled under a rack of shelves. Squatting, I shined my pen light in the narrow space and fished out an inch-long section of copper pipe with my pen. "Any idea how this got here?"

"Must be from the contractors who fixed the leaky water pipe last May. Remember I said we did an inventory in May? The leak was the reason. The paintings had to be relocated while the pipe was repaired."

"Were both of the missing paintings accounted for after the men finished the job?" Tradesmen were in a uniquely convenient position to pilfer pieces out of an establishment. Power was often disabled in the areas where they worked, rendering sensors and surveillance cameras useless. And their toolboxes and blueprint tubes offered ample cover to smuggle out a rolled canvas undetected.

"Yes and no. The correct number of pieces were returned to the vault, but the men continued to work on this level for two more days after that."

"Was the vault locked during those days?"

"Yes."

I examined the door's lock. "There aren't any scratches. Doesn't look like it's been picked. I'll bring in an evidence team to lift fingerprints from the room. Did the tradesmen have any cause to handle the storage units?"

"No. But with how many of us have been down here inventorying, I doubt any prints your team finds will prove anything."

"Where's your optimism?" I tossed her a smile, but she didn't return it. "I guess you'd rather I didn't draw attention to my investigation by bringing in a team?"

Zoe winced. "Yeah, that too."

"Well, you did the right thing by coming to me." I squeezed her arm reassuringly. "The FBI takes the theft of our cultural heritage very seriously. First of all, I'm going to need everything you can tell me about the provenance of the pieces, as well as pictures of the front and back, if you have them, so I can get the information uploaded to the Art Loss Register and the FBI's stolen art database."

"We can get all that from the office right now." She motioned me out of the room, but at the sound

37

of someone trying to open the hall door, I pushed her back inside.

"Who would come down here now?" I whispered, pushing the vault door not quite closed so I could see who came down the hall.

"No one should be. But one of the security guards might be checking to make sure the door's locked."

I waited until the tugging stopped, then scooped the lanyard that held the key card from her neck. "C'mon, I want to see who that was."

Zoe locked the vault door as I sprinted to the end of the hall and swiped the card over the lock. Bounding out, I caught a glimpse of a sneaker and a denim-clad leg on the second turn of the stairs. "Stop right there," I shouted and pounded up after him.

Rounding the landing, he ran past the first-floor door and raced up the next stretch of stairs.

"Call for backup," I shouted down to Zoe. As I rounded the landing, the first-level door crashed open and a blue streak slammed me into the stair rail.

"Got you," the same young man who'd stopped us earlier spat, then proceeded to wrench my arm behind my back while shoving my upper torso over the rail.

Zoe raced past us, crying, "Not her!"

But I didn't have time to wait for him to put two and two together. Springing away from the rail, I plowed backward and pinned him to the block wall. Then I twisted the wrist he'd caught and jabbed my elbow into his gut. "Sorry," I said, as he let out a pained *oomph*. "But I gotta go."

The second-floor door clanked open and I sprinted faster. "Native Art exhibit," Zoe shouted into her radio as I reached her. She'd planted herself at the doorway to the exhibit, hands braced on her thighs, gulping in breaths. "It's a kid. He can't be more than twelve or thirteen."

Three blue shirts appeared at the door at the other end of the exhibit, and two red shirts closed off the side door that led to another exhibit. The eager-beaver guard I'd elbowed raced up behind us. But the room was empty. "Did you see a kid pass?" I asked the other staff. "He was wearing jeans, a denim jacket, dirty white sneakers."

"He's in the tepee," Zoe said, still straining to slow her breathing.

As two guards hauled the kid out of the tepee, an unwelcome thought struck. "Get back to your posts," I ordered the rest of the staff and raced through the exhibit to the balcony overlooking the main atrium and linking the south wing to the north wing. Our little chase had commandeered the attention of at least seven staff members, leaving who knows how many potential targets unguarded. I scanned the movement in and out of the exhibits flanking either side of the atrium.

The staff at the entrance seemed to be scanning

exiting patrons extra diligently. Zoe had trained them well.

A few minutes later, Zoe and another guard escorted the kid to the reception desk on the main floor, where a harried parent, or possibly teacher, reamed into him. The man accompanied Zoe and the boy to the back of the atrium to the security office. Staff members congregated in small groups, no doubt relaying their role in the excitement. Except for the guy who tried to take me down in the stairwell—he stood by himself at the Impressionist gallery, west of the atrium. Back in the stairwell he'd been eager to prove himself.

Or was it that he had something to hide?

I did a quick circuit through all the exhibits to check out the other staff members.

One of the blue shirts who'd hauled the kid out of the teepee nodded my way. "This is the most excitement we've had since the senator's daughter had the peanut butter reaction."

Most didn't give me a second glance, which wasn't surprising since they didn't know I was a federal agent. By the time I reached the main floor, the kid who'd caused the commotion was being escorted out of the museum, and the security guard who'd mistakenly grabbed me was chatting up a young woman behind the circular reception desk in the center of the atrium.

"How were you to know?" she said to him. "You saw her running. That's suspicious."

He glanced my way as I passed and nodded sheepishly, then resumed his conversation in a softer voice.

Zoe joined me halfway across the atrium.

"What's the kid's story?" I asked.

"He said he made a wrong turn and got lost, then got scared when we chased him."

I elbowed Zoe as we headed to her office. "You're getting out of shape. You should jog with me in the mornings."

"No thanks. My knees can't take jogging, remember?"

Right. She'd wrecked her knees running for the high school cross-country team. "Take up swimming then. It's good exercise."

"Are you kidding me? Have you looked at a whale lately? All they do is swim and they're nothing but blubber."

I laughed. "Well, if you don't get your car fixed soon, you might be doing a lot of walking."

"Please, don't remind me."

As we stepped into the main security office that housed the monitors reeling the security camera feeds, I said, "Did the security footage corroborate the kid's story?"

"Yes—and yes, I checked the other camera feeds for suspicious behavior, since you clearly thought the chase was a diversion."

"You have to admit it would've been a good one."

Zoe winced, and I regretted adding salt to her already festering wounds. "The boy's teacher indicated that he was somewhat developmentally delayed and didn't process instructions well."

"Hmm."

"I know that *hmm*. You don't believe it was nothing?"

"Could've been. But the kid would make a perfect lackey. It could've been a dry run to gauge how security would respond."

"Well, if that's what it was, the guy pulling the kid's strings can count on us being more alert than ever the next time."

"Hmm."

"Again with the *hmms?* I've got enough stress without you filling my head with more scenarios." She walked into her office and snatched up a file folder from her desk. Waving me in, she closed the door and handed over the file. "This is everything we have on the missing paintings."

I leafed through the folder. "This is perfect. Exactly what I need." Although not without its critics, the Art Loss Register, a private London-based corporation's ever-expanding international database of stolen art, was our best hope of recovering the stolen pieces. "If we get lucky, a scrupulous dealer might check out the painting's legitimacy before buying it and report the seller."

Of course, lots of buyers simply chose not to purchase a painting after discovering it on the

Register. They wouldn't report it, because they didn't want to get involved. But Zoe didn't need to be reminded of that right now.

I closed the file and pulled out my notebook once more. "Earlier you said the paintings might have been misplaced. Are you thinking in the haste of moving them for the leak?"

"Actually, I was hoping they might've been loaned to another museum and the record misfiled. But"—she snatched up a memo from her desk—"admin just got back to me on the results of the database search I requested. There's no record of a request for those pieces, let alone of a loan."

"Okay, then next I'll need a list of all museum employees and contractors from the last nine months. Highlight those who could've readily accessed the vault."

"We're talking over a hundred people. Are you going to interview all of them?"

"Yes." I'd likely be looking at dozens of potential suspects. Not to mention that by now the paintings could've changed hands a few times, growing cleaner with every sale.

Zoe dropped her head into her hands and moaned. "I'm doomed."

"No, you're not. We'll get the paintings back," I said, even though the chances of success looked remote.

"You don't understand. The museum hasn't had

a theft in over thirty years. After Len died and, thanks to my seniority, the board appointed me temporary head of security, I had to do some serious selling to convince them we needed to invest in an updated security system."

"And clearly they needed it."

"Unless it happened *after* the update. Or because of it!"

"Hmm."

"Serena, you're really stressing me out with those *hmms*."

"Sorry. Okay, let me get started on putting out the word that the paintings are missing."

Zoe lurched for the file folder. "Oh, no, we don't want any publicity."

I pried off her fingers. "Not a problem. After this many months, there isn't much point in going public. But I've compiled an email list of people that it would be advantageous to alert in cases like this."

Zoe shook her head. "I don't know."

"Trust me, Zoe. I'm modeling my approach on the procedures of a couple of successful pioneer art crime detectives out of Montreal and California. They both collected contact information for art galleries, dealers, auction houses, police forces, even criminals. Basically anyone the thief might try to sell the work to. Then whenever they had a new piece they were looking for, they'd send out an email blast."

"But we've managed to keep the theft a secret from most of our employees. As soon as word of the theft gets out—"

"Word is bound to leak out, Zoe. It can't be helped. Not if you want to find out who did this and stop it from happening again."

Zoe gulped, the strain of the last few days showing in the purple smudges under her bloodshot eyes. "The board isn't going to like this."

My heart crunched at her misery. "Then send them to me. This is the best way I know to help you. And it's better that they're respected for doing everything possible to find the missing paintings than to have word of the theft come out later and be criticized for doing nothing." I zipped up my jacket, ready to head out and get started on the paperwork. "Trust me, most patrons will respect your efforts and trust that the resulting increased security will make their own loaned treasures all the safer."

Zoe gritted her teeth, not looking so sure the board would agree.

"It'll be okay," I reassured. I glanced at my watch—already close to 2:00. I still needed to return to my apartment and shower, but the museum was open until 9:00 on Fridays. "I'll head to headquarters and take care of the preliminaries, then join you back here after supper to begin interviewing staff."

She grabbed her coat and purse. "I'll drive you home."

Recalling the drive over, I held up my hand to stop her. "That's okay. I could use the walk and fresh air."

The FBI's St. Louis Division serves forty-eight counties in addition to the city, with my jurisdiction for art crime investigations extending into the lower Midwest. But I spent most of my time at the headquarters on Market Street, west of Union Station—a quick ten-minute hop on I-64 from my place, traffic cooperating.

A couple hours after I left the museum, I climbed the center stairs to the second floor of FBI headquarters. A row of conference and interrogation rooms bisected the level into two open-concept office areas, hemmed in by long walls of vertical filing cabinets to form a hallway on either side of the rooms.

Tanner leaned against one of the cabinets, his arms crossed over his chest, watching me. When I reached the top step, he steered me toward my cubicle and lowered his voice. "What are you doing here? You're supposed to be home."

Tanner was hard core. He lived and breathed the FBI, knew every last dot and dash of the handbook. He was the champion for all the innocent soccer moms and dog walkers out on the streets. And until thirty seconds ago, I'd been

100 percent sure he saw me as a kindred spirit.

I cupped my ear forward with my finger, as if I couldn't have heard him right. "You're telling me to take a day off?"

"Yes."

"*You* . . . are telling . . . *me* . . . to take a day off?"

He grimaced. "You're right. Never mind. You're probably safer here." He started to walk away.

"Whoa, whoa, whoa. What's that supposed to mean?" After almost shooting Nate in the litter scoop this morning, I'd more or less managed to talk myself out of my paranoia about Baldy. After all, smart bad guys wanted to stay off an agent's radar, not make their situation worse by targeting us and earning themselves top billing on our Most Wanted list.

Tanner did that crooked-jaw slant that meant he'd rather eat dirt than answer me, and my pulse spiked.

"What's going on?" I pressed.

He let out a resigned sigh. "We just got word that the guys you helped bust in Buffalo made bail. And not because they decided to play ball."

My pulse escalated into jumping jacks mode, and not the happy kind. "You think they'll come after me?"

"They're bound to think you were working for us. If I'd been your handler, I would've made sure you were long gone before the takedown."

Translation: he thought I was in deep doo-doo.

3

Taking a seat at my desk, I tried to act like the news that Baldy and Sidekick were out of custody didn't faze me. Thankfully, Tanner seemed to believe me.

For the most part, I worked my cases like I was self-employed, calling in support staff when needed and adjusting my schedule to suit the demands of the case. But given how many months I'd run strategies past my former field training agent, I didn't think twice when Tanner asked what I was working on.

"Don't rush into the interviews," he advised after I filled him in on the art museum theft. "Get the list of names and do background and internet searches on the people first. The more you know about them going into the interviews, the better you'll be able to read them."

I grinned.

"I've told you that before, I guess?"

"Uh-huh."

"Sorry. You're a good agent. You don't need me meddling."

"That's okay. I appreciate you taking an interest, but I really do need to get to work here." I pointed to my computer, and Tanner returned to his own desk. I prepared my email blast and documented the specs for the Art Loss Register and FBI website. Now and again, I sensed Tanner hovering nearby as if he wanted to say something, but I pretended not to notice.

Eventually, he stepped inside my cubicle and tapped my desk. "Time to call it a day."

"Yes, yes." I glanced at the clock—5:00 already?—and typed faster before I lost my train of thought. "I told Zoe I'd stop back at the museum."

Tanner let out an exasperated sigh but didn't try to change my mind before walking away.

My cell phone rang a few minutes later. Zoe.

"Hey," she said. "I just emailed you the list of employees and contractors you wanted, but can we wait until tomorrow morning to meet again? I've been here since dawn and I'm beat."

I stood and peered over my cubicle wall into Tanner's office space. It was empty. "Did Tanner tell you to call me?"

"Tanner? Your FBI guy?"

"He's not *my* guy," I said a tad too loudly, earning me a glance from an agent walking by.

"Okay, okay, keep your shirt on. No, no one called me."

"Good, thanks. I'll see you tomorrow morning."

The agent who'd been passing backed up to the opening in my cubicle wall. "Guy troubles?"

"Not you too?" Ever since Nolan in accounting got engaged to the friend I'd introduced him to, half the single guys on the floor had asked me if I had any more single friends. The other half joked they were holding out for me. As if.

He shrugged, grinning shamelessly.

I finished up at my computer and headed out to the parking lot. It was already dark, and the shifting shadows raised the specter of Tanner's warning about Baldy and Sidekick. I squashed the thought, thankful I had Zoe's list of names to keep me occupied this evening. The temperature had plummeted along with the sun, leaving a thin sheen of ice on my windshield. I tossed my bag onto the passenger seat and turned the key in the ignition.

Nothing happened.

Great. This had to be punishment for giving Zoe a hard time about her car. I checked the lights and radio, but it didn't look as if I'd left anything on that would've drained the battery. The parking lot was practically empty too. *Not good.* If I couldn't find someone to give me a boost, getting roadside assistance into the secured lot would be a feat. I popped the hood and jumped out.

A rumbly SUV crept toward me.

I shielded my eyes against the glare of its head-lights but couldn't make out the driver. Ignoring the sudden pounding in my chest, I waved anyway. The driver had to be staff. No one else could access the lot.

The window rolled down. "Trouble?"

"Tanner! Am I ever glad to see you. I need a jump. You mind?"

"No problem." In addition to being on the major crimes squad, Tanner was SWAT, which meant he got to drive a cooler vehicle to accommodate the extra equipment he might need at a moment's notice. I had no interest in being SWAT, but with a light snow starting and my own car crippled, I was seriously coveting his SUV.

He jumped out of his vehicle, cables in hand. Then his cell phone rang. He glanced at the screen. "It's your parents' number."

"Dinner! I totally forgot." Mom must still have had Tanner's cell phone number on speed dial from the months he'd been my field training agent. "She's still afraid to call me when I'm working."

"So what does that rank me, fish bait?"

I laughed. "No, you're SWAT. She probably thinks you can get yourself out of whatever disaster her call might cause."

Smirking, he clicked on his phone. "Yes, Mrs. Jones, she's right here. Hold on a sec." He handed it over.

"Hey, Mum. I'm sorry I'm late. My car won't start. Tanner's seeing if he can get it going now."

She let out a relieved-sounding sigh. "Oh, is that all? Thank goodness."

I didn't remember Mom ever being such a worrywart. Maybe she was hitting the change of life. Zoe told me that her neighbor had gotten so emotionally whacked out with it that sometimes she'd give her kids a hug good-bye and not be able to let them go until her husband pried them out of her arms.

"It's dead," Tanner announced, unhooking his battery cables as solemnly as a doctor taking a patient off life support.

"I'm sorry, Mum. It doesn't look like I'm going to make it for dinner. I'm not sure who I need to talk to about getting a loaner. Most of the staff have already gone home. By the time I get squared away with another vehicle, the beef will be cold and your Yorkshire pudding collapsed." Yorkshire pudding is a mixture of flour, milk, and eggs cooked in fat and served with gobs of gravy. And there was nothing Mom hated worse than our being too late to see it fresh from the oven in all its poofed-up glory.

"Where are you? I'll send your father to get you."

"That's okay, Mum. You know how he hates to go out again after he gets home."

"I can drop you at your folks," Tanner volunteered. He'd been there before, during my rookie days, and knew it wasn't far from his own place.

I covered the phone with my palm. "I appreciate the offer, but I have a long list of background checks to run through tonight anyway, and I'll want a car to drive home because I'm heading straight to the art museum first thing in the morning."

"The background checks can wait, and I'll make sure we get a working car to you."

I shook my head in disbelief at how insistent he was being. But last night's stint in the airport was starting to catch up to me, and a home-cooked meal did sound good. "Are you sure you don't mind driving me?"

"Wouldn't have offered if I did."

"Okay then." I gathered my belongings from my car and told Mom I'd be there in twenty minutes.

As I settled into Tanner's passenger seat, he finished tapping a text on his phone, then cranked up the heat.

"What were you working on so late?" I asked as he pulled onto the road.

"A case."

Of course. It was pointless trying to get more answers out of Tanner when he started talking in one- and two-word sentences. For someone who was always asking me about my cases, he took secrecy to the extreme on his own. I'd asked him once why he hadn't joined the CIA instead of the FBI. He'd said he couldn't stand foreign food and he liked to sleep in his own bed at night.

As we neared the corner, headlights blindsided me from the parking lot of the rundown building across the street from our headquarters. "What's he doing?" I blurted.

"Who?" Tanner made the turn.

"That pickup." I pointed, able to make it out better from the side until its headlights flicked off and it melted into the shadows once more.

"Going to the bar, I imagine."

Yeah. It had to be a coincidence that I'd noticed a black pickup circle the parking lot behind my apartment building as I stepped out of the shower this afternoon. Baldy couldn't have tracked me down this fast. If he was even looking.

Tanner took the direct route, straight down Forest Park Avenue to the parkway into University City. Passing a bakery, I made a mental note to pick up something for Nate to thank him for taking care of Harold.

My parents still lived in the same modest 1940s two-story I grew up in, made a tad more elegant-sounding by the prestigious university names of the streets. Not prestigious enough for Nana Jones, of course, who'd wanted Dad hobnobbing with the upper class. But Dad had never been the type to care about appearances or making connections. He'd just wanted to live in a nice neighborhood with a good school, within walking distance of his job.

Thankfully, my friends growing up didn't watch old black-and-white TV shows, so I was spared from being teased that my parents shared not only the same characteristics but also the same names—June and Ward—as the archetypal suburban parents immortalized by the TV series *Leave It to Beaver.*

Tanner pulled up in front of my parents' house. Only instead of stopping at the curb, he parked in the driveway, then jumped out and opened my door.

"Whoa, what's gotten into you?"

"What would your mother think of me if I threw you out at the curb?" He glanced at a car coasting past and slipped to my other side like a Secret Service agent guarding the president's exposed flank.

"Is there something you neglected to tell me about that call from Buffalo?" I asked, praying his sudden protectiveness was only my imagination.

"Watch the steps, they're icy."

The front door flew open. "She's here!" Mom beamed down at me as if I were the prodigal daughter come home at last. And from the delicious aroma wafting out of the house, the fatted calf had been cooked to perfection. She captured me in an uncharacteristic bear hug before I was in the door, and my first thought was, *Who are you and what have you done with my mother?*

True to the British stereotype, my parents were raised not to wear their emotions on their sleeves and definitely not to be touchy-feely. Although I supposed that considering how petrified Mom had been about my flying out of town, my safe return would seem like a big deal.

"Mmm, something smells good," Tanner said from where he'd paused at the bottom of the porch steps.

"Join us," Dad said, easing Mom and me inside.

I caught my jaw before it dropped. My dad was a pretty sociable kind of guy, but as a university professor, by Friday nights, he was typically worn out from teaching all week. We'd loved the fact as kids, because it meant Friday was the one night he'd agree to forgo sitting at the table for our meal and let us eat on TV trays in front of a movie.

I glimpsed the dining room table, decked out in Mom's finest china. Clearly, she had no intention of allowing a TV-tray meal tonight. The roast beef should've tipped me off.

An odd sensation rippled through my stomach. As long as I could remember, roast beef had been reserved for Sunday dinner. Had Mom really been so worried I wouldn't come home?

Dad took a turn giving me a hug, then led Tanner to the table, delving immediately into a discussion about the stock market. Much to Nana's chagrin, my dad had used his business degree to teach rather than go into business for himself. Tanner had been a student in one of his economics classes in bygone years, a fact they'd discovered in my first week as an agent under his supervision. For my dad, everything about the world and human nature could be compared to the stock market, so having someone at dinner versed in the lingo would make his day.

Great-Aunt Martha, on the other hand, who'd been living with my parents ever since the hip surgery that had prompted her to convince me to sublet her apartment, emerged from the kitchen carrying water glasses and frowned at Tanner. She set one on the table in front of him with scarcely a nod, then scurried after Mom and me back into the kitchen, her newly set blue-gray curls bobbing erratically. "What's he doing here? He's too old for you."

I chuckled. "He's not my date, Aunt Martha. He gave me a ride because my car wouldn't start."

She glanced back into the dining room, looking deeply disturbed. "Does your father know that?"

"Shush," Mom said. "She can bring home whichever young man she likes."

"He's not a young man," Aunt Martha hissed, but I scarcely registered the protest because I was still gaping at Mom. It was no secret, thanks to the recent announcement that my younger cousin was engaged, that Mom thought it was time I got myself a husband too. But not someone in law enforcement. She couldn't be that desperate to see me married. Or was she?

I studied her carefully, wondering if her paranoia over my trip had caused some kind of mental breakdown.

"Look what waiting for the right young man got you," Mom went on to Aunt Martha.

Uh-oh. I may be an FBI agent, but defusing this kind of confrontation was beyond my skills. I quickly shed my coat on the nearest kitchen chair and hurried out to the dining room with the bowl of mashed potatoes.

"You became the iconic spinster cat lady." Mom's rising voice followed me into the dining room. "And now you've gone and foisted your feline on Serena!"

Bristling, I looked at Tanner, who grinned at me. I offered a wan smile in return. I knew he knew exactly what I was thinking. I'd once made the mistake of waxing philosophical on this very topic during a stakeout.

"Why are single women called 'spinsters' after a certain age, as if no one will have them, when men are dubbed 'bachelors' and admired, as if they'd *chosen* to avoid matrimony?" I'd ranted.

Tanner had merely plucked a cat hair off my coat sleeve and raised one eyebrow in that annoying way he had.

My dad, oblivious to the undercurrents and adept at tuning out Mom and Aunt Martha's chattering, was saying something about the financial market.

Tanner and I both turned to give him our attention. Tanner cleared his throat and, amazingly, took up the conversation as if he'd been hanging on Dad's every word.

"Yes, sir. I agree completely with your analysis." He sipped his water and then looked me straight in the eye. "Astute investors find value where others don't."

He held my gaze for a long instant until, mortifyingly, I blushed—*blushed!*—and then stammered something about salad dressing and retreated to the kitchen.

What was that all about?

"Astute investors find value where others don't," I mimicked under my breath as I took the gravy boat from Mom. What did he want me to do—put it on a plaque?

Thankfully, Mom and Aunt Martha joined us at the table with no more mention of my singleness or my cat. Although Aunt Martha made a point of scooping the place beside Tanner, forcing me to sit across from him, presumably for fear our hands might graze each other when I passed the gravy boat.

Naturally, Tanner noticed and winked at me.

I ignored him.

Dad called for quiet, and we joined hands to say grace.

My grip reflexively tightened at his mention of my safe return, and Mom pulled back her hand with a yelp.

I focused on filling my plate, certain Dad had opened Pandora's box, or that my reaction had.

Only the questions didn't come. Everyone broke

into mindless chatter as they too piled food on their plates. Mom didn't even bring up the job opening at the Tums factory again. Dad talked to Tanner about new market analysis software his department had gotten, while Mom babbled on about plans for another cousin's upcoming baby shower.

Why weren't they asking me about the trip? Forty-eight hours ago, it had been all I could do to get them to stop badgering me with questions over my imagined mission.

Aunt Martha flagged me with her fork from across the table, and my pulse spiked. *Here it comes.*

"I found these fabulous new support hose at the mall," she said instead.

My mouth bobbed uselessly for a second or two. I had no idea what to say.

Oh, man, I was a worse mess than I'd thought. Here they'd gone and taken me at my word that I couldn't talk about the job, but I really needed to. Every time I thought about Baldy's glare outside the hotel room, I got the heebie-jeebies. Not that I wanted Tanner to know that. And his news flash about the pair's release hadn't helped.

My family *really* didn't need to know that. They'd beg me to quit.

I finished what was on my plate and pushed away from the table. "That was fabulous, Mum. Thank you. I'll get started on these dishes, because I'm afraid I need to leave soon. I have a new case I need to work on yet tonight."

"No, no, sit." Mom sprang to her feet and snatched the empty plate from my hand. "I made dessert."

"Mmm," Tanner hummed, laying his knife and fork on his empty plate.

I shot my dad a questioning look. Mom never made dessert, unless it was Christmas or someone's birthday or Jell-O was on sale at the supermarket. She'd always said we didn't need the empty calories but had seemed to think Jell-O was healthy, seeing as they always served it to hospital patients.

"Ooh," Aunt Martha squealed. "Does your case have to do with the art museum?"

I slanted a wary glance toward Tanner, since we weren't really at liberty to discuss cases. "Why would you think that?"

"Because I'd never heard Zoe so rattled as when she called last night to ask if I could arrange for Nate to take care of Harold." Aunt Martha squinted at me, then excitedly rubbed her hands together. "Ooh, it does have to do with the art museum!"

I shook my head. "I never said a word."

Dad laughed. "It's written all over your face. You've always been a terrible liar."

"For Serena's own safety," Tanner interjected, "and the integrity of her investigations, please don't let anything you think you've figured out leave this room."

Aunt Martha rubbed her hands together more gleefully than ever. "Was it an inside job, do you think? Are you going undercover?"

"No, Aunt Martha, I could hardly go undercover in my own neighborhood."

"But my friend Mildred phoned this afternoon, said she'd been at the museum with her grandson and saw you spying on people from the balcony. Said she didn't recognize you at first because your hair was gray." Aunt Martha tilted her head, scrutinizing my hair. "How'd you get the dye out so fast?"

Tanner chuckled.

If he hadn't been across the table, I would've swatted him. "Mildred could've been mistaken," I said.

Tanner shook his head, a full-out grin stretching his lips. "You're right. She's a terrible liar. Good thing she lies better when her life is on the line."

"What? When?" Mom blurted, almost dropping the stack of dessert plates she was carrying.

"He's kidding," I said, tossing a glare in Tanner's direction.

"I could go undercover for you," Aunt Martha volunteered. "No one pays attention to old ladies. I could wander around the museum and listen in on conversations between the guards, watch where they go on their breaks."

"I appreciate the offer, Aunt Martha, but that won't be necessary."

"I'm good at solving mysteries." She elbowed my father. "Tell her."

"It's true," Dad grumbled. "She ruins all the TV shows for me, because she guesses who done it before the end."

The truth was, my aunt was a whodunit junkie. In addition to watching endless hours of *Murder, She Wrote* reruns, she owned every Agatha Christie book ever written and pestered me for details on my cases every chance she got.

"Real-life investigations aren't like what you see on TV," Tanner cut in. "They can be long and tedious, and if you do manage to root out the bad guy, he might not think twice about shooting you before the final act."

"*Icksnay* on the *angerday*," I muttered in pig Latin as Mom returned with a slab cake ensconced in flaming sparklers.

She set it in front of me.

"What's this for?" The cake itself was covered in white icing with crazy colored squiggles crisscrossing it in a surprisingly aesthetic chaos.

Tanner rose from his chair and tilted his head for a closer look. "Looks like that painting the FBI just recovered in Buffalo."

Mom beamed, then pressed a kiss to my cheek. "As soon as I heard the press conference on the radio this morning, I knew the FBI had you to thank for the recovery. We're so proud of you, honey."

My cheeks heated at the unexpected praise. "Thank you. I was only the authenticator. But it was pretty cool to be part of the recovery."

Taking his seat once more, Tanner winked at me.

"Did you know about this?" I asked.

Dad slapped him on the back. "He was *my* authenticator. Didn't want your mother to go to all the trouble of making a cake and then find out you'd really been in Des Moines, Iowa, or something."

I watched the sparklers fizzle in stunned fascination at my parents' impromptu surprise celebration. Mom had done an impressive job of mimicking a Kandinsky with colored icing. If only I could shake the niggling notion that this was some kind of reverse psychology to get me to quit.

Aunt Martha practically danced in her seat. "Yee! Wait 'til the girls at the hair salon hear."

"No!" Tanner and I exclaimed in unison. "You can't tell anyone she worked the case," he went on. "Or that she's worked undercover at all."

A hesitant "oh" dropped from Aunt Martha's lips.

Not good. Not good. *Not good.*

Never one to tiptoe around a problem, Mom blurted a tad hysterically, "Who did you tell?"

4

"I only told Mildred," Aunt Martha said. "She's a grandmother, for goodness' sake. It's not as if she's going to go blabbing about Serena working undercover to the bad guys."

"Mildred?" I repeated. Mildred who happened to notice me in the art gallery with my chalked-gray hair? "Mildred who called you the second she got home to tell you, and who knows who else, that she saw me spying on people at the art gallery this afternoon?"

Deflating, Aunt Martha squirmed. "Well, yeah."

"Mildred," my dad interjected, "whose niece is married to that biker gang guy?"

My heart hijacked my throat.

"Yes"—Aunt Martha conceded—"but it's *not* as if she ever sees them."

Muttering something about her aunt not wanting to know what nieces were capable of, Mom snatched the sparklers from the cake she'd baked and went at it with a knife. "Isn't she already in enough danger without you having to go out and blab about her to your cronies?"

"It's not that bad," I reassured Mom. And since I was apparently a terrible liar, I convinced myself I believed it too.

"Call her right now," Dad ordered Aunt Martha. "Tell her not to tell anyone."

Tanner cleared his throat, snapping everyone's attention his way. "In my experience, that only makes people talk more. Better to tell her you were wrong. That you couldn't resist spinning the yarn since you figured no one would be able to verify it, but that really Serena had been attending a training session in Des Moines."

"She'll never believe her," I said.

"Then she produces the receipts."

"What receipts?"

"I'll take care of those," Tanner said.

"Ooh, photographs would be even better," Aunt Martha chimed in.

Tanner nodded. "I can do photos."

Okeydokey, if the FBI could make it look like I was in Des Moines, that worked for me. I devoured a piece of Mom's cake, then sped through thank-yous and good-byes, promising to be back for Sunday dinner.

Stepping onto my parents' porch, carrying leftover cake, I glanced at the driveway. "How on earth?" I closed my eyes. Gave my head a hard shake. Then looked again. "How'd my car get here?"

"I asked Nolan and Frank to deliver it," Tanner said, as if it were an everyday occurrence.

"How'd they get it running? Change the battery?"

"Nah." He started down the steps.

"Well, what then?"

"So," he said conversationally, completely ignoring my question, "remember that time I had the flu and you forced me to watch *The Sound of Music*? In my weakened state?"

"There was a price to be paid for my mother's chicken soup. And don't change the subject." Where were the keys? Surely not in the ignition, where anyone could help themselves to a new set of wheels.

"I have to admit, you were right. It was an inspiring movie." Tanner opened my car's passenger-side door and rummaged beneath the seat. "At least, there was one part in it that I really liked."

I rolled my eyes. "Yes. I have superior movie tastes. *Stop de-flect-ing*." I mentally rewound to our exchange in the parking lot and in the office before that. To how Tanner had conveniently driven up to my car at just the right moment. To the call from my mom to *his* phone.

To Tanner *helpfully* looking under the hood.

"You did something to sabotage my car!"

Tanner emerged from the front of the car with my keys, not even bothering to hide his grin. "Like I said, the movie was inspiring." He slapped the keys into my palm.

I stared at them blankly. What was with all the movie talk? Suddenly, the scene from *The Sound of Music* crystallized in my mind: one of the

67

nuns holding up the severed wires from the Nazis' car, as the Von Trapp family escaped over the mountains.

Muffling a chuckle, I rattled the keys in my hand. "If you're comparing yourself to a nun, you are more delusional than I thought."

Tanner gave me a sympathetic look. "I know it's got to be confusing for you, since I obviously remind you of Christopher Plummer."

"Remind me of . . . ?" Oh, brother. Clearly, Tanner had caught on to my habit of associating people with well-known movie actors.

"You know? Because I'm so debonair."

"*Uh-huh*. Here, I thought you meant because he's so old."

"Ouch."

If Tanner thought I'd tell him who he really reminded me of, he had another think coming. His head was already big enough without needing to know that he reminded me of the dark-haired, devastatingly dimpled firefighter in the movie *Accidental Husband*, Jeffrey Dean Morgan.

Tanner gave me his most innocent look, which naturally I didn't trust a bit. "My motives for the sabotage were honorable."

I snorted. "Right. You wanted to bum a free meal out of my parents."

He chuckled. "Tell me you weren't going to use the art museum theft as an excuse to bail on them."

I wiggled under the intensity of his gaze.

"I just did what was necessary to ensure you didn't miss out on their surprise."

I squinted at him. "My dad promised you Blues hockey tickets, didn't he?"

He grinned. "That too. But aren't you glad you came?"

"Yes, thank you." I bumped his shoulder with my own. "You know if this gets around it'll ruin your live-eat-and-breathe-FBI image."

"Ah, but you're forgetting about those tickets." He pulled the car door farther open and stepped out of the way so I could set down the cake. It had been a fun surprise and a really nice evening, despite Aunt Martha's cat-out-of-the-bag confession and Mom's . . . dating advice.

Tanner hovered so close I almost bumped into him as I straightened. Something about the cover of darkness and the fluffy white flakes drifting lazily from the sky and the niggling thought that Mom might be right made me whisper, "Do you ever have doubts about being married to the job?" before I could censor the thought.

Tanner slung his arm over my doorframe with an exaggerated sigh. "Who has time when there are rookies in need of proof they were in Des Moines yesterday?"

"I'm trying to be serious here."

His gaze softened. "You know that spinster cat-lady thing is just a myth, right?" He back-stepped toward his SUV. "Because from where I'm standing, you're a long way from spinsterhood."

I cringed, not liking that that's what he thought I was worried about. I was more worried about who might be waiting for me at my apartment that shouldn't be there. And okay, yes, it was kind of lonely going home to an empty place sometimes.

Tanner was too astute for his own good.

"No way! *You're* the FBI agent?" the male college student and part-time security guard who'd slammed me into the stair railing yesterday said as he sauntered into the office Zoe had loaned me to conduct my interviews. He spun around the chair intended for him and straddled it with all the swagger of a third-generation chauvinist.

Woohoo, my day was already picking up and it was only 10:30. I set down my coffee mug, circled to the front of the desk, and perched on the corner. "Special Agent Serena Jones." I didn't extend my hand. "And you are?"

He tried to appear as if it didn't bug him to look *up* at me, if I'd read the tightness around his mouth right. "Malcolm Wilson."

I made a show of flicking through the screens on my smartphone. "Ah, yes, sophomore at SLU, studying criminology, B student, former high school quarterback"—I tsked sympathetically—"but didn't make the cut for the SLU team. Currently unattached." I paused for effect. "Drive a car that's seen better days, former employment includes flipping burgers at White Castle and hawking hotdogs at Busch Stadium. About right?"

His forehead had scrunched steadily tighter over the course of my recitation. "How do you know all that?"

I assumed my professional, semi-warm smile and turned my smartphone his way. "Social media."

He leaned back, his expression morphing into disbelief. "No way. You couldn't have gotten all that from my profile."

I pulled up his online photo album and flicked through it photo by photo as I expounded on what they told me about him. It was a trick Tanner had taught me to convince the kid he wasn't going to be able to bluff his way through my interview. "Tell me what you know about the missing art."

"Don't you have to read me my Miranda rights or something first?"

I tilted my head. "Why? You're not under arrest. We're just talking."

He jutted his chin and attempted to cross his legs, only to be foiled by the back of the chair he'd chosen to straddle. "Oh, yeah, right. And I couldn't have taken anything anyway, because I'm only bottom-level security."

I nodded. Bottom-level security meant he monitored only public rooms and only during business hours. Considering how guys like him couldn't resist flaunting their conquests, I would have agreed that the likelihood he'd managed to sneak down to the storage vaults and pilfer a couple of paintings, and then have the self-control not to boast about it, was pretty low. Except typically only the guilty offered an immediate reason why they couldn't have committed a crime.

"What makes you think the art wasn't taken during business hours?"

He dismissed the possibility with a flick of his wrist. "We scrutinize every person walking out of the place. If someone tried to smuggle something out, we'd have noticed."

"What about employees exiting by the back door?"

His gaze drifted to the window that overlooked the main office area. "I guess employees would have an easier time slipping something out."

I followed the direction of his gaze and almost teetered off the corner of the desk. "Excuse me a minute." I hurried out of the office and through the adjoining administrative area.

Zoe, who'd been reviewing files at a nearby desk, chased after me. "What's wrong?"

I flung open the door, spying Aunt Martha's blue-gray curls bobbing past the circular reception desk in the center of the atrium, and tore after her. I caught the sleeve of her wool coat a second before she switched her trajectory toward an unwitting security guard. "No you don't."

Aunt Martha yanked her arm from my grasp and turned to glare at me, only . . .

She wasn't Aunt Martha. "I'm sorry," I stammered. "I thought you were someone else." I about-faced and crashed into Zoe.

"Hey!" Zoe rubbed the arm I'd accidentally elbowed. "Do you mind telling me what's going on?" Her voice dropped to a hiss close to my ear. "I thought you were foiling a robbery or something."

I glanced around, and realizing half a dozen staff members had circled the Aunt Martha look-alike and me, I wished I could dive under Monet's water lilies and pretend it never happened. "I thought I saw my aunt," I said.

Zoe dismissed the staff who'd run to my aid. "And that's a problem why?"

I looked at her as if she'd grown two heads. "Are you forgetting about Thanksgiving?" She'd interrogated every household on the street, all but accusing them of heisting our Thanksgiving turkey out of the garage fridge, only to return home to find Dad deep frying it in the backyard.

Zoe's eyes ballooned. "Are you telling me you told her about the missing paintings?"

"No, of course not. She guessed."

Zoe moaned.

"The good news is she's not here." *At least not yet.* By the time I returned to the office, Malcolm had reseated himself the right way and was intent on the screen of his phone—an online chat by the looks of it—with his thumbs tapping out a message at lightning speed.

"Aren't you supposed to leave cell phones in your locker before starting your shift?"

He hit the screen one last time, then shoved the phone in his pocket. "I forgot."

If every teen I knew didn't spend every spare minute on his phone, I might've been suspicious. I pulled my chair around from behind the desk and sat down. "Sorry for the interruption. Do you have any theories on how the thief got from the vault to the back door without anyone noticing them?" I leaned toward him to convey how sincerely I'd value his input. Okay, the sincerity was smoke and mirrors, but more than once, the line had given me a lead.

"Wouldn't have happened on my shift."

"How can you be sure?"

"Because I do my job. And I want to keep it."

Okay, so I was asking the wrong question. "Anyone come to mind who might be desperate enough to take the risk?" Last night's internet searches hadn't turned up any urgent motives that I could tell.

Malcolm pursed his lips, twisting them sideways. "Yeah, Linda Kempler." The derision in his voice made me wonder if she was an ex-girlfriend. Spurned partners, or wannabe partners, made for very talkative—if not always truthful—witnesses. "She was helping with the kids' programs."

"Her motive?"

"Money. She lives in The Loop."

The trendy shopping and entertainment area, attracting an eclectic mix of people, had acquired its name from the streetcar turnaround or "loop" formerly located in the area.

"Rent has to be more than what she can afford working here. I figure she only took the job to get her hands on some paintings."

"What makes you think that? A boyfriend or roommate might help pay her rent."

"Because from day one she was real nosy. Asked lots of questions like she was trying to figure out who she could trust and who she couldn't."

"Did you notice anyone in particular she spent more time talking to than the others?"

"Yeah, Cody Stafford. He was really into the art."

"Was?"

"He quit at the end of the year. She talked to the receptionists a lot too. Of course, everyone does that."

"She talk to you?"

"Sure."

"What kind of questions did she ask?"

"What I was studying in school. If I was interested in politics. If I voted in the last election. That kind of thing."

"And you found that suspicious?"

"Sure. Then, this morning, her brother shows up looking for her. Only she's called in sick."

"Thank you. I'll be sure to catch up to her."

Malcolm's swaggering smile returned, causing me to take everything he'd just said with a boulder-sized grain of salt.

"What about yourself? Students can always use money, right?"

He tugged at his collar. "Not me. My dad's a janitor at the university. My tuition's covered."

"Yes, I was able to enjoy the same perk," I admitted, hoping the common experience would enhance my rapport with him. "What about drug money? Are you aware of any employees with a drug problem?" He didn't strike me as a user, but in the last decade, art crime had become a far-too-popular means of financing drugs.

"Nah, not here."

"Okay." I stood to signal the end of our interview. "Thank you for your time, Malcolm." I offered my hand. "I appreciate your candor."

His grip was dry and firm, topsy-turvying my sense that he hadn't been altogether straight with me.

Zoe looked my way as I stepped out of the office behind Malcolm.

I gave my head a tiny shake to indicate that he wasn't likely our man. After he exited the reception area, I asked Zoe, "What can you tell me about Linda Kempler?"

"She seems nice."

"Malcolm seems to think she lives beyond her means."

"She only works here part time, so she might have a better paying job the rest of the time."

"Malcolm said she called in sick this morning?"

"Oh." Zoe scanned the schedule posted on the wall behind her. "Yes, her name's been crossed out. I can get you her contact information so you can reach her at home."

"Yes, do that. And speak to her closest colleagues. Find out what they know about her."

"The employees have been doing a lot of whispering amongst themselves since you started interviewing this morning." She turned to her computer and brought up the employee database.

"Any of them seem nervous about the prospect of being interviewed?"

"Not that I've noticed."

Irene, the plump, fifty-something, strawberry blonde administrative assistant who'd been gathering employee files for me, appeared at my side. "Henry Burke looked pretty nervous when he told you he had to leave early," she said to Zoe.

Burke. If I recalled right from my background research . . . "The sixty-four-year-old that's been here forty years?"

"Yes," Zoe confirmed. "And my most trusted

security guard. If his wife hadn't already been sick last summer when our former security chief died, Burke would be the one talking to you right now instead of me."

"Why'd he leave work this morning?"

"He said he didn't like how his wife sounded when he phoned her during morning break. She has kidney failure and has to go in for dialysis several times a week. He asked if we could spare him for the rest of the day."

"But he seemed nervous?"

Zoe flashed Irene an annoyed look. "No, upset."

Yeah, having a hot painting in his basement and an FBI agent closing in would do that.

"Upset about his wife," Zoe insisted, handing me Linda's phone number and address. "She slipped into a depression a few weeks ago when the kidney transplant they'd been hoping for didn't pan out."

"It's so sad," Irene agreed, depositing a new stack of files on Zoe's desk. "These are the employees who've left us in the past nine months."

As I perused the top file, I tried Linda's number. When it went to voice mail, I left a message asking her to call me. The top file belonged to Cody Stafford, another name Malcolm had mentioned. According to his paperwork, Cody had been a summer intern from Wash U and then stayed on part time until the end of December— more than a month before the paintings were discovered missing and conceivably before they went missing.

Had Malcolm pointed a finger at Linda and Cody because their absence made him truly suspicious or because it made them believable suspects to misdirect my investigation?

"Irene, could you get me Henry Burke's address and phone number? I'd like to interview him next."

Zoe's attention jerked up from the employee file she'd been reviewing. "You're going to his house?"

I tossed her my uh-yeah-I'd-be-an-idiot-not-to stare. "He heard about the investigation this morning when you introduced me at the staff meeting. Realizes he still has the painting stashed that he couldn't find a buyer for and decides he better get rid of it fast."

"Not Henry." Zoe slapped the file in front of her. "Think about it. The real thief would've suspected we'd discovered the paintings were missing when we started doing inventories of the vaults two days ago, or at least that the discovery was imminent. If the thief had been stupid enough to hang on to the painting, he'd have gotten rid of it long before now."

"But Burke didn't know," Irene chimed in. She handed me a slip of paper with his contact information, then walked over to the scheduling board and traced a finger along the row for

Burke's name. "He's been off the past four days. Since *before* we started inventory."

That settled it. "I'm heading to Henry Burke's. I'll finish the other interviews later." If I didn't already have my suspect in custody.

Mr. Burke lived on a quiet street in a largely Italian neighborhood south of Dogtown known as The Hill. It was becoming less unusual for a non-Italian to live in the neighborhood, but it would've been unusual at the time Burke bought his home, unless perhaps his wife was Italian. The Hill was the kind of neighborhood where people bought a house and lived in it until death kicked them out. Then the home would often be sold privately to someone else in the neighborhood who was ready to move out of Mom and Pop's place.

The thirteen-year-old Buick in the driveway and the curling shingles on the bungalow's roof were testimony to how much money his wife's medical bills must be consuming. Patrolling the museum's vaults day in and day out, knowing the staff rarely inventoried the holdings in storage, had to have been unbearably tempting. Tamping down a sudden swell of compassion for the man, I parked behind the Buick and strode to the front door.

A salt-and-pepper-haired gentleman of average height and build answered after the first knock.

"Mr. Burke?"

"Yes."

"I'm Special Agent Serena Jones. May I come in and ask you a few questions?"

He stepped on the threshold, pulled the door up close behind him, and lowered his voice. "It's not a good time," he whispered. "My wife's not well."

"Is that the police?" a wobbly female voice called from far behind him. "Let them in."

Burke gave me a pained look. "She's a little disoriented. She thought we had an intruder after I left for work this morning. I came straight home, but nothing appears to be missing or disturbed." He said it smoothly, as if it was fact, not a quickly thought-up lie.

"Did you call the police?"

"I didn't see the point. She's on heavy medication. I'm not sure she didn't imagine it."

"I want to talk to them," his wife insisted from somewhere behind him.

He sighed and swung open the door. "Come on in."

The door opened into a small living room, decorated in the pinks and blues popular over two decades ago. Generations of family photos covered the walls. No art. Mrs. Burke sat in a recliner angled toward a TV of the same vintage. Between her sallow skin tone and sunken eyes and cheeks, she looked ten years older than her husband. I walked to her chair and extended my hand. "Hello, Mrs. Burke. I'm Serena."

Frowning, she looked me up and down. "You're not a policeman."

"No, ma'am, I'm with the FBI." I pulled aside my jacket to show her the badge I'd clipped to my belt.

Her eyes brightened. "Good, good. Glad to see the old man's taking me seriously for once."

I slanted a curious glance toward Mr. Burke.

His mouth flattened into an unreadable line as he clasped her hand. "You know I wouldn't let anyone hurt you." He had thick, hairy fingers, blunt nails, heavy veins rippling the skin, nothing like the hand—

I blinked, startled by the sudden recollection. I hadn't thought I saw . . . but maybe I was wrong. Staring at Burke's hand, I tried to recapture the image that had flickered through my mind—a hand returning a book to the shelf. But the wispy childhood memory refused to resurface.

The sound of Mrs. Burke's voice snapped me back to the present. "I'm sorry, what was that?"

"I said I didn't think the FBI investigated prowlers."

"Not as a rule, no." I pulled up a chair to Mrs. Burke's side and flipped to a new page in my notebook. "Tell me what you saw."

"Oh, I didn't see anyone. I heard a noise in the garage."

My gaze snapped to her husband, who'd taken a seat beside her.

He shook his head. "She might've heard me leaving, then nodded back to sleep. All the doors were still locked when I got home. Nothing was missing from the garage. She sleeps late, so it could've been a car rumbling by or kids playing in the neighbor's yard or any number of things that startled her awake."

I nodded. "Where do you keep your valuables, Mrs. Burke?"

Her gaze dropped to her hands, now clenched in her lap. "Here." She touched the modest diamond ring loosely encircling her left finger, then reached for her husband's hand again and smiled. "And here."

"Our valuables went to the pawnshop a long while ago," he explained, "to help us stay ahead of the medical bills our insurance doesn't cover." He brought his wife's hand to his lips. "But we have each other. That's all that matters."

My throat clogged. If Burke stole those paintings, I hoped he got a decent amount for them, and then, because it was my job, I asked, "Who bought the paintings?"

Burke held my gaze without so much as a flinch. "We never owned any. Got to see all the art a soul could want working at the museum."

"You're aware some pieces are missing from the museum?" We'd deliberately kept the exact nature of the missing pieces vague during the staff meeting, hoping to trip up the thief—the only person aside from the board, Zoe, and myself who knew exactly what was missing.

His wife gasped. "No!" She turned to her husband. "They aren't blaming you, are they? You weren't even working the last few days."

He patted her hand. "No, dear. Not as far as I know." His gaze returned to mine with a silent "Am I a suspect?" in his eyes.

Oh, man, as much as my mother wanted grandchildren, she'd disown me if I arrested this poor woman's husband. "I'm interviewing *every* staff member."

"My Henry wouldn't steal a penny. You're welcome to search the house," his wife said, reaching over the side of her recliner. She opened a drawer at the back of the end table and pulled out a stack of papers—hospital bills and bank statements. "And look at these."

From the look of Mr. Burke's pinched expression, not being able to pay them was pure torture.

I flashed him an apologetic glance as I accepted the papers from his wife. Even with much of the cost covered by his employee health plan, the amount outstanding was significant, and no lump sum had recently been paid off or deposited to their meager bank balance. Although I didn't think he was foolish enough to give himself away by such a slip. I nodded at the paperwork as if it proved Mrs. Burke's defense and handed it back. "Is it all right with you if I search the house as well?"

Burke's eyes looked puppy-dog sad, like a loyal retriever who'd lost his master's trust. "Go ahead."

"I appreciate it." He followed me around as I searched, which, given the bare state of their cupboards and closets and even their garage, didn't take long. Not that I'd expected to find the paintings. Burke was too intelligent to still have them. But perhaps another clue—a key to a locker, a name or number scribbled on a piece of paper. "Do you recall seeing anyone near the museum's vaults who shouldn't have been there?" I asked him, returning to the chair I'd been sitting in. "Anyone acting nervous? Anyone looking awkward as they walked out, as if trying to conceal something?" This time of year, the small paintings would be easy enough to conceal under a coat, but not in the middle of summer.

"Only a handful of staff have access to the lower level. But last summer, a couple of tradesmen worked in that area, repairing a plumbing leak and damaged drywall. I kept a close eye on them, but . . ." He shrugged. "Maybe not close enough."

"Did these men ask you about the art? Its value? Anything like that?"

"Not directly. I overheard the younger one, Norman, I think his name was, ask the other one what he thought it was worth."

"What did he say?"

A grin teased the corners of Burke's lips. "Five to ten at the federal prison."

5

Since I had nothing to show for my field trip to Henry Burke's, I opted to circle around to Linda's apartment before returning to the museum. The Loop was a vibrant six-block section of Delmar Boulevard famous for its boutique stores, night-life, walk of fame, and Blueberry Hill restaurant, but Malcolm had been wrong about Linda living in The Loop. She lived on the other side of the tracks, so to speak, closer to the psychiatric hospital than to the trendy shops of The Loop.

When I caught sight of a dilapidated garage hugging the street not far from her building, I started to seriously question Malcolm's trust-worthiness. Linda's building was an older red-brick three-story, not run-down but certainly not luxury living as Malcolm had suggested. In a few of the windows, faded sheets passed for curtains.

The front door wasn't locked, so there was no buzzer and accompanying tenant list, but according to Ms. Kempler's employment file, she lived in apartment 2B. I headed up. I'd attempted to phone several times without success, so I wasn't optimistic I'd find her home. But with any luck I might find a talkative neighbor.

The stairs creaked under my weight and smelled faintly of stale beer. As I reached the second floor, the smell of fresh paint overpowered the less palatable odor. The moss-green color giving a fresh look to the hall would've looked really good too, if the painter had taken the time to patch the walls first.

The walls weren't exactly soundproof either. As I approached Linda's door, I could hear the rants of *Judge Judy* blaring from a TV inside. At least that likely meant she was home. A second after I knocked, the TV went silent. I waited for the door to open.

Since she was undoubtedly on the other side, scrutinizing me through the peephole, I held up my badge. "Special Agent Serena Jones, St. Louis FBI," I said, loud enough to be heard through the door and probably through the walls of the neighboring apartments. "I'd like to ask you a few questions."

I cocked my ear toward the door.

A wily old woman poked her head out of the neighboring door, clasping the front of her faded red chenille housecoat under her chin. "He just hightailed it out the back window."

"He? A roommate of Linda's?"

"No, she lives alone, but I haven't seen her in a couple days."

"You're sure?"

"Yes."

"Thanks!" I bolted down the stairwell, two steps at a time. If Linda wasn't there, who jumped out the window, and what was he doing in Linda's apartment? I charged out the front door and around the side of the building.

The guy hadn't even made it down yet. I checked my adrenaline at the curb and scrutinized the shirtless white male clinging to the brick wall like a rock climber. Only he was so scrawny he looked as if a good wind would blow him off. He shot me a panicked glance, hopefully taking serious stock of the wisdom of fleeing a federal agent.

I snapped a picture of him with my smartphone, figuring he had to have committed a crime somewhere. "What's your name?" I demanded, maintaining enough distance to draw my weapon if needed. "Why'd you run?"

His gaze shifted to the cracked pavement, decorated with smashed beer bottle fragments. "No law against running."

"True." But like the proverb said: the wicked flee though no one pursues.

His fingers whitened, clenched around the edge of the bricks, his socked foot frantically seeking a new toehold.

Okay, a guy who kicked off his shoes in a house he was burglarizing would be a new one. I ignored the fleeting thought that my "reasonable suspicion" for detaining him might not appear all that reasonable to a judge.

It'd been a long day and I was losing my

patience. I touched my gun, still holstered on my hip. "On the ground. Now. Hands where I can see them."

He skidded down the bricks, then took off at a run.

"Seriously? In sock feet?" I loped after him. Wow, did he think that was a pace? "Hey, why you runnin'? You know I'm going to catch you, right?"

He veered across the empty lot behind the building, but from the sound of his huffing, he was too busy breathing to answer.

Reaching his side before he hit the back alley, I contemplated tackling him, but figured, why risk hurting myself? "You don't have good runner's form, you know. You should lengthen your stride and pump your arms forward and back, not in front of your stomach."

His pace picked up a fraction.

I matched it without breaking a sweat. "You know, to qualify as an FBI agent, I clocked a mile and a half in under twelve minutes. And you have sock feet. Getting tired?"

He flattened his hands as if it would help him cut through the air faster.

"C'mon, let's stop and talk."

He slanted me a scowl that almost looked fierce, thanks to his reddening face, then ducked into the back of the next apartment building's lot.

"Try not to fall in that broken glass," I called after him. "Do you know what a Taser is?"

He ground to a stop and bent over, holding his chest.

I stepped in front of him, hands on my hips, barely breathing. "You're really out of shape, you know. Now tell me what you were—"

He suddenly straightened and jerked back his fist as if he might throw a punch.

"Okay, fun's over." I "guided" him into the side of a dumpster. "On your knees. Hands on your head."

"I didn't do anything," he gasped.

"Ever heard of resist, obstruct, delay?" Yeah, it was bogus, at least the implication I could charge him with it, but it convinced him to comply. I cuffed his hands behind his back and hauled him to his feet. "What's your name?"

"Stan Johnson."

I patted him down, figuring I'd find a weapon, dope, or something, since he'd been too busy breathing to toss anything as he ran. All I scored was his wallet. No money, but his driver's license said Stan Johnson, and the picture looked like a paler version of the guy still gulping air in front of me. "Your license says you're from Tulsa. You're a long way from home."

He didn't respond.

I flipped through the other items in his wallet, pausing on a photograph of him with a woman that could be Linda, based on the photo I'd seen in her employee file. "Where's your gun, Stan?"

"I don't have a gun."

The flinch in his cheek said otherwise. Back in the apartment, maybe. I was going to need backup to do that search.

"Who's your probation officer?"

"What?" He sounded indignant. "I'm not a criminal."

I pulled out my smartphone and called dispatch, asking them to send backup and to see if Stan had any warrants on him. Coming up empty, I irritably sucked air through my teeth. He was guilty of something.

"You're arresting me?"

"That depends on what you were doing in Linda's apartment." I caught him by the elbow and prodded him up the side alley. "Let's go have a look, shall we? And finish this discussion inside."

He resisted.

I narrowed my eyes at him. "There a problem?"

"Don't you need a search warrant?"

Great, I was dealing with a detective-show junkie. Time to throw out the big words. "Not in an exigency."

"A what?"

"An emergency." I tightened my grip on his elbow and "helped" him move forward.

"How do you figure?" He was limping. Probably had a cut on his foot, too.

I steered him toward the building's front door

and yanked it open. "The way I see it is, no one has seen or heard from Linda Kempler in days. I show up to check on her and you flee her apartment. Naturally I think you've hurt her. That gives me the authority to check on her welfare." Sure, the neighbor said she wasn't in there, but that was hearsay.

"I'd never hurt Linda."

I hoped that was true or I was going to really regret stalling back there.

"She's my sister."

"Sister, huh?" Malcolm had mentioned something about Linda's brother looking for her. "So why the different last name? She's not married." At least her status in her employee file had been listed as single with no dependents.

"Yeah, they told me at the museum."

"They *told* you."

"I've been out of the country. When I heard she had a new last name, I assumed she got married without bothering to let me know." He dragged his feet on the stairs, clearly not wanting me to see inside that apartment, and yup, he definitely had a cut on that foot. He left behind smears of blood. "How was I supposed to know if the badge you flashed was real or not? You hear stories all the time of people impersonating cops to worm their way into a house."

Guess my daily gym workout was paying off if I had him that spooked.

"Is Linda in some kind of trouble?"

"That's what we're going to find out." I pushed him in front of me and up to Linda's door. What was taking my backup so long? My gut told me there was no one in the apartment, at least not alive, or they would've fled too. But what if I was wrong?

I tightened my grip on Stan's arm. If I was wrong and his cohorts decided to shoot, he'd be my bullet trap. He'd be more likely to warn me that way. I gave him a moment to contemplate that, then reached around him and pounded loudly on the door. "FBI, open up."

Not a sound came from inside the apartment.

I tried the handle. Locked.

The same neighbor lady stuck her head out her door again, took one look at Stan in cuffs, and then slammed her door shut. The click of three deadbolts followed. I hoped Stan hadn't thrown the deadbolts on Linda's door, because he wasn't carrying a key. "On your knees." I pushed him to his knees in front of the door, then used his driver's license to shimmy the lock.

His chin dropped to his chest. "It's not what it looks like," he moaned.

My hand stilled on the doorknob. Okay, I didn't like the sound of that. I pushed the door in just enough to unlatch it, then I pulled him to his feet and drew my weapon. "You first."

"I was worried about her," he claimed as I

shoved the door with my foot and pushed him inside.

I didn't know what I'd expected—well, yeah, I did—but it wasn't this. A large, rolled-up rug was lying on the sofa, looking very much like a body could be hidden inside. Where it had once laid, if I went by the unfaded wood in the middle of the living room, there was a crowbar and a half-pried-up board.

Now the loud TV made sense. He'd been trying to muffle the sound of his "renovation."

I edged him forward slowly. The kitchen opened off the entrance to the left. I visually scanned it, nudged open the broom cupboard to ensure nobody was hiding, or being hidden, inside. I reached for the fridge door to do the same.

"You don't want to—"

I gagged as the smell of rotting meat caught me by the throat.

"—open that," Stan finished, too late.

I checked the packaging date on the rancid pound of ground beef—a week ago—then kicked the fridge shut. "When's the last time you talked to your sister?"

"Christmas."

I had a bad feeling about Linda's state of health and a lot of questions for Stan, but I needed to record his answers and I didn't want to let go of him until I'd finished checking the place. I quickly cleared the living room, aside from checking inside the rolled rug. Linda's tastes were spartan. Besides the sofa, she had an armchair and an end table. No stereo system. No phone, although these days that wasn't unusual. No books on the built-in bookshelf or papers in the drawers that were dangling precariously from their slots. No photographs on the walls. No art anywhere.

Of course, an art thief couldn't afford to covet what she stole.

Neither of the two bedrooms had closets. Only one had a bed. I glanced underneath it. No one hiding there. The dresser drawers were too small to conceal a person, so I didn't check them, but I had to wonder how any woman could fit her entire wardrobe into such a tiny bureau. Three outfits hung in the hall closet. A pair of sneakers sat on the floor beneath them. No other shoes or boots. No coats.

A single bath towel hung on the rack in the bathroom. A couple more were stacked on a shelf above the toilet. A small bottle of strawberry-scented shampoo occupied the tub shelf, along with a razor and dry bar of soap. A single toothbrush hung in the rusty chrome holder over the sink.

The place looked more like a hotel room than a residence.

I pushed Stan back to the living room and pulled over a hard-backed kitchen chair. "Sit." When he complied, I holstered my gun, then checked inside the rug. No body.

Good for Linda. Not so good for me. I no longer had a viable reason to detain Stan for questioning. Sometimes regulations really got in the way. I reluctantly unlocked his cuffs. *Then again . . .*

Anything found during an exigent search could be used in court, and the fact he'd been prying up floorboards in the apartment of an art museum employee had just rocketed him and his sister to the top of my suspect list.

Tanner chose that moment to race through the open doorway. "What's going on?"

"Ah, perfect timing." I pulled out a notebook and pen. "I was just about to ask Mr. Johnson a few questions." Drawing Tanner aside, I quickly caught him up on my missing suspect and Stan's claim that he was her brother, then turned back to Stan. "Is it unusual to not hear from your sister in over a month?"

He massaged his wrists, looking irritated. "Why are you looking for my sister?"

"Please answer the question."

"No, it isn't. Until six weeks ago, I'd been working overseas, so we didn't talk much."

Volunteering more information than I asked for. Interesting. His curiosity about my interest in his sister must've overpowered his desire to toss me out. That or Tanner was giving him the evil eye from behind me.

"But the last time we talked," Stan went on, "I told her I wanted to see her when I got back."

"Why?"

His gaze flicked to the pried-up floorboard. "It's none of your business."

"To kill her?"

He jolted at the accusation and almost toppled off his chair. "No! Of course not."

I tilted my head to check out the space beneath the boards—a space that could easily accommodate a rolled-up painting. "Are you in the habit of renovating her apartment when she's out of town?"

"She complained the floor was spongy."

My single slow nod said I didn't believe him. "Do you stay here?"

"Yeah, sometimes."

I shifted my gaze pointedly to the crowbar and back to him. "Sometimes, as in currently?" I avoided reminding him of the rotting meat in the fridge and could almost see the gears grinding in his head—he couldn't be accused of breaking into an apartment he was already living in.

"Yeah, *currently*."

Good, that solved my consent to search problem, since consent could be given by a person who controls something. Now to win his consent, one more time. "Do you have any dope or guns here?"

"No!" He sounded as indignant as I'd hoped.

"Mind if I check?"

His facial tic screamed "Yeah," but with a

no-skin-off-my-nose kind of shrug, he said, "Knock yourself out."

Perfect. Technically that meant I could search the common areas and his personal property. I got down on my knees and took a thorough look under the floorboards. Besides the remnants of a mouse nest, the space was clear. I turned over furniture cushions, burrowed my hand into the corners, found three quarters and a dime, and set them on the end table. I walked over every square inch of the floorboards, checking for "sponginess," and scoured kitchen cupboards and drawers. "Which bedroom's yours?"

Stan's eyes bulged in apparent panic, but he quickly recovered. "The first one."

"Stay here and watch him," I said to Tanner so I wouldn't have to worry about a knife in my back. In "Stan's" room, I checked the drawers—which were empty, surprise, surprise—then did a little cha-cha dance on the floorboards to test for other potential hiding spots. The floor was sound. The room was clean. No guns, no drugs, no art. No slip of paper with a middleman's number on it. No stash of cash.

Typically, a middleman might pay 3 or 4 percent of the painting's value to a thief, but Linda had probably counted on it being months before the theft was noticed and might've figured she had time to dispense with the middleman and go straight to a dealer, or better yet a collector.

She would've realized her time was up when Zoe started taking inventory.

I returned to the living room. "Did you just get into town today?"

"Yeah."

"Aren't you concerned that something might've happened to your sister? Most people wouldn't leave a pound of beef to rot in their fridge if they planned on being away."

"I figured she forgot. The message on her cell phone says she's on vacation."

"Really? So you didn't expect to find her here?"

He shrugged.

"Funny, because I've called her number a few times today and there was no mention of a vacation."

"I'm not lying," he blurted, and his indignant expression looked pretty believable.

"What's the number you dialed?"

He recited a number different than the one the museum had given me. There was no landline in the apartment, so why'd Linda have two numbers? I tapped Stan's into my phone, and sure enough, a female voice came on and said she was sorry she missed my call, but she was away on vacation and wouldn't be checking messages.

"Did you find her phone here?" It hadn't rung, but the battery might already be dead.

Stan shook his head.

"What did you find?"

"Nothing."

"Not what you were looking for?" Tanner piped up.

I reined in a wry grin. He'd been exercising tremendous self-control.

Stan let out an exasperated breath. "If you want to know the truth, our dad died of Alzheimer's while I was overseas. I couldn't make it back for the funeral, but I told Linda I'd be back as soon as I could to settle the estate. Only she said there was nothing left."

Hmm, that sounded like motive for murder.

"She said that the money was all used up paying for his care, but I don't believe it. She must've siphoned money out. Dad had a nice house and a good pension. Then when I got back to Tulsa, no one knew where she was. They said she'd moved away over a year ago. So what do you think I'm going to think when her phone says she's on vacation and then my friend spots her working here and discovers she's not even going by the same name?" He paused only a second. "I'll tell you what I think. She doesn't want me to find her because she's taken the entire inheritance for herself."

Okay, if that was true, she sounded like the type of person who might also steal paintings from the museum for an easy buck and then skip town.

The *Murder, She Wrote* ringtone jingled from my cell phone telling me Jessica Fletcher, aka

Aunt Martha, was calling. I let it go to voice mail, not wanting to invite any more questions about my investigation.

"You thought Linda hid the money under the floorboards?" Tanner asked.

Stan shrugged. "I felt a soft spot when I walked across the rug and thought I might get lucky. I figured she couldn't put it in a bank without me finding out. And when we were kids she used to have a loose board in the floor of her room that she hid things under."

"You really thought she'd leave a stash of money behind?" I hadn't seen a single sheet of paper in the whole place, with the possible exception of her bedroom. Not so much as a memo pad or pen or junk mail addressed to Occupant. If she'd cleared out that thoroughly, chances were she expected someone to search the place. But who? Her brother?

Or someone else?

If she'd been hired to pull the art museum heist and then decided to cut out the middleman, her handler wouldn't have taken kindly to being stiffed.

Was that why she didn't leave anything that might give away where she was headed? Or had whoever *planned* her latest trip not wanted any-one to find her?

I still wasn't sure what to believe about Stan, but my gut said he wasn't responsible for Linda's disappearance. I needed to talk to the neighbors, find out what they saw or heard. As I took down Stan's contact information, my cell phone rang again, this time signaling an incoming text from Aunt Martha's number. Only . . . it wasn't from Aunt Martha.

This is Nate. Call me as soon as you can. Urgent.

6

"Your aunt was attacked outside your apartment," Nate said without preamble.

"Is she okay?" I asked breathlessly. Aunt Martha often stopped by to visit old friends and the cat. Who would do something like this?

"Well enough to put up a stink about my calling the paramedics."

She needs a paramedic? Covering my phone's mic, I backed toward the door of Linda's apartment and looked from Stan to Tanner. "I need to go." His sympathetic nod said he'd overheard. "Can you talk to Linda's neighbors here? Find out when they last saw her and if she said where she was going and if anyone else has been here."

"Of course."

To Nate I said, "I'll be right there," and sped out the door.

"I'll wait with her in your apartment unless the paramedics decide she needs to go to the hospital."

"I don't need to go to the hospital," Aunt Martha groused in the background. She hated seeing a doctor worse than Harold hated going to the vet.

I raced out of the building to my car and headed west on Delmar, but traffic came to a standstill as I turned onto Skinker. I turned on my siren and bubble light. Cars magically moved out of my way. Had to appreciate the perks of the job when you could. Too bad I couldn't justify the trick on my way home from work at rush hour. I made it to my apartment in record time, but the ambulance driver was already climbing into the front of the ambulance.

I double-parked and sprang from my car. "Wait! My aunt? Is she in there?"

"No, still upstairs. But if she gets any worse, you should convince her to visit her doctor."

"Okay, thanks." Right. Short of handcuffing her and prodding her at gunpoint, getting her to a doctor wasn't going to happen. I headed toward the front door, only to be flagged down by a police officer.

"Hey, is that your car?"

"Oh, sorry." I hurried back to my car, drove it past the ambulance, and parked in the first available spot along the curb.

The ambulance driver must've filled the officer in on my relationship to their victim, because he was waiting for me outside the building. "You live in 2B?"

"Yes, I'm Special Agent Serena Jones. Have you caught the assailant?"

"No, he ran off before we arrived, but we've got a boot print and we're interviewing neighbors."

"You have a description yet?"

"Short, wearing faded blue jeans, mechanic's

gloves, and a large, gray, hooded parka that hid his face," the officer read from his notepad. "He was jimmying the lock on your kitchen door when your aunt shouted up the stairs at him. He raced down, knocking her over, and ran off."

"She interrupted a burglary?" I said, having a hard time keeping the relief from my voice.

"Seems so. You recognize the description?"

"No." When he started to ask another question, I said, "I'll be happy to answer all of your questions and ask a few of my own as soon as I've checked on my aunt, okay?"

"Of course."

Since an officer was still examining footprints around the outside stairs, I used the building's main entrance. To think I'd viewed the private entrance as a plus when I'd taken over Aunt Martha's lease. I let myself in to my apartment.

Aunt Martha sat at the kitchen table, her foot resting on a pillow propped on a second chair, her pant leg rolled up to her thigh, a gel ice pack draped over her knee, and Harold curled on her lap.

I lurched toward her. "Aunt Martha, I'm so sorry."

"Pfft. It's not your fault the hoodlum bowled me over. I was a silly old woman to shout at him. I should've stayed quiet and called the police."

"Or called me." Nate stood at the counter, filling my kettle with water and, in well-worn jeans and a black T-shirt, looking remarkably at home. He pulled the fine bone china teacup and saucer from my dish rack. "Do you want me to make you a cup, Serena?"

"I'm fine . . . and thank you for taking care of my aunt."

"My pleasure." He winked at Aunt Martha. "Besides, Martha's done her share of bringing me hot chicken soup when I've been under the weather."

Aunt Martha patted his arm and looked at him as if he'd hung the moon. "He's a keeper."

I tried not to read too much into what she meant by that, especially on the heels of last night's negative Tanner comments, and lifted the ice pack to examine her knee. "Are you in pain?"

"Nothing a little ibuprofen won't take care of."

"What did the paramedics say?"

"It's just bruised."

Nate swished boiling water around inside my teapot, poured it out, and dropped in a tea bag as if he knew how to brew a perfect pot. "They also said if the swelling persists she should see her doctor for an X-ray. Her blood pressure was slightly elevated and she twisted her wrist."

"There's nothing wrong with my vocal cords last I checked," Aunt Martha chided.

Nate squeezed her shoulder and leaned down, his mouth close to her ear. "I know you. You wouldn't have told her."

I laughed.

Aunt Martha shook her head at me. "You won't be laughing if your mother hears about this. She'll be after you to quit all over again."

"Why?" Nate asked. "What's your getting assaulted outside Serena's apartment have to do with her job?"

"Probably nothing, but that won't stop her mother."

I winced. What if it hadn't been a botched burglary attempt? What if it had been Baldy or one of his goons trying to break in? It was one thing to accept risks for myself, but what was I going to do if the bad guys went after my family too?

Aunt Martha patted my hand. "You should thank me for not letting those paramedics truck me off to the hospital or we'd have never been able to keep it a secret."

I gave her a warm hug. We'd shared lots of secrets over the years, but the idea of keeping one that might jeopardize her well-being made my stomach sour. "I couldn't bear it if you or anyone else got hurt because of me."

"Nonsense. Don't be using me as an excuse to quit." She patted the chair beside her. "Now sit and tell me about your new case."

"Oh, before I do that, I need to go out and answer the investigating officer's questions. I'll be back as soon as I can." And with any luck, by that time she'd be on to a new topic of conversation.

Nate splashed milk into the bottom of Aunt Martha's teacup. "No problem. I'll keep her company."

"Maybe I'll have a cup of that tea when I get back too," I said. "I have more china teacups in the cupboard by the fridge."

Nate grinned. "You were afraid I didn't know how to make a proper cup of tea, weren't you?"

Surprised by how well he had me pegged, I couldn't help but laugh. "You're right. Most guys tend to plunk a teabag in a mug and pour water over top."

"Yup, your aunt cured me of that habit. After I tasted how much better her tea tastes, I figured there had to be something to the ritual."

A pet sitter and a tea connoisseur. Nate was full of surprises.

I headed back outside, and by the time I caught up to the officer I'd talked to earlier, Tanner was already plugging him for details. "When did you get here?" I asked.

"A few minutes ago. Your suspect's neighbors weren't talking."

Figures. "Have you learned anything new?" I asked the officer.

"A neighbor saw the assailant run through the schoolyard at the end of the street. I've been advised that he may have had another motive for trying to get into your place, besides burglarizing it?"

I scowled at Tanner, who'd obviously done the advising. I wasn't about to name names. Not of suspects in an undercover investigation.

"If we had a name," the officer pressed, "we could pick up your suspect, compare his shoe treads. Put him in a lineup."

"I wish I could give you a name, but I can't." The assailant's description didn't even match Baldy's or Sidekick's anyway.

"Okay, well, I guess I don't need to advise you to take extra precautions."

"I will. Thanks." I waited while the officer climbed into his cruiser, then turned to Tanner. "What were you thinking? I can't drop the names of suspects from an undercover investigation."

"I know, but they needed to know this shouldn't be written off as some high school kid trying to score easy money."

"It could be!"

"Is that what you think?"

I wanted to. I really, really wanted to. I crossed my arms. "I don't know."

He sighed. "I'll ask Wainwright to track down your two Buffalo suspects."

I frowned. "Ask who?" I didn't recall meeting anyone named Wainwright, in Buffalo or elsewhere. I was usually good with names, but apparently I'd been too spooked, thanks to the key card fiasco.

"You know." Tanner fixed me with a speculative look. "Vin Diesel. *Fast and Furious*? The movie?"

"Oh! *Him*." Okay, I wasn't losing it. I was pretty sure no one had told me the guy's real name.

"Yes!" Tanner did a fist pump.

I stared, then blinked as comprehension dawned. "Really? You're wasting your highly developed FBI skills on figuring out which movie star I think people look like?"

"Yep," he said, looking smug.

"Well, get out of my head. It's creepy." Although . . . I had to admit he'd managed to momentarily distract me from my fears.

Tanner's look turned serious. "Just be careful, okay?"

I held his concerned gaze for a moment before looking away. "Always am." Giving him a mock salute, I headed back inside.

Nate poured me a cup of tea as I walked in and shrugged out of my coat. "Do they have any leads?"

"Not really." I repeated the rundown the officer had given me as I took the tea and sat at the table next to Aunt Martha.

"Enough about that," she said, patting my arm. "Tell us about the suspects you interviewed today."

"Aunt Martha, you know I can't talk about my cases."

"Oh, c'mon. Good detection is all about

thinking outside the box, and no one thinks further outside the box than me."

"I'm not sure where you got that quote from, but I'm pretty sure Holmes and Miss Marple would say good detection was all about keen observation and deduction."

Aunt Martha gave me her "pretty please" look.

Okay, after the tussle she'd had on my doorstep, the least I could do was humor her with a few minor case details to puzzle out. "Promise me not a word leaves this room?"

She held up three fingers. "Scout's honor."

I looked to Nate, who was leaning against the counter watching us, sipping tea, his long legs stretched in front of him. He lowered his teacup and mimicked my aunt's promise.

I gave them a sketchy overview of the crime.

"And what did the suspects have to say?" Aunt Martha asked.

I shook my head. "Sorry. Loose lips sink ships."

"Exactly, so if you loosen yours, maybe we can help you sink this guy."

"What makes you think it's a man?"

Aunt Martha's lips stretched into a gleeful grin. "You think it might be a woman?"

"Maybe." Okay, I probably shouldn't encourage her, but it felt good to see her glowing again.

"Oh, I bet she travels a lot. Smuggles paintings out of the country in her luggage and sells them before anyone knows they're missing."

Nate watched Aunt Martha's animated theorizing, his eyes dancing with amusement.

"What did she say when you interviewed her?" Aunt Martha jabbered on.

The woman was irrepressible. "Actually, the suspect wasn't home," I admitted, and then because Aunt Martha was so eager to vicariously experience the exciting life she assumed I lived, I relayed my adventure chasing Linda's brother.

"So you think she's skipped town? Are you going to check her credit card records? Find out where she's been?"

"I don't have enough probable cause to obtain a search warrant for banking records."

"But she could be long gone before you know it. If she used to be a flight attendant, she can fly for free. Might not even show up on the radar."

Aunt Martha cupped her chin and tapped her finger to her cheek, looking as if she was deep in contemplation. Suddenly she whisked her finger into the air. "I've got it. She's really a spy and her job at the museum is just a cover. You know, like that traveling shoe salesman who was really a CIA agent and his family didn't even know it."

"That was a movie. Not for real."

"But that's how they operate." Aunt Martha said this *very* matter-of-factly, as if she had firsthand knowledge of such a person.

Nate nodded. "It's true. When I applied to join

the CIA, they told me not to tell my family I was even applying."

I gaped. Nate was average height and build, not Navy Seal toned like Tanner. Then again, CIA agents were spies, not SWAT guys on atomic steroids. And with those hypnotizing blue eyes and that inscrutable smile, not to mention his tad-too-long windswept hair begging for a woman's touch, Nate could sell me shoes, state secrets, whatever he wanted. "You applied to the CIA?"

He laughed. "I'm kidding."

Only his wink to Aunt Martha left me wondering.

"Do any of the guards look good for the theft?" Nate asked, changing the subject. "That's who I'd be looking at."

I shrugged, thinking of Mr. Burke. "There's one gentleman that I almost wouldn't blame for pinching them. He's utterly devoted to his sick wife and they've long since hocked all their valuables to pay medical bills. But if he managed to steal and then sell the stolen items, there's no evidence he put the money to good use."

Aunt Martha suddenly dropped her foot to the floor and sat ramrod straight. "Sick how?"

Uh-oh. I'd tried to be generic enough in my descriptions so that the pair of them wouldn't be able to narrow in on anyone specific.

"She have cancer? Heart trouble? Alzheimer's? Need a transplant?" Aunt Martha tilted her head, her eyes widening. "She does, doesn't she? I can tell by your face."

Harold circled in Aunt Martha's lap, then, failing to find the sweet spot again, stretched long and slow, all the while giving me the evil eye, as if it was my fault.

"You can't tell by my face. And I'm not at liberty to say."

"But you know there's this band of organ thieves going around pouncing on hapless business travelers, right? They spike a person's drink, then sneak into his hotel room later and hack out the person's organ, then leave him in the bathtub with instructions to call 911 as soon as he wakes up."

I buried my face in my hands and shook my head.

"It's true!"

I shifted two fingers and peeked between them.

Nate's chest was jiggling, his lips pressed so tightly together they turned white.

Except the frequency with which Aunt Martha got hoodwinked by such stories wasn't funny. It drove my father—reasoning professor that he was—downright batty. I wasn't far behind. "Let me guess," I said drily. "You saw it on last week's episode of *Undercover CSI*."

"No, a friend emailed me a warning about it. A smart friend." She punctuated the last part with an indignant foot stomp. "Not someone who falls for those email hoaxes."

"Aunt Martha, it's an urban legend. Don't you think you'd hear about that sort of thing on the 6:00 news if it were true?"

The light blinked out of her eyes and she ducked her head. "Well, I suppose."

"I told you to always double-check those kind of emails on the Snopes website. If I recall right, in that case, what they think started the legend was a Middle Eastern man's claim that he'd had an organ stolen from him while visiting England. What investigators actually found was that he'd advertised to sell one of his organs and traveled there for that purpose."

"So people do buy organs! That's what I was getting at."

"Help me," I mouthed to Nate.

The corners of his eyes crinkled, and twin dimples poked his cheeks.

Oh, he wasn't going to be any help at all.

Aunt Martha plucked Harold off her lap and plunked him on the floor. "I know just who to ask to get an inside scoop too. Lou."

"As in Lou Petrolli?"

"Of course."

I splayed my hand over my forehead and groaned. Lou was an old family friend who happened to own an Italian restaurant on The Hill. And Aunt Martha seemed to think that anyone with an Italian name had to somehow know someone who was connected to the mafia.

Not that Lou had helped matters. When she once complained about the city ignoring her calls about blown streetlight bulbs or something, he'd said in his deep, mysterious voice that if she wanted, he *knew* people. I fought to keep my voice even. "Aunt Martha, I'm a federal agent. If anyone in St. Louis was negotiating the sale of body parts, I'm pretty sure I'd have caught wind of it."

Nate chuckled.

"But you love Lou's deep-fried ravioli." She patted her hair as if she were preparing for a date. "And his tiramisu."

Not fair. Aunt Martha knew I couldn't say no to Lou's tiramisu—layers of sponge cake soaked in coffee and liqueur with powdered chocolate and mascarpone cheese. My stomach grumbled just thinking about it, and Aunt Martha donned a smug smile.

"Nate, you should come too," Aunt Martha said in a tone that brooked no argument. "We might need a bodyguard."

His eyes danced with laughter, as he no doubt pictured being greeted by my Glock yesterday morning. "Your niece has formidable self-defense moves. I think you'll be fine."

"Please join us," I said. "My treat. A thank-you for taking care of Harold." Secretly, I hoped Aunt Martha's restaurant suggestion was merely a ploy to score an Italian dinner. Not to set me up with Nate or to go on an organ hunt. Saturday night at my parents' house was steak night, and Aunt Martha had never been a fan. Hard to chew with her false teeth, she'd once confided. But in case she actually intended to grill Lou about organ-selling middlemen, I figured I'd need a second pair of hands to keep her away from the people with the straitjacket.

7

If The Hill was a food, it would be spaghetti, or maybe pizza, or ravioli or manicotti. Well, anything Italian. The kind of food you share with a boisterous group of friends or family and that's guaranteed to put a smile on your face. As the hostess led us through the dimly lit restaurant to the last remaining empty table, I couldn't believe my eyes or good fortune. I was 95 percent certain the blonde sitting at the table in the back corner, wearing the pricey designer dress and an even pricier diamond necklace, was Linda Kempler. I pulled out my phone to search the photos I'd downloaded.

Nate caught my elbow and nudged me forward. "Everything okay?"

I looked from the photo on my phone to Linda. Yup, definitely Linda. "Yes. Thank you. Everything's perfect." I slid into the booth opposite my aunt and Nate gave me an odd look. "What's wrong?" I asked.

"Wouldn't you prefer to sit on that side?"

I glanced toward Linda's table—a perfect view. "No, I'm good. Thanks."

He slid in beside Aunt Martha. "Okay, but I thought cops never sat with their back to a room." He leaned across the table and added in a stage whisper, "Especially when their aunt might ask the wrong person the wrong question."

Aunt Martha swatted his arm. "Watch it or I'll make you pay for dinner."

He rubbed his arm, grinning. "Wouldn't have it any other way."

"No, it's my treat," I said. "Wouldn't want anyone to think you're bribing a federal agent."

"Ri-i-i-ght," he said, his incredibly expressive eyes twinkling with amusement, "because someone might think I stole the outrageously valuable paintings kicking around my apartment."

"Exactly."

"Good evening, everyone. Welcome to Lou's." A bubbly, dark-haired waitress handed us each a menu. "My name's Lori and I'll be your server this evening. May I start you off with a drink?"

"Just water for me," I said, doing a quick survey of the other customers. There was an eclectic mix of diners, from seniors and businessmen to a table of college students, who were probably here for the all-you-can-eat spaghetti, to couples like Linda and her date. His Armani suit and polished shoes screamed *wealthy,* and from the look of the pale line circling his slender ring finger, he was either recently separated or pretending to be.

"Someone you know?" Nate asked.

"Just a museum employee I didn't get a chance to interview today."

"A suspect?" Aunt Martha chimed in. "Because,

in case you hadn't noticed, she couldn't have paid for that outfit on a museum salary."

Oh, I'd noticed all right.

"More likely she entices rich boyfriends to treat her," Nate said, his voice tinged with disgust.

Aunt Martha flashed him a sympathetic look.

Okay, what was *that* about? Nate was hardly the kind of guy who'd have his heart broken by a gold digger.

The waitress cleared her throat.

"Oh, hot water and lemon for me," Aunt Martha said, then excused herself to go to the restroom.

Nate tapped the top of his menu to mine, snagging my attention again. "So, when did you first decide you wanted to be a federal agent?"

"A few months after 9/11. The day the FBI recovered the Norman Rockwell painting of the Boy Scouts, with the World Trade Center in the background. Did you know that over a hundred million dollars worth of fine art was destroyed during 9/11?"

"No, I had no idea, but I imagine a lot of the offices were decorated with valuable paintings."

I nodded, my gaze straying back to Linda and her date. He looked like the kind of guy who'd have expensive art on his walls. "Their loss was nothing compared to the lives lost, of course, but the art that survived became compelling symbols for many people."

"Including you?"

His soft question jerked my attention back to his face.

He looked at me expectantly, his gaze as soft as his question had been, almost as if he knew he was treading into risky territory.

"Yes, including me."

He nodded. "I remember seeing pictures of a sculpture still standing amidst the rubble of Liberty Park. It was of a businessman looking into his briefcase, and it became a kind of makeshift memorial."

"Yes! It was a J. Seward Johnson sculpture called *Double Check*. Every time I saw it, I cried." Tears welled in my eyes just thinking about it. I blinked them away. "The businessman reminded me of my grandfather, I guess. He'd been a business-man, but he also loved art and nurtured my love of it." The recollection drew my gaze back to Armani guy's hands.

"He gave you a special gift. Art shows us ways of seeing the world that science can't."

"Exactly! Most law enforcement officers don't put a high value on art crime investigation, because they think only the rich are losing, but we all lose a piece of our common heritage. For me, the return of that Rockwell painting helped reclaim a small piece of the American ideal we all lost that horrible day."

"And the day your grandfather died."

"Yes," I admitted, flinching at how easily he'd

read my thoughts. Apparently I needed to work on my poker face with more than just my family. "My grandfather used to say, 'Life beats us down and crushes the soul, while art reminds us that we have one.'"

"I think Stella Adler said it first," Aunt Martha said, returning to the table at the same time Linda's date pulled his linen napkin from his lap and stood.

"Would you excuse me a minute?" I said as Nate slid over to make room for Aunt Martha. "I see someone I need to talk to." I waited until Linda's date turned away from the table, then strolled over and handed her my business card. "Hi Linda, I'm Special Agent Serena Jones. I need to ask you a few questions."

Like a heat-seeking missile, her impeccably dressed dinner date did a midair flight adjustment and stalked back toward me. "What's this about?"

I straightened, and thanks to the extra two inches my boots lent me, we stood eye to eye. "I'm sorry, sir. This doesn't concern you. Could you excuse us for a few minutes?"

A vein in the middle of his forehead bulged. Literally bulged. For a second, I thought he was going to bust an artery right in front of me. Instead he growled, "Do you know who I am?"

He didn't wait for a response before he strode away, which was probably good. Because he would've been disappointed that I didn't have a clue who he was. Although I knew his type—the type that assumed everyone would kowtow to his whims.

"What's this about?" Linda lowered her voice as I slipped into the man's vacated seat.

"Let's start with your brother."

"My brother? Is he in trouble?"

Funny how the pair of siblings both assumed the other was in trouble. "I guess that depends on what you think of his renovation to your apartment."

"My apartment?" Her voice edged higher. "He was in my apartment?"

"He said he's staying there," I relayed, as if I'd had no cause to disbelieve him.

"Oh, of course," she lied, although she covered it well. "I was unexpectedly called out of town and only just got back."

That explained the rotting meat in her fridge.

"But he knows he's always welcome in my home," she added.

"That's interesting, because he thinks you changed your name so he wouldn't be able to find you and recover his share of your father's inheritance." If not for the attack on Aunt Martha, I might've stuck around long enough to point out to him the inconsistencies in his two claims.

"He told you that?" Irritation edged her words. "I told him all the money that wasn't lost in bad investments went to Dad's care. If I'd known

Stan was back in the country, I would've met with him."

"It was kind of hard for him to let you know, considering you'd changed your name and phone number and moved to another state."

She shook her head. "I did all that because I had a possessive ex-boyfriend who wouldn't stop harassing me. Stan didn't need to call the feds."

She was a good liar. I'd give her that. She'd caught herself twirling her hair and made a point of stopping, same with avoiding eye contact, but I'd been watching her talk to her date before I came over. She'd talked with her hands a lot. Now, when they weren't twisting in her lap, they were subconsciously moving objects between us, such as her water glass and the Prada clutch that had been sitting on the other side of her plate.

"Your brother didn't call me. I'm investigating a theft from the art museum." I swept my gaze over her outfit. "And considering you have a part-time job for wages that are nothing to write home about, I'm struggling to make two and two add up to a fifteen-hundred-dollar dress."

Her fingers tapped a nervous rhythm on the stem of her wine glass. "Doug likes to take care of me."

I assumed Doug was the date, now watching us from the bar, who'd just pocketed his phone. My smartphone rang the *Daah, da-da-duh* . . .

Daah, da-da-duh daah of the *Dragnet* theme song reserved for my supervisor. "Excuse me." I cupped my phone to my ear. "Special Agent Serena Jones."

"Jones, have you interrupted the senator's dinner?"

"The"—I gulped, lifted my gaze to Linda—"senator?"

She nodded.

Okay, that explained . . . a lot. "Uh, yes, sir. I guess I did." It figured he'd know how to reach my boss after hours. They'd probably hobnobbed at the MAC—Missouri Athletic Club—like all society's movers and shakers. "His companion is a witness in a case I'm working on."

"An art crime investigation with a trail colder than the Mississippi does not justify you interrupting a public official's private dinner."

"No, sir." The senator headed our way and I stood. "Leaving now, sir." I hung up and tapped the business card I'd handed Linda earlier. "Please call me when it's convenient." I nodded to Doug. "I apologize for the interruption."

"I guess the senator wasn't happy about you interrogating his date?" Nate asked as I returned to the table.

"That obvious, huh?" Oh, man, what kind of FBI agent didn't recognize a state senator, when even my building super had? I really needed to pay more attention to politics. I did a double take on the empty seat beside him, my pulse quickening. "Where'd Aunt Martha go now?"

"To say hi to Lou."

I looked at him as if he'd grown a third eyeball—one my organ-donor-seeking aunt had just swindled off an unsuspecting diner! "You let her out of your sight? Are you nuts?"

His mouth bobbed open and closed like he was a fish out of water.

I whirled to my feet and nearly sent the waitress's tray of drinks sailing.

She did a graceful turn and managed to slide the tray onto the table the second time around. "Is something wrong?"

"My aunt. Have you seen her?"

"Yes, she's talking to a gentleman at the bar."

"Oh no." I raced to the bar at the front of the restaurant, probably looking as if I was the one in need of a straitjacket, and arrived in time to hear Aunt Martha say, "If I needed a kidney, say, the donor wouldn't even have to be dead, right?"

"Aunt Martha!" I grabbed her arm and tugged her away. What had I been thinking, indulging her detective kick? The guy she'd been talking to bore a striking resemblance to that bulbous-nosed actor who always portrays a mobster in the movies and—my heart thumped—he looked as if he was seriously contemplating Aunt Martha's request. "I'm sorry she bothered you. She forgot to take her medicine this morning."

"What are you doing?" Aunt Martha struggled against my hold. "That was Carmen Malgucci. He could've helped."

"If you don't come back to the table this instant," I hissed under my breath, "I'm leaving."

By the time I dragged Aunt Martha back to our table, a platter of deep-fried ravioli appetizers she must've ordered sat in the center.

"I told the waitress we'd need a few more minutes to decide on our entrees," Nate said, then turned his attention to Aunt Martha. "Is your knee swelling again?" he asked, probably thanks to the way I'd "helped" her back to the table.

"No, it's fine." Aunt Martha dipped her chin toward a Godfather lookalike in a dark double-breasted suit, sitting next to the window across from a heavyweight who looked like he'd break your leg if you welched on your debts. "Now, *he* looks like a man who could get you an organ if you—"

"My aunt will have what he's having," I said loudly enough to drown her out as the waitress returned to our table. "I'll have a lasagna." I mentally scheduled fifty extra sit-ups and another mile into my morning exercise routine . . . if I survived tonight. Or more precisely, if my job did. My first annual physical fitness test was next month, but from the scrutiny I felt pinging the side of my head from the general direction of Linda's dinner date, he'd have my boss questioning more than my *physical* fitness for the job.

● ● ●

I awoke with a start and yanked the blankets to my chin. As my eyes adjusted to the scant light filtering through my bedroom curtains, my pounding heart slowed a fraction. Horror movies had nothing on Aunt Martha's wild imaginings.

Between nightmares of meat-cleaver-wielding butchers in bloodstained aprons snatching me out of bed and the knocks and rattles of the radiators jolting me awake, I felt as if *I'd* been the one knocked over by yesterday afternoon's would-be burglar.

I squinted at my digital clock. 5:30. I still had an hour and a half before I had to start figuring out what I was going to do about Aunt Martha's sleuthing and how I'd go about questioning Linda again without incurring my supervisor's wrath.

Something crashed. I yanked open my night table drawer and reached for my gun before the sound registered as dishes in my kitchen. "Must be the cat," I whispered to no one in particular, but I loaded the gun and grabbed my flashlight anyway.

Harold grunted from the foot of the bed.

Okay, not the cat. I jumped up and pressed my back to the wall next to the open door, listening.

Another dish rattled.

What was the guy doing? Making himself breakfast?

Righteous indignation at what he'd done to

Aunt Martha surged up my chest, galvanizing my courage. I padded down the hall, then, flicking on the flashlight and pointing both it and my gun toward the sound, shouted, "Freeze!"

Beady little eyes glinted in the beam of light.

Really little eyes.

The mouse froze for all of half a second, then had the nerve to not only scurry away but also brazenly take the bread bag he'd been scavenging with him.

I stalked back to my bedroom and slammed on the overhead lights.

Harold blinked indignantly.

"What kind of cat are you? There's a mouse in the kitchen helping itself to my breakfast and you're in here snoring."

Harold stretched one paw out in front of him, then the other, and arching his back, let out a bored yawn.

"That's it. It's time you earned your keep." I laid my gun on the bedside table, scooped Harold off my bed, stalked down the hall, and plopped him on the kitchen floor next to the crumb trail left by the mouse. "Find it." I nudged him with my slipper. "Now!"

Harold tapped a breadcrumb with his paw, then proceeded to bat it around the kitchen floor like he was the Blues hockey team's next star center.

"Wait until it starts stealing your food, then you'll change your game plan."

Harold stopped mid-swipe and looked at me as if the prospect of a mouse daring to touch his kibbles seriously miffed him. He sat on his haunches and cast glances to every corner of the kitchen.

"I think he ran under the stove," I said.

Apparently not up on his appliance names, Harold swiped a paw under the fridge.

A gray, furry body slid across the floor.

"Way to g—" I took a second look as Harold proudly pranced off to the living room carrying his prey. "Hey, that's not a real mouse. Where did that come from?"

A shadow crossed the window above the outside stairs leading to my kitchen door.

I snapped off the light and raced back to the bedroom for my gun, then, gripping it with both hands, edged toward the side of the door. The lone parking lot light scarcely pushed back the lingering darkness, and the fridge motor kicked in, muffling any sound I might've heard, save for Harold yowling at his phantom toy mouse. Or maybe that was the blood screaming past my ears.

Suddenly, a face pressed against the door's window, hands cupped around the eyes.

"Nate? What on earth?" He must've overheard the mouse commotion. Dropping my gun hand to my side, I unsnapped the deadbolt. Pulling my gun on Nate was becoming a bad habit.

As I opened the door, a linebacker-sized figure

charged up the stairs and slammed Nate into the rails.

My outside landing was a good fifteen feet above the driveway, and the safety rail caught Nate at the small of his back. The assailant gripped his collar and kept shoving until Nate's upper body teetered precariously over the rail, a gun in his face.

"Freeze," I shouted, steadying my Glock with both hands, my feet braced. Sleet found the open door, pinging my bare limbs.

The gunman's head cocked my direction. "I got this, Serena. Wait inside."

I blinked. "Tanner?"

"Yeah, wait inside," he growled.

Maybe it was the sleet freezing my limbs solid. Maybe it was the sight of Tanner's gun shoved into Nate's chin. But my own gun stayed aimed at Tanner's center of mass. "Stand down," I ordered. "That's my apartment superintendent."

Tanner scrutinized the man caught in his grip, his gun easing back only a fraction. "What's he doing peering in your window in the middle of the night?"

"I heard a commotion," Nate said in a surprisingly steady voice, considering Tanner's finger was a quarter of an inch away from blowing his brains out. "I came up to make sure she was okay."

I suddenly wished I was carrying a hammer-fired pistol so I could cock back the hammer and send a chill down Tanner's spine with the sound that said I was primed to take him out. "Stand down, now!"

"Okay, okay." Tanner holstered his weapon, and with his other hand still fisted in Nate's jacket, tugged him off the rail.

The instant Tanner released him and backed off a step, Nate's fist connected with Tanner's jaw. Tanner scarcely flinched.

I couldn't help it. I burst into laughter.

The man had four or five inches on Nate, plus at least fifty pounds and hours of SWAT training a month, but all he did was smirk and rub his chin. "I guess I deserved that."

Meanwhile, Nate was shaking his hand and massaging his knuckles as if the punch hurt him more.

"Get in here," I said to both of them and shut the door behind them. I slammed my gun onto the counter, amazed I could pry my frozen fingers from around the grip. At the sight of both men's gazes slipping to my attire, I yanked on the jacket I'd left hanging over the back of a kitchen chair the night before. "I'm pretty sure this is *not* what my mom meant when she said I needed more men in my life!"

The kitchen suddenly felt very small with two testosterone-pumped, would-be heroes competing for space.

"Okay, I know what Nate's doing here." His apartment was below mine, after all. "I'm sorry I woke you. It appears we have a mouse problem. The commotion you heard was it knocking a dish on the floor. I appreciate you coming up to check." I shifted my attention to Tanner, my eyes narrowing. "But what are you doing here?"

He stood at the other end of the kitchen, a vantage point that gave him a view of the living room and hallway to the bedrooms, and his stony, unreadable expression did *not* give me the warm fuzzies. But it took another second to clue in that he must've been watching my place for no good reason.

Except Tanner always had a good reason for everything he did.

I crossed my arms, tucking my hands under my armpits to hide my trembling—a mix of bare feet on a cold floor, my adrenaline crashing, and the unwelcome thought that my paranoia was actually justified. "What aren't you telling me?"

His head tilted, his gaze shifting to the living room. "Looks like your cat took care of your mouse problem."

My derisive snort snapped his attention back to me. "It's a toy. He found it under the fridge. I have no idea where it came from."

Tanner chuckled. "Maybe you've got smart mice. Planted decoys to keep the cat busy chasing the wrong thing."

Nate glanced around the doorway at Harold prancing about with the toy mouse dangling from his mouth. "Your aunt brought that for him yesterday afternoon."

The cat's proud swagger and his rod-straight tail stretching toward the ceiling reminded me of the college student I'd interviewed today. My mind whirred at that thought. "What did you say?"

"I said, your aunt—"

"Not you"—I shifted my attention to Tanner—"you. What did you say?"

"The mouse planted decoys?"

"Yeah . . . That's it."

Tanner and Nate exchanged glances, clearly both thinking I'd been sniffing Harold's catnip.

"I'm thinking suspects. I interviewed this employee yesterday morning and right from the start I figured he was slippery, but he gave me good information. Pointed a finger at a woman who looked like she could be a prime suspect."

"A decoy," Tanner said, getting where I was headed.

"Yeah, maybe."

"Do you think *he's* good for the job?"

"I think I need to talk to his friends, because he's the kind of guy who wouldn't have been able to resist bragging about it."

Tanner whipped out his smartphone. "What's his name?"

I glanced at Nate, reluctant to name suspects in

front of him. Of its own volition, my gaze dropped to his bare chest peeking past his unzipped coat.

"Name?" Tanner prodded.

Name, right. I took Tanner's phone and thumbed Malcolm's name into the social media search bar Tanner had already opened. When I'd connected to the right Malcolm and seen that he'd actually gotten smart after our little tête-à-tête and tightened his privacy settings, I handed the phone back to Tanner. "Him."

"Could this guy have figured out where you live?" Nate cut in. "Sent a buddy to break in while you were at the museum?"

"Yeah." Tanner's thumbs tapped away on his smartphone. "If he wanted to sidetrack your investigation, giving you a break-in to deal with would be smart."

In a strange way the theory was almost reassuring. Better than thinking Baldy had put a hit on me. But . . . "I don't see how he'd have figured out where I live so quickly. I don't have a landline so my number's not in the phone book, and I'm subleasing the place from my aunt, so my name's not likely on any other kind of register." Which should boost my confidence that the whole break-in thing was random. "I haven't even gotten around to changing my address on my driver's license yet."

Tanner turned his phone screen my way. "Do you know this woman? She looks like someone a guy would try to impress with a little boasting."

It was a picture of Malcolm in a bar, with his arm slung around the back of a dark-haired beauty, posted six hours ago. "She works at the reception desk at the museum. How'd you access his photos?"

"His friend posted it."

Clearly another non–privacy-savvy friend.

"Do you know her name?"

"She's not tagged?"

"No."

I closed my eyes, straining to put a name to the face. *Petra.* My eyes popped open. "Petra Horvak. I'll have to move her to the top of today's inter-view list, find out what Malcolm's been saying to her."

Nate hitched his thumb over his shoulder toward the door. "I'd better get going. Leave you two to your investigating."

"Thanks for checking on me." I gave him a quick hug. At least it was meant to be quick. I wasn't even sure why I hugged him. It wasn't as if I came from a huggy family, which probably explained why the unexpected zing that jolted through me as his arms encircled my waist and his bristly cheek grazed my hair short-circuited my brain.

"Yeah," Tanner added. "I'm sorry I roughed you up." Although he didn't really sound sorry.

Nate stepped back, gave Tanner a terse nod,

his jaw squared, clearly not appreciating the reminder, then returned his attention to me. "I'll bring you a couple of mousetraps later."

I eyeballed Harold, who'd fallen asleep with the toy mouse tucked under his paw. "Good plan."

As I held the door open for Nate, Tanner glanced at the lightening sky. "I should go too. We can follow this up on Monday."

I shut the door before he could wedge through. "Not so fast. I want to know what you were doing outside my apartment in the wee hours of the morning."

Tanner leaned back against the counter, crossing his long legs in front of him.

"Oh, you know. I had a sudden burning urge to figure out which movie actor your apartment maintenance man looked like. It was giving me insomnia."

"Cute." I crossed my arms.

"No, I don't think he is." Tanner rubbed his jaw as if in deep thought. "In fact, now that I've gotten to know him a little better, I'm gonna go with . . . Shrek."

"Ha ha." Nate was a long way from a green ogre. "Answer the question."

He sighed, dropping his pose. "Fine. I was making sure your burglar didn't come back."

"Oh." I wasn't sure how to feel about that. Part of me wanted to be irritated with Tanner for watching my place, as if I couldn't defend myself.

But another part of me turned warm and fuzzy at the thought.

I squelched that part as fast as it rose. "So you don't think the attempted break-in was simply a crime of opportunity?" I asked.

"I don't like coincidences."

"Neither do I. Oh, you won't believe who I found at Lou's restaurant last night."

"Who?"

"Linda Kempler. Unfortunately, before I could get much information out of her, her date called Benton."

"Who was her date?"

"State Senator Doug Reed." I still couldn't believe I hadn't recognized him.

Tanner whistled. "The image her brother painted of her is looking truer by the minute. She sounds like a real gold digger."

"Yeah, I just hope she doesn't have plans with the senator today too."

"Take the day off. If she's the senator's girl-friend, she's not going anywhere."

I rolled my eyes. "This from the man who spent the night sitting outside in his freezing cold vehicle watching my door."

He shrugged.

"Can you spell *double standard?*"

Tanner squeezed my shoulder. "What you need to do is take the day off. It's Sunday. Twenty-four hours isn't going to make a difference on a case this cold. Go to church. Have dinner with your folks. Start fresh first thing Monday morning."

"The museum's closed Mondays. I need to do more interviews today."

"No. You don't. If you harass Linda on a Sunday and the senator's there, guaranteed you'll get another call from Benton."

"What I need is less unsolicited advice and someone to keep an eye on my aunt. Last night she asked a mobster where she could get a kidney donor."

Tanner burst into laughter.

"I'm not joking. I don't know what to do with her. If she's not careful, *she* could wind up the donor." I choked up on the last word, despite making light of it. Lately danger was hitting way too close to home.

8

"Hey, Miss Jones, hold up."

I stopped in the middle of the church parking lot and turned to see who'd called after me. A middle-aged guy with a receding hairline waved, helped a young girl into the minivan he was standing next to, then hurried toward me. He was five ten, five eleven maybe, neatly dressed in tan jeans and a white dress shirt under a brown leather bomber jacket. I'd attended the church for a few months now, but I didn't recognize him, so how did he know me?

He thrust out his hand. "We haven't met. I'm Dave Sparrow."

I shook his calloused hand. From all appearances, he was a hard-working family man. "How may I help you?"

"My wife pointed you out to me. I work for Russ Bailey's General Contracting. He said you'd want to talk to me because I worked at the art museum last summer."

"Yes, I do. Thank you for introducing yourself. I hadn't received the list of names yet from Mr. Bailey." Which made me wonder if Bailey was worried one of his subcontractors had lifted the paintings and alerted them to give them time to get rid of any evidence if they hadn't already. I pulled a notebook and pen from my purse and jotted down his name. "When would be a convenient time to meet with you?"

"You're welcome to join my family and me for lunch if you don't already have plans."

"Oh." Mr. Sparrow was growing more unpredictable by the second. I ignored the niggling memory of my promise to Tanner to take the day off. Interviewing Sparrow in front of his family was not ideal, but then again, children had a way of conveniently exposing the truth when their parents least wanted, and it wasn't *really* working so much as accepting a fellow church member's hospitality. "I'd love to join you. Thank you."

He rattled off the address and invited me to follow their van. The house was a modest bungalow in West County, an area favored for its high-quality public schools. His furnishings were nice but not high-end. The art on the walls was the kind one would pick up from Walmart, not an art museum. All very tasteful and innocent. From all appearances, he looked like a squared-away family man that I'd be able to move to the bottom of my suspect list.

Over dinner, we talked about the Blues' latest win—his girls were avid hockey fans—and their upcoming winter retreat with the church's youth group. When they started to quiz me on what it was like to be an FBI agent, their dad shooed them off to do dishes so the adults could talk.

I consider myself a pretty good judge of character and even better at reading body language, so I got straight to the point. "Did you steal the missing pieces from the art museum?"

They both laughed. Not a nervous I-have-something-to-hide laugh but a genuinely amused laugh. "Dave's conscience won't even let him walk out of a store if the clerk gives him too much change," his wife explained.

"My father got really sick when I was a young boy and my mom had to take on two jobs to get us through. One of them was working at a gas station, and one day a punk drove off without paying. The station's owner took the money out of Mom's pay. Money we needed." Dave shook his head. "I was furious. Wanted to go out and steal food to make up for it. But my parents made me promise that I'd remember how much the theft hurt us and that I'd never steal, no matter how easy it looked."

"Who else were you working with at the art museum?"

"Norman Fellowes."

I wrote down the name. "You see him do anything suspicious?"

Dave exchanged a look with his wife, then scrubbed his palm over his whiskered jaw as if trying to come to a decision. "I didn't see him take anything."

Okay, that sounded like an evasion if I'd ever

heard one. Tilting my head, I studied him in silence.

He soon started squirming. "I'm not saying he couldn't have done it. He could've hid a canvas between the scraps of drywall he carried out or something. But I didn't see him do it."

"Norm has problems," Dave's wife chimed in, and Dave sent her a silencing glare.

"What kind of problems?" I pressed.

Dave let out a resigned sigh. "He has a bit of a drinking problem. And I suspect gambling. I don't work with him that often, but when I have, he's been a good worker. Doesn't slack off like some do."

His wife gave him a tell-her-the-rest look.

"I figured if Russ told me you'd want to talk to us, he'd also tell Norman, and . . ."

"That I should talk to him sooner rather than later."

He flinched. "Yeah, maybe."

His wife reached across the table and squeezed his hand. "Dave doesn't like to speak ill of anyone."

Dave gave his wife an appreciative smile. "Growing up poor, I was accused more than once of being in on something I wasn't. Makes me hesitant to rush to judgment."

"I understand. I appreciate you seeking me out. Do you know where Norman lives?"

"In Dogtown. With his girlfriend, Cara O'Brien. I don't know the address." I jotted down the girlfriend's name. I thanked him and his wife for lunch and said good-bye to the girls, then sat in my car and called dispatch. "Can you run Norman Fellowes through NCIC, see if anything pops? He's a tradesman. Lives in the south end." I looked up Cara O'Brien and plugged her address into my GPS, then, just for fun, changed the voice to a male Australian. Nothing like the lilt of a masculine foreign accent to make you not mind so much being told where to go.

Not that I had to interview Norman now, but if I didn't, I wouldn't be able to get him out of my head.

The dispatcher checked back in as I turned onto his street. "He looks clean."

"Okay, thanks." Unfortunately, I couldn't say the same for the street, which was surprising, because for the most part St. Louis was an impressively clean city. Instead the street looked like the day after St. Patty's Day—Dogtown's favorite holiday, thanks to its Irish roots. A local party must've gotten out of hand last night and spilled onto the sidewalks, because the houses themselves were small, neat bungalows, probably of post–World War II vintage, sitting on raised lots separated by the quintessential white picket fence—or in Norman's case, graying.

I climbed the cement stoop to his door and knocked.

A woman in spandex workout pants and a tank

top swung open the door as she took a swig from a water bottle.

"Is Norman Fellowes home?"

Her gaze swept over me, her straw-colored hair bobbing in a high ponytail that exposed her dark roots. "Who's asking?"

"Special Agent Serena Jones." I slid my badge from the outside pocket of my purse and held it at eye level.

She laughed. No, roared. A bent-over, knee-slapping roar. "What'd he do? Renege on a debt to Manny the Masher?"

Manuel Lamonte, affectionately known by those who avoided him as Manny the Masher, was St. Louis's most notorious loan shark. Although it was never proven, he'd allegedly crushed more than one deadbeat client with the compactor at his wrecking yard. A reputation that had served him well in ensuring his current clients made timely payments. If Norman was in debt to him, that'd be a prime motive to snatch the paintings. "Is Norman having financial problems?"

The woman snorted. "He makes enough money. But he's a lousy gambler." She took another swig from her bottle. "Ain't my problem no more. I kicked him out when he didn't pay his share of the rent."

"How long ago was this?"

"Friday night."

"Do you know where he's living now?"

"Don't know and don't care. But by now you can probably find him at O'Shaunessy's, watching the football game with the boys. You can't miss him. He's six six and as skinny as a rail."

"When Norman left, did he leave behind any belongings? Clothes? Furniture? Art?"

She spurted water as she let loose another laugh. "Norman, art? His idea of art is a poster of a shiny red muscle car. You're welcome to it. It's still on the wall in the basement."

"He never showed you, or mentioned, any paintings?"

She squinted, her gaze drifting. "Now that you mention it, when he was doing the job at the art museum, he did say he was gaining a whole new appreciation for art." She shook her head. "He showed me pictures he'd snapped of his favorites."

"Can you describe them?"

"Let's just say my mother would've fainted dead away if I'd let him hang them on the wall."

Okay, so not pastoral landscapes. But if he'd been noticing paintings and Manny the Masher was putting the squeeze on him, he could have been tempted to make off with a couple.

I drove around to O'Shaunessy's. Cars lined both sides of the street for a block. Stake a cop at either end, and the place would be a ticket gold mine by the time the Super Bowl ended. I parked on the next block and walked.

The bar was loud and dimly lit and smelled like a locker room. I spotted a tall, slim man at the end of the bar, his gaze fixed on the big screen.

I weaved around the packed tables and sauntered to his side. "Norman Fellowes?"

He spared me a half-second glance. "Who's asking?"

For a heartbeat, I was tempted to not mention what I did for a living, to cozy up to him and feign interest in his plans for after the game. From the smell of his breath, he already had one sail to the wind. A little sweet talk would no doubt loosen his lips.

But that half-second glance told me that as long as there were men in twenty pounds of padding smashing into each other on the big screen, the act would be lost on him. And it was still the first quarter. I flashed my badge. "Special Agent Serena Jones."

The guy on the stool next to me paused with his long-neck bottle halfway to his lips, took one look at me, and vamoosed.

I slid onto the stool he'd vacated, between Norm and the big screen. "I need you to answer a few questions."

As providence would have it, the network chose that moment to break for a commercial.

"What about?" Norm scooped a handful of peanuts from the bar, seemingly undisturbed by the prospect of being questioned by an FBI agent, which made me wonder if he'd even registered what I'd said.

"Items missing from the Forest Park Art Museum."

His head jerked back, his eyes wide, a frown tugging down the corners of his lips. "I don't know anything about any missing paintings."

"I didn't say they were paintings."

He choked on a peanut, then stalked to the restroom, pounding his chest.

"Hey, you okay? I don't want you choking to death in there." Remembering what Burke said, I wondered if he was choking on the idea of doing five to ten in the federal pen. I stationed myself outside the door, figuring as long as I could still hear him coughing, he hadn't pulled a Stan-out-the-window on me.

Cheers rose from the bar and Norman raced out, still zipping his pants. "What'd I miss?" He reclaimed his stool at the bar, tossing me a glare as if I was to blame.

"Listen," I said in my friendliest I-want-to-help-you tone. "If you cooperate, I'll talk to the prosecutor, see if he'll cut you a deal. I'm just interested in recovering the items. Tell me who you sold them to and—"

Norman surged to his feet, knocking his stool into my leg in his hurry to put distance between us. "I didn't steal nothing."

All eyes shot our way.

I didn't care. "I know you're in deep with Manny the Masher."

"Shh." He looked around, waved nonchalantly to those still looking, and sat back down.

Okay, so apparently *Norm* cared. Interesting.

"You talked to my ex-girlfriend?" he hissed. "She doesn't know what she's talking about. I paid Manny back."

"With a painting?"

"No! I don't know nothing about any painting."

Of course, what else would he say? Trouble was, I believed him. Believing people was becoming a bad habit and getting me nowhere in this investigation.

By the time I got home Sunday afternoon, I was more than ready to R & R with my paintbrush and canvas. Pablo Picasso once said that "art washes away from the soul the dust of everyday life," and my soul was feeling very dusty.

I dropped my keys and purse on the kitchen table and put a mug of milk in the microwave to heat up for hot cocoa, but as I reached for the handle of the cupboard where I kept the cocoa tin, visions of a twitching nose and beady eyes popping out from behind it flashed through my mind. "Harold!" I strode to my bedroom and found the freeloader curled up in the middle of my bed. I scooped him up and carried him back with me to the kitchen. "Here's the deal. I ward off

149

two-legged intruders. You handle the four-legged ones. Okay?"

Harold meowed, but it didn't sound like he agreed.

Too bad. I was trained to take down two-hundred-pound men, not two-ounce rodents. I held Harold up to the cupboard and gingerly opened the door.

Nothing moved inside. And thankfully there was no telltale evidence that anything had paid the cupboard a visit. "Okay." I dropped Harold to the floor. "You're off the hook for now, but no more Stuart Little videos for you. Mice are not a part of this family."

I headed to the bedroom to change, rethinking having kicked off my shoes at the door as my gaze swept the hall for any kamikaze mice tempted to cross my path. My unwelcome houseguest turned out to be smart enough to stay out of sight. I dragged on a pair of faded blue jeans and an old Wash U jersey. "Time to relax," I said to Harold, who'd reclaimed his spot in the center of my bed and gave me his I-was-relaxing-fine-until-you-came-home look. Must be nice to be a cat and not feel guilty about lazing around doing nothing but shedding fur.

Not that I should feel guilty. I returned to the kitchen and fixed my hot cocoa. I'd put in way more than my quota of hours for the week. It wasn't as if I was racing against the clock to save a kidnapped child or track down a serial killer.

I carried my hot cocoa to my easel in the living room. Sipping the cocoa, I compared the photos I'd taken of the bridge over the river near the Grand Basin in Forest Park with the scene emerging from my canvas. I wasn't sure why, but something about bridges and water spoke to me more than any other image.

I mixed ultramarine blue with a touch of black and added shadows to the river beneath the bridge.

A squeak from the vicinity of the floor made me jump, sending a streak of muddy blue across my canvas.

"Harold, get in here!" I shouted as our mouse dashed across the living room.

Harold zoomed past my easel and slapped his paw on the mouse's tail. The mouse skidded to a stop, and then Harold seemed at a loss to know what to do next.

"Hold it." I ran to my bedroom for a shoe box.

The doorbell rang. Shoe box in hand, I peeked out the peephole and yanked open the door. "Nate, am I glad to see you. Is that the trap?"

"Yes." I reached for it, but Nate swung it out of my grasp. "Unless 'trap' is some kind of code for 'ambush'?"

"Huh?" He held it easily out of my reach as—hello?—the mouse was probably making his getaway.

"Your *personal security detail* isn't just around the corner ready to take me out?"

My personal *what?* Oh, he meant Tanner. "Cute." *Men!* Could they not focus on priorities? I snagged the bottom of the trap and pulled it out of Nate's hands.

"I brought a live trap, because I hate the idea of killing the poor little guy if we don't have to."

"Aw." He was nothing but a big softie. Who could stay annoyed with that? "In here," I said, hurrying toward the living room.

Except apparently Harold shared Nate's sentiment about killing, because at the sight of Nate, he lifted his paw and let the mouse escape. "No!"

Harold sprang on it again, and I kind of felt sorry for the little guy.

Nate snagged the shoe box I'd tossed. "Hold still, Harold."

That was Harold's cue to lift his paw. Maybe he and I had more in common than I'd realized. I'd been tempted more than once to release a quaking, desperate-eyed suspect. Then again, I doubted it was pity that caused Harold to let up on our mouse.

Thanks to Nate's quick reflexes, the mouse soon had a shoe box cell. "I'll relocate him outside, but you'll probably want to set the live trap along a kitchen wall in case he's left buddies behind."

"Right."

Nate's head tilted sideways, his gaze on my painting. "Interesting."

"That"—I motioned to the swipe of muddy blue springing from my river onto the bridge—"wasn't deliberate. It's the mouse's fault."

A mischievous smile curved his lips. "Wasn't it Beecher who said, 'Every artist dips his brush in his own soul, and paints his own nature into his pictures'?"

My eyes widened of their own volition. I knew the quote, but I was amazed Nate did. A pet sitter, a tea connoisseur, and an art enthusiast. The surprises kept coming.

To think when I bailed on tonight's dinner with my parents, my mother had complained that I never do what she wants. Yet right now, I couldn't help but think Nate would be a fun guy to date. Something that would please my mother very much. Far too much. Except . . .

My gaze slid to the ruined painting as his words—*paints his own nature into his pictures*—sank in. I planted my hand on my hip. "What are you saying? I'm a mess?"

He chuckled. "More like unreinable."

I frowned. "I don't think that's a real word." Although at least he'd said it like it wasn't a bad thing.

9

I checked my watch—still an hour before I had to meet an informant—and strolled into the living room. Sipping my tea, I assessed the bubbly froth I'd added to yesterday's oops streak on my painting. It almost looked as if a mischievous boy had thrown a rock into the river to watch the splash. I pictured a younger version of Nate standing on the bridge, dropping the biggest rock he could lift over the side. "Unreinable, indeed."

A rap at the door jolted the tea out of my cup. For crying out loud, what was with me? I'd never been this jumpy. "Just a minute," I called, hurrying to the kitchen to rinse the tea from my hand. Who would visit on a Monday morning? If I hadn't worked all weekend, I'd already be on my way to headquarters. I peeked out the peep-hole.

A rainbow-colored, multi-pom-pomed ski beanie filled my field of vision. Either Aunt Martha had gotten a new hat or the circus was in town.

I threw back the dead bolt and opened the door. "Aunt Martha, what are you doing here?"

"I thought we could shop for Janessa's baby shower gifts. You didn't forget it's this Friday, did you?"

My *younger* cousin was having a baby—how

could I forget that? "I'd love to shop with you, but I can't this morning. I have to work."

Aunt Martha pushed her way in. *"Peeshosh. What are you going to do? The museum's closed Mondays."* She tugged off her crazy hat, then hunkered down on the floor and dangled the pom-poms in front of Harold, who swatted at them like they were the greatest thing since catnip.

"I do have other cases, Aunt Martha."

"Makes no never mind. You deserve a day off. You worked Saturday. And . . ." She waggled her finger at me as if I'd been a naughty girl. "Sunday afternoon."

"I was painting yesterday. That's why I didn't make it for dinner."

"That's not all you were doing."

"How would you know what I was doing?" My gaze snapped to the dieffenbachia she'd also left behind with the apartment. I wouldn't put it past her to plant a bug—the listening kind—in the plant.

Aunt Martha laid a finger alongside her nose like the TV detectives she aspired to be. "Mrs. O'Riley's son said he saw you at a pub in Dogtown." Aunt Martha arched a penciled eyebrow. "You telling me you're a hoyden?"

"A hoyden? What on earth's a hoyden?"

"A carefree, boisterous girl. Didn't Mr. Sutton tell you?"

Ah, the newest word of the day.

"He says using it in a sentence will help you remember it." She wrestled a pom-pom away from Harold. "If you were a girl," she cooed to the cat, "we could call you a hoyden. You should have seen Serena when she was a girl. Oh my, she was a hoyden and a half."

"Okay, I think you've mastered the word already. And yes, I mean no, I'm not a hoyden. Yes, I briefly interviewed a suspect at the pub Sunday afternoon."

"Then your boss shouldn't mind if you do a little shopping this morning."

"Aunt Martha, I—" My ringing cell phone interrupted. I glanced at the screen. "Excuse me, I need to take this."

"I have news on the Monet," one of the dealers who'd received my email blast said in a thick French accent.

"Perfect. What do you have?"

"A dealer in Paris bought it on January 5th."

I snatched up a pen and paper. "What's his name and address? Does he still have it?"

Aunt Martha clapped her hands. "Isn't this exciting, Harold? We have a lead."

"*Non*," my contact on the other end of the line responded. "He sold it to a dealer in Nice who-o-o—how do you say?—was not happy to learn it was stolen."

"Does that dealer still have it?"

"*Non*, and he claims not to know who bought it."

It wasn't uncommon for art collectors to make purchases anonymously to keep paparazzi, other collectors, thieves, or even museum curators courting donations at bay. "Okay, I appreciate you digging up this much for me. Could you give me the names, addresses, and phone numbers of the two dealers?" I jotted down the information and hung up.

"You got a break in the case?" Aunt Martha sprang to her feet without the slightest hitch, despite Saturday's scuffle.

"Yes, the Monet turned up in Paris last month." And if Linda told the truth on the message she'd left for her other number, that vacation she'd been on may very well have been in Paris. Linda, who was dating a senator with a direct line to my boss. I muffled a groan. Why did my strongest suspect have to be the one my boss didn't want me to bother?

"So do you get to fly to Paris? I've always wanted to go back to Paris. Eat frogs' legs." Aunt Martha nuzzled Harold against her chin. "You'd like those."

Harold purred his agreement as if he'd been around during her globetrotting days as a business tycoon's personal assistant.

"No, I need to make a phone call." Paris was seven hours ahead of us and it was already past 9:00, which meant it was—I did a quick calculation in my head—after 4:00 in the afternoon there. I scrolled through my contact list and put a call in to the FBI Legal Attaché—*legat* for short—in France and explained what I had. The legat had no actual authority to investigate the crime and interrogate witnesses, but he could liaison with the local police.

"*Oui*," the legat agreed. "I'll call the *Police Nationale* to arrange to interview the dealer here in Paris. It's unlikely I'll have any information for you before tomorrow."

"I understand."

"Then it will be a couple of days more before I can get to Nice to accompany the local police to interview the second dealer."

Yeah, I itched to hop on a plane and do it myself. Although if there'd been any trail to be found, the dealer had probably already taken measures to eradicate it, because worse than the quarter million he'd be out if he had to reimburse his client was the tarnish to his reputation if word circulated that he'd sold a stolen painting in the first place.

Aunt Martha clicked off her cell phone as I disconnected my own. "Get your coat."

"What? Why?"

"You want to know if that suspect of yours was in Paris too, don't you?"

Great, now Auntie Sherlock was listening in on my phone calls. "How do you propose we do that?"

"By asking Nate's travel agent. He's on his way up now."

I tried to imagine how an apartment superintendent had the time or funds to travel frequently enough to have a travel agent and decided some things were better left unasked. "Aunt Martha, I'm a federal agent. All I have to do is ask CBP to look her up."

"CBP?"

"Customs Border Patrol."

"Oh." She looked crestfallen. "I'd really hoped we might hit a few shops for that gift after paying the travel agent a visit." Her hand drifted to the knee she'd twisted in Saturday's attack and massaged it as if it'd started to hurt again. No wonder, with the way she'd been down on the floor with Harold a moment ago.

I wanted to believe it was a ploy to guilt me into playing hooky for an hour, but I felt guilty just thinking it. "I'll tell you what. I have to meet someone at the mall in"—I glanced at my watch—"half an hour. You can come along and start scouting potential gifts while I talk to him, and then we can select something together. Sound good?"

"Him?"

"What?"

"You said you were meeting a *him*."

I rolled my eyes. "Not that kind of him."

Surprisingly, her face brightened.

Okay, there was no figuring out my aunt. "I just need to make a quick call to headquarters before we leave." I connected with CBP and filled the contact in on what I needed on Linda. By the time I got off the phone, Aunt Martha was explaining our change in plans to Nate at the door. "I appreciate the offer, though," I added as I grabbed my coat.

He smiled. He had a nice smile. One that lit his eyes and made the corners crinkle. "Anytime," he said on his way out.

Aunt Martha gave Harold one last tussle with her hat, then tugged it back on her head. "Nate's nice, don't you think?"

"Yes." I turned the deadbolt to lock the hall door and grabbed my purse, trying to ignore the twinkle in Aunt Martha's eye. "Let's go out through the kitchen."

The shining sun intensified the feeling bubbling up inside me that I might be on the verge of breaking the case. The informant I'd arranged to meet had given me good information in the past.

Midmorning traffic was light, making the trip to the mall a quick one, but Aunt Martha still found enough time to catalog all the nice things Nate had done for her over the years she'd lived in the apartment. She was as transparent as an empty picture frame, and I couldn't help but wonder if she'd availed Nate of a laundry list of my noble acts too. I cringed to think about what might make

Aunt Martha's list for me. Hopefully not the time I tried to cheer her up when she was sick by sticking straws over my eyeteeth and pretending I was a walrus.

I dropped Aunt Martha off at the mall entrance, figuring there was less chance of her spying on my meeting that way. "I'll find you in the baby boutique in about twenty minutes, okay?"

"Sure thing." She closed the car door and waggled her fingers. "Cheerio!"

To be on the safe side, I opted to walk in by a different entrance. My informant—a pawnshop employee who'd gotten caught fencing stolen property for a buddy—was already reclining on a bench by the fountain, eating a chocolate bar.

I fished a coin out of my pocket and tossed it in. "You think wishes come true?" I asked for the benefit of anyone who might be listening.

He shook his head. "Nah, I wouldn't waste your money."

"Ah, c'mon, you've never had a wish come true?" He wasn't in jail, so the way I saw it, he'd had at least one, even if he didn't like the conditions so much.

He shrugged.

I surreptitiously glanced around to ensure no one was paying any attention to us, then took a seat on the bench beside him and pretended to search in my purse for a cough drop. "What have you got for me?"

"The week before Christmas, a blonde tried to sell my boss a Monet. She didn't mention a Rijckaert."

"But you saw the Monet?"

"Yeah. Looked like the one in your email. The woman wanted twenty grand for it, and I could tell my boss knew it was the real thing, but he tried to convince her it wasn't and offered her a grand."

"What did she do?"

"Said she already had an antique shop willing to give her fifteen, so if he didn't want it, she'd go. He said he might have a client who'd be interested and asked her to come back after Christmas."

"Did she?"

"Not that I saw."

A sudden movement at the edge of my peripheral vision caught my attention—Aunt Martha, in her rainbow hat, hurrying to the restroom. It'd be just like her to try to eavesdrop on the conversation.

I pulled a tissue from my purse and pretended to wipe my nose. "You catch her name?"

"She didn't leave one."

"Can you describe her?"

"Classy looking. Real tall, except maybe that was 'cause of her high heels." He pointed a few inches down his arm. "Her hair was about to here, wavy, pinned up on one side with a gold clip."

So far she sounded a lot like Linda. "Body type?" I asked, returning the tissue to my purse and continuing my make-believe search of the contents.

"Slender, but curvy. She had a great body. Wore this clingy kind of dress that . . . well . . ."

I looked up from my purse. "Kept you from paying much attention to the painting?"

With an "Mmm-hmm," he popped his last square of chocolate into his mouth, then crumpled his wrapper and tossed it into the trash.

Aunt Martha emerged from the restroom without a glance my way and headed toward the baby boutique. Maybe she hadn't seen me after all. "Did you see what the woman was driving?" I asked the informant.

"No."

I resisted the urge to pull out my cell phone and show him a picture of Linda. I needed to do it right, give him a photo lineup of blondes to pick her out from. Since Linda had a senator for a boyfriend, I couldn't afford any slipups. I thumbed a lozenge out of its packet and zipped closed my purse. "And were you able to find out anything about Norman Fellowes?" When the informant called last night to ask for a meeting, I'd decided it wouldn't hurt to see what he could find out about Norm's debt situation.

"He worked out a deal with Manny the Masher."

"What kind of deal?"

"He's paying off his debt by remodeling the guy's kitchen."

"You're sure?"

"That's what one of Manny's lackeys told me."

"Thanks. I'll be in touch." I walked off without another glance his way, just in case someone had been watching. Popping the lozenge in my mouth, I visited the restroom to jot down the information while it was still fresh in my mind. If Linda had been determined to hold out for at least twenty grand, it was conceivable she'd opted to fly to Paris with it herself, maybe figuring she'd get even more.

I thumbed in the number for headquarters as I headed to the boutique to meet Aunt Martha. "Hello, Jones here. Can you put me through to the CBP officer?"

"Hold please."

Aunt Martha waved from the checkout counter. "Over here. Look at these." She held up a Winnie the Pooh crib sheet set and a baby mobile. "Aren't they adorable? And these can be from you." She held up a selection of outfits in unisex colors.

"Wow, that's great. I've never seen you pick out gifts so quickly."

"Nonsense." She shoved her credit card at the cashier. "I know you're in a hurry to get to work. I don't want to keep you."

Headquarters came back on the line.

"Excuse me a sec." I turned and walked to a quiet corner. "Hi, yes, this is Serena. I was wondering if you have an answer for me on Linda Kempler."

"Jones, this is Benton."

My heart jumped to my throat at the sound of my supervisor's booming voice.

"I want to see you in my office ASAP."

"Sir?" My voice quavered. Crud. This couldn't be good. He must've heard about my request for information on Linda's recent trips. Only his objections had to go a lot deeper than not wanting me to interrupt a senator's Saturday night date. "Is there a problem?"

"We'll discuss it when you get here."

"Understood. On my way."

Aunt Martha joined me with her shopping bags. "What's wrong?"

"Nothing's wrong." I clipped my phone back on my hip and forced a cheerier note into my voice. "My supervisor wants to see me when I get in is all."

"Oh my, then you should go straight there. I can take a bus back to the apartment to get my car."

"Don't be silly." I steered her out of the store. "I'm not going to make you take a bus."

"I don't mind. In fact, I insist. I'm the one who dragged you away from work in the first place. I'm not going to let you get in trouble with your boss."

"I'm not letting you take a bus," I repeated adamantly.

"But"—she glanced from store window to store

window—"I saw a gorgeous outfit as I came in that I still want to check out."

We had a staring contest as I debated the professional repercussions of making my supervisor wait.

"Go. I'll be fine," she insisted.

Only something made me a tad uneasy about her eagerness to get rid of me.

For some reason as I left the mall parking lot, my car didn't turn where it was supposed to and before I knew it, I was outside Linda's apartment building. It was on the way to headquarters . . . in a roundabout sort of way. And if Benton was about to tell me to lay off the senator's girlfriend, this might be my last chance to question her without defying a direct order.

The museum was closed and the senate was in session, so chances were good I'd find her at home.

According to DMV records, Linda drove a Honda, but there was no sign of it on the street. I walked to the corner and looked both directions. Okay, this wasn't looking hopeful. But I was here now. Maybe she'd mentioned to a neighbor where she was headed. I returned to the building and reached the second floor just as a man carrying a gun breached her door. I drew my weapon. "FBI. Freeze."

The guy turned to me, his arms raised, a dead

bolt, not a gun, in his right hand. "What's your problem, lady? I work here. I'm fixing the lock."

"Did you advise the tenant you'd be entering her premises?"

"What's to advise? She canceled her lease. A couple of guys with a van moved her stuff out this morning."

No, no, no, no. *No!* I holstered my weapon. I knew I should've come back here yesterday. "Was her brother still here?"

"How do I know?"

"Did she leave a forwarding address?"

"Nope."

"Okay, thank you." I headed back to my car. Linda was looking guiltier by the minute. During the drive to headquarters, I tried to get Tanner on the phone. It went to voice mail. *Terrific.* Our supervisor was as straight as an arrow. At least that's what I'd always thought. I couldn't believe that if he knew the senator was mixed up with a thief, he'd tolerate a cover-up. Then again, putting a stop to my interrupting the senator's dinner smacked of an old boys' loyalty that had already hampered my investigation. And what else would he be summoning me to his office to discuss?

An image of Baldy and Sidekick flickered through my mind. *Okay, that wouldn't be good either.*

I parked near the back door and hurried up the stairs, two at a time. Shedding my coat as I walked, I detoured past Tanner's desk, but he wasn't there. Benton must've spotted me, because he stuck his head out of his corner office and waved me over. I dropped my coat on Tanner's chair and approached Benton on wobbly legs. Facing him suddenly felt ten times worse than being holed up in a hotel room with Baldy and Sidekick, wondering when my backup would show.

Oh, right, that's because this time, I had no backup.

My hands were sweating. My heart was pounding. And I didn't even know what I'd done wrong.

Besides having the nerve to suspect a senator's girlfriend of stealing a pair of priceless paintings.

"Sit down, Jones."

"Yes sir."

Maxwell Benton was in his late forties, with a full head of white hair that made him look like Richard Gere. I'd been told the hair was a side effect of his first divorce at twenty-nine. He'd had two more divorces since then and had a teenage daughter he rarely saw.

I'm not sure why that thought ran through my mind, except as a vain search for common ground to meet him on.

He removed his reading glasses and studied me over steepled fingers. "You're a good detective."

"Thank you, sir."

"Tenacious. I like that."

Sensing a "but" coming, I held my breath.

"But you're on the wrong track with Linda Kempler. She's not your thief."

I exhaled slowly. "If that's the case, then the evidence should bear it out."

"I'm afraid she can't afford to have you digging around in her life. You'll have to take my word for it that she's not involved."

I planted my feet firmly on the floor and sat taller in my chair, gripping the armrests. "With all due respect, sir, how can you know that? I have an informant who said a woman fitting Linda's description tried to sell a Monet at the pawnshop where he works."

"It wasn't Linda."

"Are you aware that she hasn't been back to work since the paintings were discovered missing? That she's vacated her apartment? That according to her phone message, she was away on vacation when one of the missing paintings turned up in Paris?"

Benton's eyes widened. "You've already located one of the paintings?"

I relayed the details of this morning's new developments.

"Excellent work."

"Why can't I talk to Linda? If she's innocent, the—"

"Not going to happen. You need to look elsewhere."

169

My gaze skittered over the commendations and related photo ops plastering his wall as I tried to convince myself that the request wasn't motivated by friendship or politics. Nope, I couldn't do it. "What is she afraid I'll find?"

"This conversation is over," he said more sternly, "as is your investigation of Linda Kempler. Do I make myself clear?"

"A simple analysis of her phone, banking, and travel records would go a long way to assuring me that I'm not turning a blind eye to one of my prime suspects."

"She's not your thief. You have my word on that."

"But—"

"That needs to be good enough. Dismissed."

I had a staring contest with him for another three seconds, then gritted my teeth and let myself out.

Tanner was waiting for me in my cubicle, looking concerned. He handed me the coat I'd left on his chair. "You okay?"

"Peachy."

"Want to talk about it?"

"I wish I could." Somehow I didn't think Benton would appreciate me telling anyone he'd ordered me to stop investigating my prime suspect. I wasn't surprised the senator was pushing his weight around. A politician couldn't afford a scandal. And while dating a woman accused of swindling her brother out of his inheritance might be forgiven by the public, dating a woman who stole half a million dollars' worth of the city's paintings, money that opponents would speculate had been funneled into his next campaign, would finish him. "Have you ever investigated a public official?"

"Are we talking Linda Kempler's state senator?"

I let out a ragged sigh and slanted a glance over the wall of my cubicle toward our supervisor's office. "Benton's crossed her off my suspect list."

"Huh."

"*Huh?*" My voice pitched up a couple of octaves. "That's all you've got for me? She was my prime suspect. And let me tell you, the fact she vacated her apartment and has probably already left town doesn't make her look any more innocent."

"You don't have any evidence against her, though, right? Yesterday it sounded like you were thinking the guy who pointed the finger at her might be worth a second look."

"That was before the Monet turned up in Paris around the time Linda was traveling abroad."

"You know that for a fact?"

"No, Benton gagged CBP on me too."

"So you only have her brother's word on it? And that Malcolm kid from the museum?"

"An innocent person doesn't skip town two days after a federal agent approaches her for questioning."

"Maybe she has something else to hide." Tanner lowered his voice. "Maybe she's in witness protection and she was afraid all the attention wouldn't be safe. It would explain why Benton's being cagey."

"Be serious. A person in witness protection would have to be an idiot to date a politician. There's no escaping the cameras, especially come election time."

"Speaking of idiotic dating choices . . ." Tanner did that single eyebrow raise he was so annoyingly good at.

"Meaning . . . ?" I raised a disdainful eyebrow of my own. Or maybe two.

"Your handy-dandy superintendent/guard dog buddy."

"Nate? What are you talking about? We're not dating."

Tanner snorted. "Does he know that?"

"Of course he does!"

"Uh huh. At any rate," he went on in that irritating superior tone, "I've known plenty of idiot witnesses. Interview the other employees. Follow the leads you can. Something else will turn up."

Great. Apparently, Tanner had gone and joined the old boys' club too.

10

By Monday night, a big fat zero had turned up. I'd caught up on all my case notes and reviewed the backgrounds of a couple dozen more art museum employees in preparation for another day of interviews tomorrow, and none screamed "I did it."

Never mind that I wouldn't have suspected Linda from her background check either. But she was running now, and my boss didn't find that suspicious.

I yanked on my sneakers, needing to run off my own pent-up frustration.

"I'll be back in thirty minutes," I shouted to Harold as if he had a clue how long that was. Is that what spinster cat ladies did? I slammed the door, not really wanting to know.

I crossed Skinker Boulevard to run the loop around Forest Park. It was already dark, but the sidewalks were dry and well lit.

"Hey, Serena!" Jax, a fellow runner who lived a couple of streets over from me, waved from across the street, then immediately skirted traffic to join me.

"I didn't know you ran at night," I said, setting the pace. We would occasionally cross paths during our morning runs and pace a couple of miles together.

"I had a day I'd like to forget."

"I hear ya." Jax was an assistant circuit attorney, which probably meant he got saddled with the grunt work. "Tough case?"

"I'd rather talk about anything else than my day. How was yours?"

"Not one I want to talk about either."

He laughed. "We make a fine pair." He motioned me to take Government Drive into Forest Park.

I didn't usually run through the park after dark, but Jax was no pipsqueak. Between the two of us, I figured we'd be safe.

"Have you been skating yet this winter?" he asked.

"Not in years." There was an outdoor rink at the other end of Forest Park. As teens, Zoe and I had hung there a lot, getting ridiculously giddy whenever a boy would ask one of us to hold hands and skate around to the music in the moonlight.

"I was thinking of going sometime. You want to join me?"

"I doubt my skates would fit me anymore."

He didn't say anything more, and as good as the streetlights were, they weren't bright enough for me to tell what he was thinking. Had he been asking as in . . . like . . . a date? We jogged together a lot and had occasionally crossed paths at the local coffee shop, shared a table, but . . . did he think I was interested in him *that* way?

I mentally flipped through my Rolodex of friends. "I should introduce you to my friend Marissa. She loves to skate."

"That's okay." He chuckled, but it sounded like one of those fake chuckles you make when you don't want the other person to know you feel embarrassed.

We ran in companionable silence for a half mile, my mind mulling over Benton's edict. I'd have an easier time taking his word on Linda's innocence if I could at least take a gander at her financial and cell phone records. Then as we raced up the hill past the art museum, a brain wave struck. "Can I ask for your legal opinion on something?"

"Sure."

What I needed was probable cause for a search warrant that my boss couldn't ignore. Jax wasn't a federal prosecutor, but he could give me a solid legal opinion of what I'd need to make the request fly. "Can you tell me if this is enough to convince a federal judge to give me a warrant?" I recited everything I had on Linda.

Jax's pace slowed. "You think this person stole paintings from the art museum."

"Yes."

"Has the Paris dealer made a positive ID?"

"My cohort in France won't have a chance to talk to him until tomorrow at the earliest."

"Then why not wait to see what he says?"

"My suspect has already vacated her apartment and for all I know, plans to flee the country."

Jax nodded. "How do you think she took the paintings?"

"There are dozens of ways she could've slipped them out of the building."

"Such as?"

From Jax's tone, I had a bad feeling my chances of convincing a judge to give me a search warrant were going south faster than Linda's next flight. "She could have hidden them in her book bag."

"Aren't employees' bags checked as they leave?"

"Security can easily be distracted."

"Do you have a witness who saw this person leave with a book bag? Or surveillance footage?"

"No," I said, fighting to keep my tone even.

"There are dozens of explanations for her actions that are a hundred percent legal. What about a motive?"

"She has expensive tastes."

"*I* have expensive tastes. Doesn't mean I stole a painting." He shook his head. "I'm sorry. I know it isn't what you wanted to hear, but I couldn't get a state judge to buy this request, so I doubt your people could find a federal judge that would. It looks too much like a fishing expedition."

"That's what I was afraid of. And unfortunately the suspect has friends in high places."

"How high?"

As we circled the roundabout onto Lagoon

Drive, the all-too-familiar churning returned to my stomach with the fear I'd already said too much. "Pretty high."

"Well, federal judges are appointed for life, so you don't have to worry about political intimidation."

Easy for Jax to say. It wasn't the judge possibly being intimidated.

"But you need something a lot more solid than this. You got a friend who can access the banking records for you?"

I practically fell over in shock that he'd think I'd do such a thing. "If I had that, I wouldn't need the warrant," I joked.

"Well, if you wanted to use the information in court you would. But what I was getting at is if a friend checks the records and sees something incriminating and tells you, then you could request the warrant on the strength of your"—he made air quotes—"confidential informant's information."

That didn't sound terribly legal. Not that it mattered, since I didn't have a confidential informant. Unless . . . I asked Kristal.

Kristal was a childhood friend who grew up across the street from me. She'd searched banking records on the sly to help the head of the high school reunion committee locate almost everyone from our class to invite them to the upcoming ten-year reunion.

"Any teller could probably look up the info for

you." Jax tossed a smile at me. "Pick a male one. A woman as beautiful as you won't have any problem getting him to look to see if your suspect's had any large deposits go into her account."

Oh, wow. He was talking as if he thought I'd do it. Okay, admittedly I was a little obsessive when it came to following rules, but I thought in law enforcement of all places it would be appreciated. Yeah, okay, I clearly hadn't been paying attention to all those cop shows I'd been watching.

"I can't lie to the prosecuting attorney about a CI I don't have." Let alone ask a perfect stranger to risk his job to look up information for me on some vain hope that he might be able to go out with me. Thank goodness I didn't run into Jax while Aunt Martha was with me. She'd already be down at the bank pestering Kristal.

"A CI doesn't have to be listed by name in a warrant," Jax reassured.

"You actually think I should do this?" I had a hard time keeping the disbelief from my voice.

He shrugged. "That's your call. How far are you willing to go to seek justice?"

I wasn't *pusillanimous,* I told myself for the dozenth time as I parked in front of the museum Tuesday morning. The instant I'd stepped out my door this morning, Mr. Sutton had assaulted me with the synonym for *cowardly*—his word of the day—and it had felt like some sort of divine judgment, which was ridiculous. I was obeying my boss. Following the rules. Doing what I was supposed to do.

As I stepped out of the car, my gaze strayed to the rugged stone bridge at the bottom of the hill—the one depicted in my painting. Remembering Nate's take on it, or rather what it said about me, I shook my head. He didn't know me at all.

If I was unreinable, I wouldn't have thought twice about defying my boss and marching down to the bank to sweet talk some hapless teller into giving me the lowdown on Linda Kempler's bank account.

An unreinable person would be unstoppable, a force of nature that would breach the riverbank and jump the bridge and not let something like her boss's pesky cease-and-desist hamper her from getting to the truth.

No, I was pusillanimous.

I slammed the car door and stomped up the stairs to the museum. I had no proof Linda was guilty, I mentally reasoned. Never mind that she and the senator, with his private little calls to Benton, were acting as if she was. Zoe had two dozen more employees lined up for me to interview today, any one of whom could prove to be our thief.

I strode into Zoe's office and dumped my coat and bag on her chair. "Okay, let's do this."

I'd called Zoe last night and updated her on the latest developments, but from the bags under her eyes, the update hadn't helped her sleep. "I'll get Petra."

Right. I'd almost forgotten about my momentary hunch Sunday morning that Malcolm's finger pointing in Linda's direction had been a decoy to take the heat off him. Hopefully, his latest conquest—Petra Horvak—could settle the suspicion one way or the other.

According to her background check, Petra's parents immigrated to the United States from Croatia soon after her birth. Five years ago she married in Raleigh. Since her subsequent divorce a year and a half ago, she'd worked a variety of unskilled jobs throughout the state. She was a dark-haired beauty who had a few years on Malcolm, although you wouldn't know it to look at her.

Zoe's assistant handed me a mug of coffee. "I can't believe Malcolm finally convinced Petra to go out with him. He's been angling for a date with her for months."

"Really? What do you suppose tipped the scales?" A sudden influx of cash from the sale of stolen paintings?

"She must've broken up with her boyfriend and Malcolm caught her on the rebound. The guys are total opposites. I'd have personally picked Malcolm from day one. But I've never understood women's attraction to those motorcycle-driving, bad-boy types."

Petra shuffled into the room. "Am I being fired?"

"Why would you think that?"

She glanced from Zoe to me. "Because Miss Davids is chief of security. Security escorts people out when they're fired."

"No, Miss Horvak, you're not being fired. Please have a seat. I just want to ask you a few questions." I waited for her to settle into the chair on the other side of the desk I was borrowing. "How well do you know Malcolm Wilson?"

Her eyes widened. "Why? Is he a suspect?"

"Please just answer the questions."

"Not well," she said, ducking her head.

"But well enough to go out with him Saturday night?"

She grimaced. "That's because he'd been pestering me for months. And he'd offered to treat." She gave a one-shouldered shrug. "Everyone's got their price, right? I figured he wouldn't read too much into it, since a bunch of us from here went together. It wasn't supposed to be a date."

"What did you talk about when you were out?"

"He talked about what he's studying at college," she said. "Criminal justice. Kind of ironic, huh? If he's a suspect, I mean."

"What else did he talk about?"

She looked off into space as if visualizing the evening, then shook her head. "I'm afraid I didn't pay that close of attention. We were in a pretty noisy bar."

"Did—" I caught myself before asking if they'd discussed the missing paintings. Interrogation 101—don't ask questions that have a simple yes or no answer. "What did he say about the missing art pieces?" I rephrased.

"He mentioned you were interested in Linda, probably because I was the one who'd told him she called in on Friday."

Okay, that was news. "How well did you know Linda?"

She shrugged. "Not well. We talked on breaks a few times. We don't run in the same circles, if you know what I mean."

I glanced at her file in front of me. "I see from your résumé that you started here last summer, and in the year or so before that, you bounced through five different jobs across several towns. Why so many moves?"

"My husband and I split." She squirmed in her seat, studied her fingernails. "I had a hard time getting past it."

"I'm sorry. I can only imagine how difficult that must've been."

Her head snapped up. "He's an accountant. So it's not that I was hurting for money or anything," she said, clearly concerned that I thought she might've been desperate enough to steal a painting. "He pays me alimony."

"Of course." I grilled Petra with the requisite questions about access to the museum vaults without any flags being raised, a pattern that repeated itself the rest of the day.

At 3:30—which was 10:30 p.m. Paris time—the call I'd been waiting for from the legat finally came in. I waved away Zoe, who'd been escorting in the next employee. "What did you learn?"

"The dealer who first bought the Monet wasn't much help. He said the seller was a dark-haired American male who claimed to be an agent of a financier who wished to remain anonymous."

"He must've gotten the agent's name."

"John Smith."

"You've got to be kidding me."

"That's what the agent told him. He said he had no reason to doubt him."

"Hmm." More like he saw the opportunity for a sweet deal and didn't want to doubt him.

"He said he checked the Art Loss Register," the legat went on.

"It wasn't yet listed."

"Yes. He also said the agent gave him the impression his client needed to sell the painting due to financial distress."

That could've been a ploy to make him feel it would be rude to question the provenance. The old days were long gone when once a painting crossed the ocean, it didn't matter whether a painting was stolen or not, it was cleansed, which demanded a great deal more diplomacy on the dealer's part to cultivate the often delicate relationships with clients. I let out a heavy sigh. It didn't help that too many wealthy collectors couldn't produce their papers if they wanted to, because they were irresponsible when it came to keeping records of transactions. "I suppose he figured he'd done enough to be able to claim that he bought the piece in good faith."

"Perhaps. I'll be in touch again once we speak to the dealer he sold it to in Nice."

"Thanks, I appreciate it."

Zoe must've clued in that the call was from my contact in Paris, because when I went to the office door, the next interviewee was nowhere in sight.

"Well?" she asked excitedly. "Do they know where it is?"

"Not yet, sorry. A John Smith sold it to the Paris dealer, if you can believe it."

Irene, the administrative assistant, joined us. "Did you say Paris?"

"Yes."

"One of our former interns is studying there. Left after Christmas." Irene slipped past us and sifted through the stack of employee files. "Here he is. Cody Stafford. His application says he's studying international relations at Wash U, but e was passionate about art. Sounded as if he'd taken a number of art history courses."

"Oh, I remember him," Zoe chimed in. "I didn't know he was going to Paris, though."

International relations and art history were a useful combination for an art thief. Remembering Malcolm's observation that Cody and Linda had talked a lot, I asked, "Was he friends with Linda Kempler?"

Zoe looked to Irene.

"I don't know."

I scanned the information on his application in the file. The address was for a dorm room that would no longer be applicable if he was on an exchange program. I tried the phone number and got a "no longer in service" message. "Do you know where he's from?"

"Illinois, maybe," Irene said. "That's where he was heading after the farewell party we threw him his last day. I assumed he was going home for a few days before heading to France." She turned to Zoe. "You were off that week, which is why you probably didn't hear about his trip. That last week, all he talked about was going to the Louvre."

"Do me a favor," I said, "and ask around to see if anyone has current contact information or knows where his family lives."

"Sure thing." Irene hurried out as I put a call in

to the analyst at headquarters helping me with background checks and asked her to move Cody to the top of her to-do list.

Zoe skimmed through Cody's file. "Do you think he and Linda were in cahoots? Or are you rethinking your suspicions of her?"

I snapped a pic with my cell phone of the intern's photo from the file. "Too early to say. But hopefully the legat will be able to find out once I get him this photo and an address." I glanced at my watch. I still had time to visit the registrar at Washington University before her office closed.

I hurried to my car and sped toward Lagoon Drive. The university's main campus was only a few minutes west of Forest Park. I snagged a parking spot off Brookings Drive in front of Brookings Hall, and as I pushed open my car door to step out, a pickup truck almost took it off. "Watch where you're going," I shouted after him.

He stopped and hooked his arm over his seat, looking like he might back up and try again.

Way to shoot off your mouth to Mr. Road Rage, Serena. I veered onto the sidewalk, but that didn't stop the guy. He revved his engine and reversed toward me.

"Are you nuts?" I screamed, diving behind a tree. Okay, asking a crazy person if he's nuts when he was speeding toward me wasn't smart either.

186

The truck lurched to an abrupt stop, the driver's laughter drifting through his window. He sped off before I made out a single number on his mud-smeared license plate.

And here Mom was worried my job would kill me.

11

I hiked across campus to the Women's Building where the Office of the Registrar was housed. Clusters of students hurried in and out, backpacks slung over their shoulders.

Doreen squealed the moment I stepped through the door. Doreen was an institution in her own right at the university. She'd been in the registrar's office for forty years. Knew everything about everything. She also happened to be a long-time friend of the family. She scurried from behind her desk and drew me into a bear hug. "So good to see you." Holding me at arm's length, she surveyed me from the tip of my sensible shoes to the top of my head. "You don't look any worse for wear. Still pretty enough to catch any boy on campus. You enjoying the job?"

"Very much."

"I'm glad to hear it. I chatted with your mom at the Christmas party and she wasn't so sure you were."

I laughed. "I think that might've been wishful thinking on her part." Brits may have a reputation for their stiff upper lip, but the gene seemed to have skipped my mom.

"She just wants you to be happy. So what brings you here?"

"I'm hoping you can help me locate a student."

Her smile fell. "One of our students is on the wrong side of the law?"

"I need to question him, but I don't have a current address. The last address his employer has on file was the dorm room he likely occupied in the fall semester."

"Well, I can tell you what's currently listed in the directory information as long as he hasn't blocked its public release." She slid back into her office chair and tapped on her keyboard. "They do have the right to block the information. It's all about rights these days. We have to be so careful."

"I understand." But based on Jax's nefarious plan to score me a confidential informant yesterday, I couldn't help but wonder if anyone else but Doreen had been on duty whether I could've gotten more information out of him.

"What's the student's name?"

"Cody Stafford, studying international relations. He's studying in France this semester on an exchange, I was told."

Doreen studied her computer screen and nodded. "Yes, that's right. I don't have a current address for him in Paris. But I can call their registrar first thing in the morning and see if they do." She jotted an address on a memo pad. "This was his home address and phone number at the time of enrollment." She ripped off the small pink page and handed it across the desk.

The phone number was the out-of-service one I'd already tried, but the home address would likely score me what I needed. "This is perfect. Thanks. If you do get his address in Paris, please call me on my cell phone right away."

"Sure will."

The other staff in the office began shutting off computers and gathering their belongings. I reached across the desk and squeezed Doreen's hand. "It was good to see you again." As I headed back to my car, I texted the analyst running background checks for me and asked him to hunt down a current phone number for Cody's old address or for wherever his parents might've moved.

"Serena, what are you doing here?" Dad hurried over, shifting his books to his other arm, and leaned in to kiss my cheek.

"Tracking down a witness."

A smile played across his lips, reinforcing my suspicion that Dad secretly admired my career choice despite appearances to the contrary when Mom was within earshot. Maybe he, like me, hoped that one day I'd solve the mystery surrounding his father's murder. "Were you successful?"

I held up my hand, still holding the pink slip of paper. "I think so."

"Guess you don't have time to join us for dinner then?"

"What's on the menu?" Almost anything my mom served would be better than what I'd pick up en route to Cody's last known address, and the driving would be easier if I waited until after rush hour, but it never hurt to ask.

"Bubble and squeak."

Almost being the key word. "Mmm, tempting."

Because rechristening leftovers with a cutesy name made them *so* much tastier. Especially when in Mom's kitchen, brussels sprouts were inevitably involved in insidious ways.

British cuisine. World renowned since . . . never.

Dad laughed. "I'll take that as a no."

I tried to look grateful for the offer, even as the flashback seared my brain: my brother's earnest face as he told me that if I held my nose while I ate my sprouts, I wouldn't be able to taste them. Followed almost immediately by sly glee when Mom thought I was insulting her cooking and made me do the dishes by myself that night.

Which, come to think of it, was probably his goal in the first place.

Maybe he should have been the agent in the family.

I'd never wished we had a dog more than the nights Mom cooked sprouts. Although something told me that not even a dog would've eaten them. The only thing worse than eating sprouts by themselves was eating a whole plate of mashed potatoes, overdone carrots, and dried-out meat that had been fried with them and thereby acquired their unappetizing flavor.

I shivered, then kissed Dad's cheek. "I'll try to stop by tomorrow."

"Before you go, do you really think someone in St. Louis is running a black market in spare organs?"

"What?"

"Aunt Martha said—"

"Oh, right. Well, you know, lots of churches are replacing their organs with contemporary worship bands, but I can't imagine there'd be much of a market for them, black or otherwise."

Dad grinned. "Another of Aunt Martha's wild theories?"

"Let's hope so." My phone rang and I glanced at the screen. Zoe. "I need to take this. I'll talk to you later."

Dad waved and headed off.

I pulled up my collar against the rising wind and hurried back to my car with my phone to my ear. "What's up, Zoe?"

"Irene was asking around about Cody, and I think you'll want to hear what one of the staff members had to say."

"Is he still at the museum?"

"It's a she. And yes."

I glanced at my watch. Five minutes to 5:00. "I know you're closing, but does she mind waiting? I'm only a few minutes away if traffic cooperates."

I could hear the muffled sound of Zoe talking in the background, then, "We'll wait."

I parked at the curb in front of the museum fifteen minutes later. *Rush hour* was the ultimate misnomer, since no one got anywhere fast at that time of day.

Zoe was waiting at the door to let me in. "This is Cheryl. She's one of our gallery monitors."

The young woman looked to be about twenty, dressed in the navy blue slacks and monogrammed polo shirt that identified her as staff.

"Let's talk in a conference room," I said and accompanied them through the empty, three-story-high atrium, our footfalls echoing. My gaze drifted up to the balcony where a night watchman was keeping his eye on us. He nodded and moved on.

Zoe led us into a small conference room.

I took a chair opposite Cheryl and pulled out y notebook. "I appreciate you staying late. I'll try not to keep you long. Why don't you start by telling me what you told Zoe?"

"A few days before Cody finished his internship, I heard him and the guard—"

"Which guard is that?" I interrupted.

"Mr. Burke. The older gentleman with the sick wife."

I recorded the name. "Okay, continue."

"They were arguing in the lunchroom. I couldn't hear what they were saying, except I did hear

Mr. Burke tell Cody he was crazy. As soon as I walked into the room, they clammed up. Right in the middle of a sentence. And didn't say another word to each other."

"Did they seem agitated? Excited? Angry?"

Cheryl seemed to think a moment, then said, "When I first overheard them, Cody sounded like he was trying to convince Mr. Burke to do something. When I walked in, he looked pretty intense too. You know"—she leaned toward me, her posture tense—"like this."

"How did Mr. Burke seem?"

"Upset."

"This was the last week of December?"

"Yes. Cody's last week with us. I think it was the Wednesday."

"Did you notice them talking at any other time?"

"Yes, on Cody's last day. We all stayed a little late to wish him well. Had cake in the lunchroom, that kind of thing. Mr. Burke didn't come. I figured he'd wanted to hurry home to his wife. But when I walked out to the parking lot later, I saw him and Cody talking by Burke's car."

"Did you hear what they said?"

"No, but Cody put his hand on Mr. Burke's shoulder, looking really intense. Then Mr. Burke batted it off and climbed into his car and sped away."

"What did Cody do then?"

"Watched him drive off, not looking too happy. He held his head like this." Cheryl pushed her fingers through her hair and clasped the sides of her head. "And he looked worried. I remember he slung his backpack over his shoulder, walked to where his bike was chained, and kept looking back toward the museum as he worked the lock."

Interesting. Maybe I could take my boss's word on Linda's innocence after all. "What did you do then?" I asked Cheryl.

"I got in my car and drove home and didn't think any more about it until Irene asked about him this afternoon."

"How well did you know Cody?"

"We chatted a time or two during lunch breaks."

"Did he talk about his plans to go to France?"

"Oh, yeah. It was all he talked about. He was psyched about going to the Louvre." She bit her bottom lip. "Do you think he took the paintings?"

"Do you?"

Her tortured lip scrunched to the side. "He doesn't seem the type."

"What do you mean by type?"

"You know. He wasn't materialistic. Wouldn't know the difference between a Boglioli and a Sears special."

Okaaaaaay. Since I had no idea what a Boglioli was, I simply nodded.

"He rode his bike everywhere too. Didn't seem to care that he didn't have a car. And I didn't get the impression he blew his money on partying like a lot of the college guys do."

I thanked Cheryl for taking the time to talk to me and joined Zoe in escorting her out. "What do you think?" I asked Zoe after the door closed behind Cheryl.

"As much as I hate to say it, it sounds like maybe Burke saw Cody take the painting and Cody bribed him to keep quiet."

I nodded. "Except from Burke's reaction in the parking lot, it didn't sound as if he wanted to play along."

"But he must have. He never reported Cody."

"Assuming they were talking about the theft at all."

"It makes sense. Cody wouldn't have had money to pay Burke until he sold the painting, and if he planned to do that in France, he had to convince Burke that he could trust him to send the money once he had it." Zoe motioned to the night watchman that we were leaving too. "Maybe that's what had Burke so upset. He'd be the one still at the museum when and if the painting was discovered missing, and he only had Cody's word that he'd send him the money."

"*If* Cody stole the painting."

I snatched off the ticket flapping under my windshield wiper outside the art museum. Only it wasn't a ticket. It was a coffee shop receipt with a message scrawled on the back in black ink: *All work and no play makes Serena a dull girl.*

I glanced up and down the hill and at the statue dominating the center, not sure who I expected to see. Maybe Tanner poking fun at me for all the times I'd razzed him about working too much. But aside from Zoe, who needed a ride, thanks to her sputtering car finally surrendering to the inevitable, no one was around. Everything but the skating rink on the other end of the park was already closed for the day. There were no cars, joggers, or dog walkers meandering the chilly, shadowed streets. But that didn't stop the creepy-crawly feeling tingling down my spine.

"You arrest some city worker's cousin?" Zoe motioned to the note, which she must've thought was a ticket too, and laughed. "Payback time."

I stuffed it into my pocket and climbed in the car. "Hazard of the job." Part of me wanted to confide in Zoe about this on-again, off-again feeling that someone was watching me. What was I saying? Clearly someone was watching me. He knew my car. Had to assume my going into the museum after hours meant I was working.

"You going to talk to Burke tonight?" Zoe asked.

"Yeah. By tomorrow morning, I should have Cody's address and phone number in Paris. I'd like to know everything there is to know about him before I make contact."

"Can I come with you? Then we could have supper together before you drive me home."

With the anonymous note burning a hole in my pocket, the idea of having company held appeal. "Sure. What do you feel like?"

"Chicken?"

Yup, that's exactly how I felt.

I pulled into Burke's driveway fifteen minutes later, but the curtains were drawn and not a single light filtered past them.

"Looks like they're out," Zoe said.

"Yeah, it's too early for bed. I'll peek in the garage to see if his car's home."

Burke's neighbor emerged from his garage with a dog in tow. "You looking for the Burkes?"

"Yes, do you know where they are?"

"An ambulance came about an hour ago and took Ella to the hospital."

"Thank you." I hurried back to the car. "Looks like the questions will have to wait."

"Why? What's going on?"

"Burke's wife is in the hospital."

"Then we go there."

I slung my arm over the seat to back out of the driveway. "It's not that urgent. The man will be stressed enough without me adding to it."

Zoe shook her head. "You're too soft. You've got to think like a hard-nosed cop."

"You've been watching too much TV."

"No, think about it. If he's already stressed, and

you turn up the heat another couple of notches, he's more likely to say something he doesn't want you to know."

I gaped at her. "You want me to put the thumb screws to him when his wife could be dying? I thought you liked him."

"I do. But if he's innocent, once he gets over being ticked that you still suspect him, he should admire you for leaving no stone unturned."

"And if he's not innocent?"

"He's bound to give himself away. Right?"

I backed onto the road, my hood pointing in the direction of the hospital. She had a good point, as insensitive as it sounded.

"Besides," Zoe went on, "if the doctors are treating his wife, he'll have lots of time on his hands to talk. And if, God forbid, she dies tonight, you'll be glad you talked to him beforehand, rather than have to harass a grieving widower."

I stepped on the gas. "Okay, okay. We'll go now." On the drive, I silently prayed that Mrs. Burke wasn't on death's door, and while I was at it, I added a prayer that my cohort in France would locate the missing paintings. I'm not sure if I could look the other way and let a thief go. But if Burke was the thief, I think I'd have a hard time sleeping at night either way.

I showed my badge to the receptionist manning the desk in the ER and learned that Ella Burke had already been admitted.

Zoe punched the Up button on the elevator.

"Let's take the stairs," I said, pinching her coat sleeve and tugging her with me.

She dragged her feet. "She's on the *fourteenth* floor, and unlike you, I have heels on."

"C'mon, it's good exercise."

"Don't start that with me again."

"Okay, okay." I let go of her coat sleeve and tugged open the stairwell door. "I'll meet you up there."

"What? You can't be serious. Serena, it's a big elevator. You'll be fine."

I waggled my fingers and let the door close between us, then sprinted up the stairs and reached the fourteenth floor as the elevator doors opened, except Zoe wasn't inside.

She tapped me on the back. "You didn't really think you could beat me, did you?"

"Hey, for all you knew it could've wound up stopping on every floor on the way up," I said a tad defensively, to which she just rolled her eyes.

We found Mr. Burke pacing the hall, back stooped, his well-worn cardigan sagged open.

Zoe hurried up to him. "Henry, how is Ella doing?"

He lifted his gaze, his ragged expression morphing to surprise. "How'd you—?" His gaze shifted to me. "Oh."

My empty stomach tanked. He was involved. He had to be.

Zoe must've seen it too. "We need to ask you some questions about Cody," she explained.

His face blanched. "Can't this wait? My wife's . . ." He hitched his thumb over his shoulder toward the room, his voice petering out.

"My questions won't take long." I motioned toward the visitors' room. "Why don't we sit in there?"

Burke let out a resigned sigh and shuffled to a chair inside.

I sat down and got straight to the point. "One of the stolen paintings has been tracked to Paris. We know that Cody is going to school there. We also know that the two of you were overheard arguing on at least two occasions."

Burke didn't look at me. His gaze was focused on a smudge in the center of the tile floor. He wrung his hands in his lap, the fingers turning bloodless.

I struggled to harden myself against the sympathy welling in my chest. Oh, man, I wished we hadn't come tonight. Even if he was involved—and his reaction sure made him look guilty—his wife could be on death's door in the next room. The last thing I wanted to do was add to his torment.

Zoe caught my gaze and gave me a get-on-with-it prod.

Drawing a deep breath, I mentally reviewed Cheryl's claims about the arguments she'd over-heard between Burke and Cody. "If you know something about Cody's involvement in the theft, I suggest you come clean now. I would hate to have to arrest you for withholding evidence when your wife clearly needs you at her side."

His head snapped up, the furrows in his forehead the size of craters. "I don't know what you're talking about. I didn't see Cody take any paintings."

I searched his eyes as he clearly fought the urge to look away. "Okay, what did you see?"

He dropped his gaze once more. "I didn't see anything."

I exchanged a frustrated glance with Zoe. Why couldn't the man see that I was trying to give him an out?

"What *were* you arguing with Cody about?" Zoe asked.

"How am I supposed to remember? We talked lots of times."

"On these occasions, you were arguing. Why were you angry with Cody?"

Burke shook his head. "I don't know what your spy *thinks* he saw, but it wasn't me getting mad at Cody."

"I can understand how someone drowning in unpaid hospital bills would be tempted to accept a small payment to look the other way. If you cooperate—"

Burke sprang to his feet. "How dare you? I did no such thing. Now if you'll excuse me, I need to be with my wife." He stomped out of the room.

Zoe leaned back in her chair, arms crossed. "Do you believe him?"

"I'm not sure."

12

"What now?" Zoe asked, climbing into my car in the hospital parking lot.

I checked the text I'd missed—an update from the analyst at headquarters on what she'd found on Cody. "A field trip."

"Where?"

"Cody's former address in East St. Louis. His stepfather still lives there."

"Go to East St. Louis now? Are you nuts? No one in her right mind drives into East St. Louis after dark. Someone gets killed like every other week in that place."

"Yeah, but didn't they have a murder last week? That means we're good."

"I'm serious, Serena. They've got guys stealing manhole covers right out of the ground for scrap metal. Drop a wheel into one of those babies and they'll probably spring from the shadows to hijack the car too."

"You're exaggerating."

"I'm not. I read a story about the manhole cover thefts in the paper. Besides, East St. Louis is in Illinois. That's not even your jurisdiction."

Well, yeah, technically, since it was on the other side of the Mississippi in St. Clair County, it was the Fairview Heights Resident Agency's domain, but . . . "I don't see the point of bothering anyone else when I'm only going to see if Cody's step-dad has current contact information for him." Besides, I was a whole lot closer than the other agency's office.

"Have you heard of the telephone? I know it's kind of a new invention, but letting your fingers do the walking really saves on wear and tear on the old car tires."

"Yeah, tried that. The analyst couldn't track down a number for him. And this way I can interview the neighbors too."

"At least wait until morning."

"Everyone will be at work in the morning. If you don't want to go, I can drop you at home."

"No way, I'm not letting you go there alone. What kind of friend would I be?"

"Okay then." I turned toward the highway.

She grabbed the dash. "Wait!"

Yup, I figured she'd only offered so I'd change my mind to spare her life. "Change your mind?"

"No, but if we're going to do this, we need to stop by my place so I can change into something I can run for my life in if needed."

I laughed. "Fair enough. I'll drop you off and drive around the corner and pick up take-out chicken while you change."

By the time I had our dinners, a light snow had started, and I felt like I was flying a spaceship with stars swooping past the windshield at warp speed. Not the best conditions for driving, but maybe it would keep the murderers indoors for the evening.

I pulled up to the front of Zoe's place and she skipped out of the house, bundled in a black parka and ski hat, wielding a flashlight the size of a billy stick. Add face paint and she'd be all set for Night Ops 101.

"What's with the getup?" I asked as she opened the passenger door.

"I figured if I looked like I ruled the streets, the riffraff would think twice before messing with me." She pulled something from her pocket. "If not, I brought my stun gun."

"You can't carry a stun gun into Illinois unless you have a FOID card."

"A what?"

"A Firearms Owner's Identification issued by the Illinois State Police."

"Really?"

"Really."

"Okay, just a second." She jumped out of the car and dashed back into the duplex she shared with her parents. She left the doors open, and I could hear her shouting, "Mom, I need your pepper spray!" Ten seconds later, she came dashing back out, victoriously holding up a small aerosol can. "Got it."

As I shifted into Drive, she said, "We need to stop at my cousin's around the corner. Number 14."

Her cousin was ex-military and an army surplus junkie. "What's he loaning you? Night vision goggles?"

"That's a good idea! I bet he has some of those."

"I was kidding. It's not as if we're breaking into a house on a dark, deserted street."

I parked in front of number 14, and her cousin Billy sauntered to the curb, a jacket slung over his shoulder and dressed from head to toe in black urban camo—all six feet four inches.

His arms and chest were a lot thicker than I remembered, and I was pretty sure it wasn't thanks to the sleek combat shirt hugging his chest like a second skin. Didn't the man know it was snowing outside?

"Forget the pepper spray," I teased Zoe. "Just bring your cousin."

Zoe reached behind her and released the lock on the rear door. "That's the plan."

"What?" I sputtered as Billy opened the back door and climbed in.

"Hey, Serena, good to see you again."

"Billy." I cleared the squeak from my throat. "Hey, good to see you too." Billy was two years older than us, and I'd had a colossal crush on him ever since I was eight and he'd rescued me from their tree fort after his brothers hid the ladder. A few years later, when half the world feared our country's infrastructure would collapse at the stroke of midnight because all the world's computers would suddenly go berserk, "thinking" it was 1900 instead of 2000 or some such thing, and my biggest fear was that the world would end without my ever having kissed a boy—not counting kissing tag in kindergarten—I'd confided the fear to Billy at Zoe's New Year's Eve party. Less than half an hour later, he caught me under the mistletoe and allayed my fears.

Deep down, I knew it was a mercy kiss, but I hadn't cared. It had made me tingle right down to my toes and pray fervently that the world wouldn't end at the stroke of midnight.

Of course, by the time I was deemed old enough to date, he'd already worked his way through every girl in his senior class and was halfway through the junior class, and my hero worship had dimmed considerably.

Zoe poked her elbow into my arm. "We can go now."

"What?" I tore my gaze from Billy's devastating dimples. "Oh, right." What was it about those dimples that still had the power to make my tummy dissolve in flutters and to make me feel fifteen again—*before* I figured out that he wasn't a girl's dream come true? More like my worst nightmare, if I had the misfortune of falling in love with the Casanova.

I stepped on the gas a tad more forcefully than necessary, and Billy let out a deep-throated chuckle that rumbled through the interior of the cab. Suddenly having the ox-man in the backseat didn't make me feel safe at all.

Having lost my appetite too, I passed my take-out box back to Billy and turned on the radio to cover the racket my pounding heart was making.

"Why do you think the senator voted against his own bill?" the radio announcer asked.

I reached for the knob to change the station.

"No, I'd like to hear this," Zoe said. "It was weird, don't you think? It's as if he's Dr. Jekyll and Mr. Hyde. He spent months pushing for support of his bill to limit foreign adoptions with his 'we need to make it easier to help our own orphans and unwanted babies before we bring them in from overseas' rhetoric that capitalized on his own unhappy stint in the foster care system. Then he goes and votes against it."

I kept my opinions of the senator's questionable choices to myself. But as far as I was concerned, any senator who would use his political clout to interfere with a federal investigation couldn't be trusted.

"This is proof," an oddly distorted caller's voice came over the air, "that everyone has a price. The senator made himself out to be this champion of foster kids, but clearly someone with a different agenda must've gotten to him."

"What a crock," Billy chimed in. "The senator's vote one way or the other didn't change the outcome. The bill still passed."

Reaching the Illinois border, I turned off the radio and turned on my GPS so the rugged Australian drawl of my GPS man could guide me the rest of the way.

Of course, that earned me more laughter from the backseat. "Do women really get off on guys with an accent?"

I glanced at Billy through the rearview mirror. "Let's just say if I have to put up with a guy telling me where to go, I'd rather he didn't sound like my brother."

Billy flashed me another of his dimples. "Or my captain. Yeah, I can relate."

Cody's old address was near the nuts and bolts factory. A blue-collar section of town. Not the worst. Not the best. But neither was saying much. Row houses dominated the streets. Front yards were so shallow a resident standing on their front porch could shake hands with a passerby on the sidewalk. Not that it looked as if many people walked these streets, at least not for fresh air and exercise.

"So who we going to see?" Billy piped up from the backseat.

"*I'm* going to see the stepdad of a college student I'm trying to locate. You and Zoe can wait in—" The car lurched and thumped and then made a real racket.

"Pull over," Billy ordered.

"It's one of those manholes. I told you." Zoe's

voice rose hysterically. "We can't stop here. That's what they want us to do."

"Chill," Billy said. "Sounds like a tire. You got a spare in the trunk?"

"Yes. And if you don't mind changing it, I could pay my visit while you work. The address I need is half a block up."

"Sure, no problem."

"What do you mean *no problem?*" Zoe screeched. "He's supposed to be our body-guard." Her panic would've been comical if three guys in ratty jeans and tattooed leather jackets didn't pick that moment to swagger out of the shadows.

"See!" Zoe yanked her black ski hat over her ears and palmed her can of pepper spray.

Billy climbed out of the backseat, dwarfing the trio. "Can I help you boys?"

The "boys" postured, throwing a glance in the car as I debated whether flashing my badge would make the situation better or worse. They must not have liked their odds, because they moved on with nothing more than a hand gesture in Billy's direction.

Billy poked his head back into the car. "Let me change the tire, then I'll walk you two in."

I joined him around the back of the car, where he was busy kicking a pile of bent nails off the street into a storm drain. I glanced to the corner, my heart doing a nervous dip. "I guess Zoe was right about it being a setup," I said, unlocking the trunk.

"Looks that way."

"I appreciate your help."

Billy pulled out the spare and the jack. "You can wait in the car."

"No, I think I'll stay here and watch your back. Those guys didn't get past the corner."

He squinted in their direction, then dipped his chin in a single nod. I imagined he'd seen a lot worse threats on his tours, but he didn't try to talk me out of the offer. "Zoe says you work art crime cases."

"That's right."

"Any leads on your grandfather's killer?"

My heart jolted. It'd been over a decade and a half since my grandfather's murder and ten months since I'd qualified as a special agent. And not even anyone in my family had seemed to make the connection. Or if they had, no one had dared voice it.

When I didn't answer, Billy stopped cranking the jack and peered up at me.

"Not yet, no."

He nodded and returned his attention to the tire, this time taking the lug wrench to the nuts. "You will."

My throat clogged at the confidence in his voice as my gaze settled on his wind-chapped hands working at the bolts, that vague image of the intruder's hands flitting through my thoughts. I'd done everything I knew to do—reported Granddad's stolen painting to the Art Loss Register, distributed its picture and provenance to all my contacts with the date it was stolen—so yes, one day Granddad's painting might turn up. It wasn't uncommon to recover stolen art a generation later, after the original purchaser had passed away and the person who inherited it approached an auction house to determine its value. Of course, at that point, the chances of tracing the trail back to the thief would be remote. And as sweet as it would be to recover Granddad's painting, I was more interested in nailing the man who took it—the man who killed my grandfather.

Zoe climbed out of the car. "You guys almost done?"

"Yup." Billy lowered the jack, then tossed it and my flat into the trunk. "Let's park closer. Then"—he glanced toward the corner where the three guys were still lurking—"I'll wait by the car while you two go in."

Cody's address was a three-story apartment building at the end of the block. A single glass door opened into a lobby sporting two rows of mailboxes with numbers but no names. Half the boxes looked as if they'd been jimmied open. The walls were cement block, the floors were chipped tiles—the same kind my public school replaced when I was in grade six.

"I'm impressed that a kid from here got into Wash U," Zoe said.

"Yeah, if he made good on selling the painting, apparently he doesn't believe in sharing the wealth with his folks."

The heavy bass of rap music reverberated through my chest as we walked the hall. Thankfully, it wasn't emanating from apartment 124. I knocked, and a clean-cut man in a white dress shirt and navy blue slacks opened the door. "Mr. Caldwell?"

"Whatever you're selling, I don't want any." He started to shut the door.

I blocked it with my foot and produced my badge. "I'm Special Agent Serena Jones. I'd like to ask you a few questions."

He opened the door again but didn't invite us in. "What's this about?"

"We're looking for Cody Stafford."

"Is he in some kind of trouble?"

"We need to talk to him."

"He's not here. Moved out two years ago."

"To attend university, we know, but do you have contact information for him?"

"No."

"When's the last time you heard from your stepson?"

"He ain't my stepson anymore. His mother walked out on me two months after the kid left."

"Can you give us her contact information?"

He recited her cell phone number from memory. "At least that's what it was two years ago. I haven't talked to her since she left."

"He returned to town on New Year's Eve. Can you give us the names of friends he was likely to visit?"

"Haven't got a clue. Is that all?"

"Yes, thank you for your time." I tried the number he'd given me, but the maddeningly familiar "You have reached a number that is no longer in service" message immediately responded.

A neighboring door opened and an elderly man poked his head out, his gnarly hand clutching a walking stick. "I couldn't help overhearing your questions about Cody."

"And you are?"

"Jethro Wiley."

"Do you know how I can get in touch with Cody, Mr. Wiley?"

His whole body seemed to jitter, likely from Parkinson's or simply old age. "You should ask Ariel in 234. She's friendly with most everyone, if you know what I mean."

"Ariel." I jotted down the name and apartment number. "Okay, thank you for your help."

As we headed upstairs, I glanced out the entrance's glass door. Billy was leaning against my car, arms crossed, looking every inch a bodyguard.

Ariel answered her door in a skimpy outfit, blowing on splayed fingers. "I'll be a few minutes," she said, turning away from the door without making eye contact. "My nail polish isn't dry yet."

Clearly she'd been anticipating someone else. I explained who I was.

"Sorry, can't help you. Cody wouldn't give me the time of day, much less a forwarding address. He thought he was better than everyone else. Never came to the parties. Nothing."

"Do you know who else he might've come to town to see?"

"I can't imagine."

"Okay, thank you for your time." I handed her my card. "If you see him or hear anything about his whereabouts, please give me a call."

"Yeah, whatever." She carefully pinched the card between her thumb and finger, being careful not to let it touch her wet nails.

"I wouldn't hold your breath," Zoe whispered as we headed down the stairs. "What kind of teen says no to a girl like that?"

My shoe slurped off a sticky step. "One with standards, maybe." Or something big up his sleeve.

"But if he didn't come to town to party with old friends for New Year's Eve, why'd he come?"

I glanced back at her. "Maybe he didn't. We only have Irene's word on it."

Zoe grabbed my arm and pointed out the glass door. "Look."

My heart tripped. Billy—big, strong, built-like-a-tank, here-to-protect-us Billy—was backed up against my car, his arms in the air.

13

"What do we do now?" Zoe hissed in my ear, her back glued to the stairwell wall in Cody's former apartment building.

I couldn't see who was holding Billy at gunpoint beside my car, and I sure didn't want him to see me before I had a plan. I motioned Zoe to stay back and, with gun in hand, edged closer to the glass door.

Billy turned toward my car and braced his hands on the snow-covered roof.

"What on earth?" I stepped closer. "It's a cop!" Two actually. I holstered my gun and pulled out my ID. One cop held a gun on Billy as the other cuffed him. Not that I blamed the cop for the preemptive measure. I'd want Billy cuffed before I frisked him too. The man was built to do serious damage. The Barney Fife lookalike holding the gun looked a little too edgy to risk charging out, so I raised my hands, my badge clearly visible, and slowly pushed through the door. "Excuse me, officers. What seems to be the problem? I'm FBI agent Serena Jones and that's my car."

Fife swung his gun in my direction, not looking like he believed me. "You're not from this district's agency."

Really? A beat cop knew the agents that well? "No, I'm from St. Louis."

The cop who'd been frisking Billy took my ID and scrutinized it under his flashlight beam. He wore a winter jacket, but his hands and cheeks were red. "What are you doing in East St. Louis?"

"Questioning the stepfather of a missing witness."

"We caught this man breaking into your car."

"Actually, he's a friend, William Cox." I motioned to Zoe huddled inside the apartment's entrance. "He and another friend came along to keep me company. Bill volunteered to stay with the car after we noticed a group of shady-looking teens hanging around the street corner. The car is FBI issue. The ownership's in the glove box. You're welcome to check it, Officer . . . ?"

"Davidson." Officer Davidson returned my ID, then opened the passenger door and rummaged through the glove box. He emerged a moment later and nodded to his partner to holster his weapon. "We're sorry for the trouble, Special Agent. People who drive cars this nice in this neighborhood and who have bodyguards the size of this guy are usually drug dealers."

"Please, call me Serena, Officer Davidson, and no need to apologize. I appreciate your diligence."

He grinned. "Name's Phil. Who you looking for? Maybe we can help." He unlocked Billy's handcuffs, and Billy threw me a scowl as he turned around, rubbing his wrists.

"I'd appreciate any help I could get. Our witness is a nineteen-year-old Wash U student, Cody Stafford, who used to live in this building with his mother and stepdad. I'd been hoping to find someone who's still in contact with him."

"We've got yearbooks at the precinct for all the local high schools. If he was on a sports team or part of a club, you might track down the other members and ask them."

"That's a great idea."

Zoe must've figured it was safe to come out now that Billy was uncuffed. "What's a great idea?"

"Officer Davidson suggested we look for friends of Cody in the high school yearbooks."

"Tonight?" Billy asked, his irritable tone declaring he'd lost his enthusiasm for the game.

"No, it can wait until tomorrow." If Doreen came through with Cody's new contact information in Paris, I might not need to bother at all.

Officer Davidson pulled a notepad and pen from his pocket. "If you want to leave me a number I can reach you at, I can take a look through the books at the end of our shift and call to let you know what I find."

I fished a card from my wallet and pressed it into his hand. "Thank you, Phil. That would be a tremendous help."

He tucked the card into his inside coat pocket,

then tipped his hat. "No problem. Drive carefully. The roads are getting slick."

Officer Davidson and his partner waited for us to climb into my car and start the engine before heading to their cruiser parked a few car lengths away.

I glanced at Billy in the backseat. "Sorry about the manhandling."

He shrugged. "When you cooperate, they treat you decent enough."

As we cruised past the officers, Davidson waved.

Zoe shook her head and made a disgusted snort. "How do you do it?"

"Do what?"

"Make men trip over themselves to help you?"

"I'll tell you," Billy spoke up from the backseat. "She looks us in the eye when we're talking to her. And she remembers our names and smiles when she uses them."

"Really?" Zoe half turned and looked over the seat at him as if hanging on his every word.

"Sure. Most guys figure any woman who smiles at him is interested."

I squirmed at the suggestion. Was that really what guys thought? I choked on a gasp. Was that what Tanner had been getting at with his does-Nate-know-you're-not-dating question?

Zoe shifted her attention to me. "Do you do that on purpose?"

"No!"

Billy's low-throated chuckle rumbled through the car. "You sound like you don't want a guy to be interested."

"She doesn't," Zoe said. "I always figured it was the challenge that made guys swarm around her."

"Could be." Billy met my gaze in the rearview mirror. "Men do like a challenge."

I arrived home to frightened squeaks and Harold hovering over a mouse in the live trap. "You're clearly not as big on challenges as Billy," I grumbled. Another mouse was the last thing I wanted to deal with right now. But I wasn't about to hand it over to Harold on a stainless steel platter. And unless Nate figured out how the critters were getting inside, the little guy would probably be back by morning if I plopped it outside.

I dropped my bag on the counter, then hunkered down beside Harold and scrutinized our captive. "I think it's the same one we caught before. Don't you?"

"Me-ow-ow," Harold said. Translation: yeah, let me show this intruder the door permanently.

I slipped my keys into my coat pocket and picked up the trap. "Not on your life. I've seen you in action. You've got the shakiest gun in the west. We'll let Nate handle it." I bypassed the elevator in favor of the stairs and knocked on Nate's door on the floor below mine.

"Hey." Nate's eyes lit as his gaze touched mine. "What can I do for you?" His gaze dropped to the trap. "Oh, we caught another one, did we?"

"I'm not so sure he isn't the same one. See that nick in his right ear? The first one had that too. Otherwise, I would've just let him outside myself."

"Huh, okay, I guess I'll have to take him to Forest Park tomorrow to help him find a new piece of real estate."

"And figure out where he got in."

"Yeah, which could be tougher than I'd thought."

Voices drifted through his open door, and I cocked my head to listen, FBI nosiness on auto-pilot. Then I smiled. "No way. You're watching *The Great Escape*?"

"Yeah. You know it?"

"Sure do. I love old movies, Nate."

"Yeah?" He propped an arm against the door-jamb, making irresistible look way too easy.

I suddenly realized I was committing the grave sin of smiling and using a man's name, and I faltered.

"Uh, yeah," I said, mentally cursing Billy. "My grandfather was a movie buff and we used to watch one every weekend. *The Great Escape* was one of his favorites."

"Cool." Nate's smile crinkled the corners of his eyes.

Oh, crud, now I probably sounded like I was hinting to join him! Hastily, I thrust the trap toward him. "You better not let Squeaky watch it. Might give him ideas."

Oh, that was brilliant. Yeah, I was *so* suave with men. *Not.* Billy and Zoe were deluded.

Nate's laugh rumbled through my chest as he stepped back, fully opening the door. "You and Squeaky should join me. Movies are always more enjoyable when you share them with someone."

I wavered, my arm still outstretched, holding the cage that Nate hadn't relieved me of. It was getting heavy.

"C'mon," Nate prodded. "I'm pretty sure I even have popcorn."

"Deal," I said, against my better judgment. Watching an old movie sounded like exactly the kind of distraction I needed. Nate finally took the trap, and I trailed him through the door. Wow, a pet sitter, a tea connoisseur, an art enthusiast, and an old movie buff. This man could be dangerous if I wasn't careful.

Blitzing Billy's voice from my brain, I shrugged out of my coat. The layout of Nate's apartment mirrored my own, except instead of being painted in bright lemony yellows, he'd done it in earthy greens and taupes. I liked it. I peeked into the living room and was drawn to a pair of Impressionist landscapes on the far wall.

"Can I get you a drink? Coffee? Tea? Hot cocoa?" Nate called from the kitchen.

"Water's good, thanks," I said, hesitating halfway across his living room.

He joined me from the other end of the galley kitchen, water glass in hand, and following the direction of my gaze, smiled. "You like them?"

"They're amazing. I love the way the light plays off the leaves. And the translucence of the colors is as stunning as the Blacklock my grandfather used to have." The paintings were real too. Not prints. How did an apartment superintendent afford them?

"My great-grandfather was a collector," Nate said, as if he'd heard my unvoiced question. "He left each of us a couple of paintings. My brother sold his at auction and bought himself a Porsche and a speedboat."

"So you weren't exactly kidding at the restaurant when you mentioned the outrageously valuable paintings kicking around your apartment. These have got to be worth a few hundred thousand easy."

He shrugged. "I guess. Not that it matters. I'm too sentimental to part with them."

"You've done a great job of caring for them." The humidity in the room was perfect, unlike my too-dry apartment that guaranteed sparks would fly every time I touched a doorknob. And he'd mounted them on an inside wall, avoiding the temperature fluctuations endemic on outer walls in old buildings like this one. And they were out of direct sunlight, but . . . "Aren't you afraid someone will steal them?"

Grinning, he punched a code into a discreet security panel near the light switch, then motioned me closer to the painting. "First of all, a thief breaking into the apartment of the building's super isn't going to suspect that the art on the walls is priceless. If he didn't know anything about art, he'd probably leave it hanging where it is. If he tried to snatch it"—Nate grabbed the frame and gave it a hard tug—"he'd find himself out of luck."

"He might slice the canvas from the frame."

"True. But by then, the alarm sensors would have already alerted the police."

Sensors? I hadn't even noticed them. I ran my fingers along the frame, surprised by the level of security he'd managed to attain so discreetly. "Impressive." Apparently, I could add security expert to his list of accomplishments too.

"Well, I wouldn't call myself a security expert," he said, picking up the remote and rewinding the movie, seemingly oblivious to his uncanny ability to read my thoughts. "Or I wouldn't have so much trouble keeping the four-legged riffraff *out* of the building."

The mouse squeaked from his box.

"I don't think he appreciates being called riffraff," I teased.

Nate sat on the love seat and propped his feet up on the coffee table. "Coming?"

226

My insides somersaulted. The love seat was the only chair in the room facing the TV, and he clearly expected me to sit beside him. Worse than that, the idea appealed to me more than it probably should.

I was really beginning to wish I'd let Barney Fife run Billy in.

14

The next morning I ate cold cereal over the sink, lubed with OJ instead of milk because I forgot to pick up more after dropping Zoe home last night, which also nixed my usual morning tea.

Harold sat in the center of the kitchen and yowled at me.

"Your bowl is half full," I griped, in no mood for his idiosyncrasies after seeing every hour on my bedside clock last night.

I don't know what preyed on my mind more, how edgy Billy's unnerving tour into the male psyche had made me around Nate, or the thought of having to arrest Henry Burke for accessory after the fact if my suspicions of Cody ended up playing out.

Harold yowled again.

I slapped down my bowl, picked up his, gave it a little shake until the kibbles covered the bottom of the bowl, and set it back down. "You've got to be the finickiest cat on the planet. There are starving cats in China who'd—"

Ugh. Did those words really just come out of my mouth? I didn't have my own kids yet, and I'd already become my mother. Thankfully, Harold was smart enough not to give me any lip about sending the stale food to Chinese cats if they were so hungry.

Or maybe he knew what they did to cats in China.

He sniffed at the food and then ate it half-heartedly.

"It can't be any worse than orange-flavored corn flakes."

Harold sat on his haunches and yowled something that sounded very much like "oh yeah?" then batted his paw under the stove.

"Oh, please don't tell me we have another mouse."

He batted a folded piece of paper out from under the stove and took a bite out of it.

"What have you got there?" I nabbed the rest of the paper before he could eat any more. It had writing on it, but not mine. *Sorry I missed you.*

My heart slammed my rib cage, my mind veering to last night's anonymous note on my windshield. I waved the paper at Harold. "Where did you find this?"

He stretched out his front paw and proceeded to lick it.

"Okay, I'm being paranoid." It could be a note any one of my friends slipped under the door. Except when I read it, I didn't hear a cheerful "Sorry I missed you!" with light, airy Beach Boys music playing in the background. I heard a deep-throated "Sorry I missed you . . . I won't next time," followed by a devilish laugh with scary sawing violin kind of *Psycho* sounds in the background.

I dug the other note out of my coat pocket and compared the two. The one from my windshield was printed in pencil. The one Harold found was written in cursive ink. I squinted at it more closely. Were those initials at the bottom? "T. H."

I gulped back the corn flakes inching up my throat. "The bald guy who sold me the painting in Buffalo had the initials T. H., Trent Hodges."

The phone rang, making me jump clear across the room. For a second, I didn't pick it up, thinking it was him. *Don't be stupid.* I snagged the phone and edged around the kitchen wall into the hall, out of sight of the windows. "Hello."

"Did you forget about me?" Zoe asked.

I glanced at my watch. 8:00 already! "Sorry, I lost track of time. I'm leaving now." I raced to the bathroom and quickly brushed my teeth, then grabbed my purse and coat. My hand froze on the doorknob. What if he was out there?

I peeked out the kitchen window. No sign of anyone lurking in the parking lot. I snatched up the two notes, stuffed them into my coat pocket, and left by the hall door, then circled the building the opposite direction anyone watching would expect me to come from. The parking lot appeared clear, so I scrambled into my car and headed to Zoe's.

"You look like a wreck," Zoe said as she climbed into the passenger seat.

"Good morning to you too."

"No, I'm serious." She clicked on her seat belt, looking very concerned. "What happened?"

I debated lying, but the blender whirring in my stomach wouldn't let me. I grabbed the notes from my coat pocket and plopped them onto her lap. "Those happened."

"Is this what was on your windshield last night?" she asked after silently reading the "All work and no play" note. "Not a ticket?"

"Yes."

She unfolded the note I'd commandeered from Harold and read it aloud. "Sorry I missed you. T. R." She laughed.

"R? No, it's an H, and what are you laughing about?"

"Because a gorgeous guy's trying to get you to notice him and you're petrified."

"What? No!" I shot her a glance across the seat, swerved into oncoming traffic, and got barraged by horns as I swung back into my own lane. "What are you talking about?"

"Tanner R. Calhoun. Your special agent field-training buddy. I've seen the way he looks at you."

"You're crazy. He's ten years older than me. The only way he looks at me is in disbelief that I'm slow on the uptake."

Zoe laughed again. "Exactly. And ten years is not all that much."

"No, no. The initials are T. H., not T. R. Besides, Tanner doesn't call himself T. R."

"His business card says Tanner R. Calhoun." Zoe scrunched her lips and studied the note again. "And this looks like an R to me."

The knot in my stomach loosened a hair. "You think so?"

"Why? Who's T. H.? Another prosecuting attorney who spotted you across a crowded courtroom? Another field agent who can't stop himself from asking you out for lunch every chance he gets? Or wait, my favorite, another would-be felon trying to sweet-talk you out of arresting him? You know, any other single woman would be tap-dancing over getting notes like these. If you really don't want to date, maybe you should stop playing so hard to get."

"I'm not playing hard to get." I stuffed the notes in my pocket. "Forget I said anything."

"Ah, c'mon. I'm sorry. You know I'm just jealous. I haven't had a date in weeks, and you have to beat them off with sticks."

"Hardly. But hey, would you want to go ice skating?"

She grinned. "Yeah, I miss our guy-hunting escapades there."

Oh boy. "I know this great guy Jax who's looking for someone to skate with. Maybe I could set you up."

"Really? Sure, I'm game. But don't think I

haven't noticed you're evading my question. Who's T. H.?"

I tightened my grip on the steering wheel as I flipped on the turn signal at the intersection to pull into Forest Park. "T. H. are the initials of a guy I arrested."

"Oh." Zoe was silent for a long moment, and then her voice dipped into another long *Oh*. "What are you going to do?"

"I don't know. He hasn't made any threats. I haven't even seen him. I just get this feeling that I'm being watched sometimes."

"Was that who knocked your aunt down outside your apartment?"

"The description didn't fit, but it could've been someone he sent."

A horn honked behind me. Glancing up at the green light, I turned.

"You should report him. Have someone tail him."

My gaze skittered over the pine trees lining the road—perfect cover for a sniper. "What if I'm just being paranoid? My boss will think I'm not cut out for the job."

"He's not going to fire you. You're a great agent."

"How would you know?"

She grinned. "Because your aunt keeps telling me every chance she gets."

Gotta love Aunt Martha. My cell phone rang as

I pulled up in front of the museum. I tapped the screen. "What have you got for me, Doreen?"

"Bad news, I'm afraid. Cody never showed up at the university in Paris. Hasn't been to any of his classes or checked into his residence."

Yes! I mentally fist-pumped the air. Not that I was happy about not knowing where he was, but his going AWOL smacked of not wanting to get caught. He must've figured Burke would squeal on him. "Okay, thank you, Doreen. I appreciate your help."

"Why do you look happy about this?" Zoe asked the second I disconnected.

"Is Burke scheduled to work today?"

"Yes, I think so."

"Good." I turned off my car and unfastened my seat belt. "I think I'll have another chat with him." I'd been replaying last night's interview over and over in my brain. I could buy that he wouldn't remember exact conversations he'd had six weeks ago, especially with all he had going on at home. And maybe I was reading too much into his defensiveness. Confronting him outside his wife's hospital room had been pretty low. But criminals at their lowest were the easiest to flip.

As we climbed out of the car, Zoe pointed down the road. "I think that's him."

He was facing the other way, wearing a parka that hid his body shape, but his size and the color of his hair matched. And I didn't like the look of the duffle bag in his hand. "Mr. Burke, hold up a minute."

The man's step faltered infinitesimally, but he didn't glance over his shoulder and kept on walking.

I darted across the street after him.

A motorist slammed on his brakes and horn, then flashed me a rude gesture as he cruised past. Burke didn't even react, except maybe to move faster. He tossed his bag across the seat of his car and jumped in.

I sprinted for the passenger door and caught the handle just before he pulled away from the curb.

He sped off anyway, taking two of my finger-nails with him.

"Argh. Stupid flip handles." Nothing to get a decent hold on. I streaked past Zoe back to my car. "Check your surveillance cameras. Find out what he stuffed in that duffle bag." I jumped into my car and yanked it into a U-turn in front of another honking motorist. Burke's car had already disappeared. I sped down the hill, a tight second to my racing heart. At Government Road, I glimpsed his aqua green sedan turning onto Washington Drive. If he wanted to disappear, he should've picked a less distinctive getaway car. Rather than flip on my siren and lights to pull him over and risk him speeding through Forest Park to get away, I lagged behind to see where he was headed.

He wound through the park roads to the east end and soon pulled into the hospital. Okay, hospitals had come a long way in sprucing up their interior designs, but I was pretty sure the admin wouldn't accept a hot painting as payment for his wife's hospital bills. Now that my pounding heart had notched down a few hundred beats, I supposed thinking he'd walk out of the museum with another painting in the middle of an ongoing investigation was . . . extreme.

I snatched a ticket from the parking meter, tapped my thumbs impatiently on the steering wheel as I waited for the bar to rise to admit me, and then parked nose-to-nose with Burke's car. His gaze met mine through the windshields, and for a second I thought he might do something really stupid. Then he seemed to deflate and turned off his ignition. I jumped out of my car and walked around to his door.

He hesitated a fraction of a second before lowering his window.

"Why didn't you stop back at the museum?"

"I don't have time for more questions."

"What's in the duffle bag?"

"Huh?" He glanced at the bag sitting on the passenger seat. "Is that what you chased after me for? You think I stuffed something in the bag?"

"May I search the bag, sir?"

He yanked it from the seat and shoved it through his window. "It's the contents of my locker. I went into work to ask for a leave of absence so I can be with my wife."

I pawed through the bag, which contained a Clive Cussler paperback, a couple of granola bars, a polo shirt, and a pair of polished black shoes. "Thank you." I handed it back through the window.

"Can I go now?"

"Cody never showed up for his classes in Paris."

Burke's fingers dug into the fabric of the duffle bag. "He didn't?" A gamut of emotions flitted across his face, from wariness to confusion to relief, at which point his fingers seemed to relax a fraction.

It'd been over a month since Cody allegedly sold the painting. If the kid hadn't already paid up, Burke wouldn't be holding out any hope he still would. So since he wasn't chirping like a bird, I had to assume Burke had already been paid and that learning the kid had gone to ground had inspired relief he wouldn't crumble under interrogation.

"Don't you find that strange?" I asked. "Everyone I spoke to about him said the trip was all he'd talked about."

Burke nodded, a tiny *v* forming between his eyes. "Yeah, he was real excited about it."

"Makes sense, though, if he was worried we'd find out about the theft."

Burke's gaze drifted to the hospital building. "I can't believe he stole anything."

"What do you believe?"

His cheek muscle twinged. "That I failed as a security guard." He returned his attention to me, his gaze intense. "But I don't want to fail as a husband. Can I please go see my wife now?"

I opened his door for him. "Yes. I'm sorry to have kept you."

He motored the side window closed, then pulled his key from the ignition and climbed out. "You're doing your job. I understand that."

"Okay, what did you find?" I groused, joining Zoe in the surveillance room back at the art museum. Yes, I was steamed. I was pretty sure Burke knew more about the burglary than he was saying. And I didn't want to believe he was involved.

Zoe confirmed that Burke had come in to request an immediate leave of absence.

I squinted at the monitor for the camera feed she was rewinding. "What else did he do while he was here?"

"He was in the locker room for three minutes, talked in passing to two room monitors on his way to the lobby, and then stopped at the reception desk and talked to Petra."

"Really? How long did they talk?"

Zoe rewound the feed and compared the time stamps. "Five and a half minutes. Looks as if she's trying to encourage him that everything will be all right." Zoe pointed to Petra on the screen. "See, you can read her lips."

"Burke looks upset. Is there another camera view that caught his face?"

"No, her head is in its way."

"Okay, I need to get to headquarters and follow up on some things."

I stopped by the reception desk on my way out. "Good morning, Petra."

"Oh, hi! How can I help you today?"

I smiled at her zeal. If Burke had been half as eager to stay on my good side, I might already have an indictment for Cody's arrest. "What did Mr. Burke talk to you about before he left?"

Her eye contact faltered, her gaze shifting to her co-workers around the lobby, as if she was trying to figure out who'd talked to me about her.

I tipped my finger toward the camera on the ceiling.

She laughed. "Ah, I see. Sorry, I guess we're all a little paranoid we're telling tales on each other."

"Mr. Burke?"

"Oh, right. He was really upset, because his wife took a turn for the worse. I was trying to tell him everything would be okay, but I don't think he believes it anymore. The poor man. I feel so sorry for him."

"Yes, it must be hard for him to know a kidney could save his wife's life and yet be powerless to make that happen."

Petra let out a heavy sigh. "Yeah, if my husband had been half as devoted, we'd still be together."

"Oh?"

She flushed, shook her head. "I really wanted a baby. He didn't. Not enough, anyway. Hardly compares to what the Burkes are facing."

On the way out of Forest Park to drive back to headquarters, I radioed dispatch to have CBP look into Cody Stafford's travel history. Except with open borders between the European countries, I wasn't sure how helpful it would be. He could've easily slipped out of France without being detected.

As I pulled onto I-64, I was about to put in a call to the legat in Paris when a black pickup charged up behind me. What was it with guys in black pickups?

I lifted my foot off the gas, but the driver kept hugging my bumper. "C'mon, guy, the highway's practically empty. Pass me already." I squinted in my rearview mirror, but he was too close for me to make out his plate. "Buddy. You picked the wrong car to play this game with today." I flipped on my lights and siren.

The truck slowed.

I flashed a smug smile at my rearview mirror. "Yeah, I thought you'd see it my way." I flipped off my equipment and flicked on my turn signal for my exit ramp. The next instant, the idiot clipped my rear bumper, throwing me into a spin.

15

The instant my car swerved into a spin, my defensive driving training kicked in. Yeah, would've helped if it'd kicked in a mile back. I tunnel-visioned the direction I wanted to go and steered, resisting the impulse to overcompensate. My instructor's voice echoed in my head— "power, power, power"—and I realized I'd reflexively eased off the gas. I lowered my foot and the car pulled out of the skid and up the ramp. *Yes!*

I pulled over on Jefferson Ave., my heart clamoring to make a jailbreak from my chest, and radioed in a description of the idiot's vehicle. Then I gave myself another two minutes to coax my blood pressure out of the burst-a-valve zone. Drawing a deep breath, I dropped my head and thanked God for protecting me. My gaze landed on one of the notes Zoe had left on the passenger seat—*Sorry I missed you.*

My throat thickened. He hadn't missed me this time.

I shifted the car back into Drive. It was time to talk to Tanner.

I climbed the stairs to headquarters' second floor a tad slower than usual. Tanner backed up around the corner he'd just turned and gave me a once-over. "You look like—"

I leveled a silent warning at him not to finish the thought. "We need to talk."

He trailed me into an empty conference room and closed the door behind him. "What's going on?"

I tossed the notes on the table. "You write these?"

"No." He separated them on the table with the eraser end of a pencil and scrutinized them.

I don't know what unnerved me more, his silence or the flinch in his cheek muscle.

"Where did you find them?"

"I found the 'All work and no play' one under my windshield wiper last night, outside the art museum, shortly after closing. My cat was batting the other one around my kitchen floor this morning. I assume someone slipped it under my apartment door, but I have no idea when."

"Who else has handled them?"

I hadn't thought about preserving fingerprints until Tanner pulled out his pencil. "Me and Zoe."

"Any ideas who T. H. is?"

"Thank you, I told Zoe it was T. H. She thought it was T. R., and since your middle initial is R . . ." I let the rest of the explanation trail off. I'm sure he got the picture.

"Who is T. H.?" he pressed.

"Right"—I reined in my stray thoughts—"Trent

Hodges is the name of the guy I bought the Kandinsky from in Buffalo."

"So he's found you already?" Tanner captured my gaze, his own both softly concerned and fiercely warriorlike. "Toying with your mind."

I stifled a shiver. "I think we might be past mind games."

"You mean the attack on your aunt?"

"Yeah, that too."

"What do you mean 'too'?" The hard edge to Tanner's voice would've been almost amusing if my heart hadn't started doing that prisoner rant on my rib cage again.

"A guy in a black pickup just tried to run me off the road." I raised my hand to cut off the questions I could see coming. "I called the police, but I didn't get the plate number and I can't ID him, so I'm not holding my breath. I suspect it was the same guy who tried to take me out yesterday."

"What? Why am I only hearing about this now?"

"Because at the time, I thought it was a case of road rage, not personal. Now I'm not so sure. Two incidents involving a black pickup, two days in a row, is a little too coincidental."

Tanner flexed his hand open and shut, his jaw working back and forth in time with it. "We can send the notes to the lab to see what they can pull off of them." He turned the note that had been under my windshield wiper over with the tip of his pencil. "This one was written on a coffee shop receipt. The shop probably doesn't have a security camera, but nearby businesses might." He pulled out his notepad and jotted down the date and time from the receipt. "I'll check it out. You check Hodges' file. Call Buffalo. Find out if they've got eyes on this guy. Known associates. You know the drill."

Yeah, I knew the drill.

I did the research, made the calls, all the while managing to disassociate myself from the thought that the creep I was trying to track down was tracking me. It hadn't made me feel any better to learn that Baldy hadn't left Buffalo in the past five days. Guys like him hired muscle to teach their lessons. Although it did make me wonder about the initials on the note. Maybe the note had been innocent. Maybe old Mrs. Hudson on the first floor had stopped by for a cup of tea. Her name was Katrina, but her husband always called her Trina—T. H.

I shook my head. The intentions of that pickup driver hadn't been innocent.

"Serena."

I whirled my chair around at the sound of my name, with the sinking feeling it wasn't the first time Tanner had said it.

The concern in his eyes intensified. "Aren't you going to answer that?" He motioned to the phone on my desk.

The *ringing* phone. I snatched it up. "Special Agent Serena Jones."

The customs agent on the other end of the line informed me that Cody Stafford hadn't left the US at all, at least not legally.

You've got to be kidding me. I curled over my desk and buried my head under my arms.

"Serena, you okay?"

Tanner. I uncurled and swiveled my chair around.

"I take it that wasn't good news?"

"Apparently my prime suspect never left the country." I shook my head at my pipe dream. "The only reason I'd suspected him was because he was supposed to have been in Paris at the time the Monet was sold. I didn't have a shred of evidence to connect him to the actual theft." Except that curious argument with Burke, and Malcolm's claim that he'd been chummy with Linda, neither of which was proof of anything.

"But you've got other leads, right? And an analyst is going through the names on your suspect list."

I let out a heavy sigh. "I've got other theories, but without hard evidence, that's all they'll ever be."

"Hey, don't beat yourself up over it. No one really expects you to catch the guy. Art crime investigation is primarily about recovery."

Yeah, what had made me think I could change that reality?

"And you've already got a lead on where the Monet is," Tanner went on, but my brain was still stuck on the no-one-expects-you-to-catch-the-guy part.

I'd trained for this job to track down my grandfather's murderer. If there was no hope, why was I here?

In middle school, there'd been a kid who made it her mission to make my life miserable. She'd trip me during intramural soccer games. She'd bump me in the cafeteria, making me spill chocolate milk all over my clothes. She'd sabotage my art projects. And all the while she'd innocently proclaim to the teacher that these were accidents.

This went on for weeks until my classmate, Matt Speers, came up with a brilliant plan to bait her into acting when the teacher would see her. These days Matt patrolled the streets for the St. Louis PD, so I figured that by now, he'd probably become a pro at baiting and netting. He'd sounded eager to give it a shot when I'd called him, anyway.

I climbed into my car behind FBI headquarters, my stomach as fluttery as it'd been fifteen years ago as I'd waited for the teacher on yard duty to round the corner.

I rolled up the street to turn onto Market and surreptitiously scanned every which way for signs of the black pickup. Matt was idling in an unmarked cruiser in the small lot in front of the main entrance and raised a single finger from the top of his steering wheel as I passed by.

Not spotting any suspicious vehicles, I merged onto I-64 and got off at Forest Park to circle around past the art museum—the second most likely place the guy would watch for me.

No black pickups, and along the way, I'd apparently lost Matt too.

I parked in front of the art museum where anyone looking wouldn't miss my car and then called his cell phone. "You still with me?"

"Yup. You going inside?"

"Yeah, I thought I'd give him a chance to make a move."

I crossed the street and glanced at the view of the Grand Basin from the museum steps. The fact I still couldn't see Matt's car had me a little unnerved. If black-pickup dude was as adept at hiding, we might not spot him until it was too late.

I meandered into the museum and eyeballed employees' reactions to my appearance. Some nodded, then turned their attention elsewhere. Some pretended not to see me at all. Malcolm swaggered right over to me and asked how the investigation was going.

"It's coming along." I headed to Zoe's office and caught her up on the new development, then perused a few employee files to kill more time.

After ten minutes I strolled back outside. Across the street a crowd of tourists spewed from a trolley bus. Still no sign of a pickup, black or otherwise. I took a detour to the lookout, leaned on the rock wall, and faced up to the futility of my not-so-brilliant idea. This wasn't junior high. And black-pickup dude wasn't an impetuous twelve-year-old. Who knew how long he'd bide his time before he acted again?

If he acted again.

Speers couldn't spend the next twelve, twenty-four, forty-eight hours following me around on the off chance the guy might take another run at me. He had a wife and two kids who expected him home at night, not to mention real police work to do. I dialed his number to end the exploit.

"Didn't they teach you anything at the academy?" Speers barked back, then muttered, "First Bunch of Idiots," his pet name for the FBI. "Bad guys have been known to change cars, you know. Tan, two-door sedan at your nine o'clock. Parked three cars behind yours. Guy followed you inside, then came back and sat in his car."

"A sedan?" I pulled out my car keys and surreptitiously glanced down the street, but I couldn't see the driver, thanks to the sun's glare on the windshield. "Did you run the plate?"

"I couldn't make it out on my drive-by."

"Okay, just a second." I turned and tossed my

head with a laugh as if he'd said something hilarious. "L, nine, H—"

The driver sprang from his car.

"Stan? You've got to be kidding me."

Stan Johnson slammed the door of the car in question and stalked toward me.

I pocketed my phone without explaining who the guy was. After all, what was I supposed to say? That he's the brother of a suspect I've been forbidden to investigate? "Hey, Stan, what's up?"

"Where's my sister?"

Matt pulled up alongside Stan's car, blocking it in, and jumped out.

I lifted my hand to signal him to stand down, then ran my fingers through my hair so Stan wouldn't notice. "I don't know."

"You're lying," Stan seethed, and Matt started toward us.

I shot him another glance that arrested his forward momentum. "If you want me to help you, Stan, calling me a liar isn't the way to do it. Makes me think that Linda's hiding from you for a reason. Like maybe she's scared you'll hurt her."

Stan visibly deflated. "I just want what's mine. She said you talked to her. Told her I was looking for her. She said she'd meet me back home in Kansas. Then she never showed up, and by the time I got back here, she'd cleared out her apartment."

"I'm afraid I don't know where she disappeared to any more than you."

"They told me inside she took a leave to care for a sick aunt."

I nodded.

Stan threw up his arms. "We don't got an aunt!" He stalked back to his car.

Matt pulled his car ahead of mine to allow Stan to leave, then sauntered over to me. "Wrong guy?"

"Yeah, he's harmless. I'm sorry to take up so much of your afternoon. We might as well call it quits on my crazy plan."

"Let me see you home. That's where the creep's more likely to wait for you. Although he'd probably prefer to catch you after dark."

My heart hiccupped. "Are you trying to scare me?"

He shrugged. "Just call 'em how I see 'em."

I let out a loud sigh. "Yeah, okay. It's not far. Let's go." I pulled onto the road, and Matt let a couple of cars fill the space between us before following. Of course, if black-pickup dude had been watching me back there, he'd have made Matt and wouldn't be paying me a call now. Turning onto my street, I scanned the interiors of the cars parked curbside. All empty.

I turned down the driveway and spotted a guy in gray dress slacks and an overcoat standing on the iron stairs outside my kitchen door, three floors up. He turned and waved.

Jax? What was he doing here? I slowed and pointed to the back lot to indicate I had to park first. I wedged my car between Mr. Sutton's '77 Buick and the fence. If Jax was hankering to go ice-skating again, perhaps I could steer him in Zoe's direction and end her dateless streak. I tore a page from my notepad and jotted down her name and number before climbing out of the car. Jax's head bobbed into view over the roof of a car. Then he disappeared with a loud *wumph*.

Thinking he'd slipped, I rushed out from between the cars. "Are you okay?"

Billy had Jax pinned to the ground with his knee digging into Jax's back.

"Billy? What are you doing? Get off him."

"He was coming after you."

"He was coming to talk to me. He's a friend."

"You sure? He's been casing the joint for the last twenty minutes."

Jax reared up, knocking Billy off balance. "I was waiting for her to come home, moron."

Billy drew back his fist, looking ready to plow Jax to the next county.

"Freeze," Matt yelled, his Taser bobbing from Jax to Billy.

Billy's fingers immediately stretched into flattened palms. Jax didn't seem to think the order was directed at him as he disgustedly swiped at bits of gravel and mud on his slacks and over-\coat.

251

"It's okay, Matt. I know these guys too."

Matt shook his head and jammed his Taser back in his holster. "Is there any guy in this city not trying to impress you?"

I gave an exaggerated shoulder shrug. "What can I say? I'm popular."

He rolled his eyes. "I'll leave you to them. Give me a call if you spot the truck trolling the area."

"Will do."

Jax spun toward me, looking aghast. "Some guy is following you?"

"Yeah, I imagine that's who Billy thought you were."

I introduced the pair and they grunted hellos as they reluctantly shook hands. Except . . . "Billy, how did you know someone's been following me?"

"Ma overheard Mable telling Mary Margaret at the hair salon that her husband heard on his police band radio that a guy in a black truck tried to take you out on the highway this morning."

Jax's face paled. "Are you okay?"

Did I look okay? I felt about as okay as my mouse must've felt dashing across the living room in front of Harold. Maybe worse, considering Harold was a wuss at mouse catching. "Sure," I said. "I'm fine."

"Liar," Billy whispered behind my back.

Ignoring him, I kept my attention on Jax. "Why were you wanting to see me?"

"I was wondering how you got along with that search warrant you were after. I guess you didn't get my note."

"Your note?" My heart thumped. "When did you leave a note?"

"Monday night. You weren't home yet, so I slipped it under your door."

"Oh, J. K." What I'd thought was a cursive capital T was really a J, and K and H were pretty similar. "That explains a lot. I thought it was signed T. H. so I didn't know who sent it."

"I guess I have to work on my penmanship."

"Did you leave the note on my windshield outside the art museum too?"

"Yes, sorry, I had no idea you didn't realize they were from me. I saw you go in when I was heading to the skating rink."

"Oh, that reminds me." I pulled Zoe's number from my coat pocket. "My friend Zoe was just telling me how much she missed skating at Forest Park, and I mentioned you."

Jax's expression went rigid, his gaze fixed on the slip of paper in my hand.

What'd I say wrong?

I looked helplessly to Billy.

"You talking about Zoe Davids?" With a wink, Billy snatched the paper from my hand, sounding utterly smitten. "Oh, man, if you don't want to take her out, I will. She's gorgeous."

I snatched the paper back and swatted Billy's

arm. "Somehow I don't think she'd agree to that."

"Ah, don't tell me she's looking for one of those happily-ever-after kind of guys. Why can't more women be like you?"

Jax tugged the slip of paper from between my fingers. "I'll give your friend a call. Another night of skating sounds like fun." He strode away with a quick wave.

I blinked. "What just happened?"

"Hello?" Billy knocked on my head and made a hollow tapping sound with his tongue against his cheek. "The guy was leaving you notes like a lovesick sixth grader. He wanted to go out with *you,* not your girlfriend. But you have to admit my happily-ever-after line was pure genius."

"Huh?"

"As soon as I saw his interest perk, I knew pointing out you *weren't* the happily-ever-after kind of woman would make him see the light."

"But—" I wanted to be that kind of woman. One day. When there wasn't a maniac in a black truck trying to run me down and my grandfather's murderer was behind bars. I fisted my hands in my pockets. "Why are you here?"

He shrugged. "When I heard what happened, I figured I'd make sure the jerk didn't show up here."

"That's sweet."

"Nah, I'm bored to death waiting for my new job to start. You going to be okay?"

"Sure."

"Give me a call if you want to get rid of any more wannabe boyfriends."

Laughing to hide the heat that flooded my cheeks, I saluted and headed inside.

Harold was meowing at his bowl of kibbles.

I shook it so the entire bottom was covered again, and he eagerly tucked in. "Are all cats as particular as you?"

Harold didn't respond, so I combed the cupboard and fridge for my own comfort food. "I may be as inept at reading a man's interest as reading his notes, but the pickup driver's message was loud and clear."

Finding nothing that would lift the funk I'd worked myself into, I closed the fridge.

In those bleak junior high weeks when Bully Betty had been on my case, the one bright spot I could always count on was coming home to Mom's sympathetic ear and fresh baked cookies.

And if ever I needed a cookie day, today was the day.

16

Mom burst out the front door the instant I pulled into my parents' driveway. "Are you okay? Lois called and said someone tried to run you off the road."

"How on earth did Lois hear that?"

"So it's true?" Mom's voice hit a new high.

Suddenly, coming home didn't seem like such a smart decision. Mom would latch on to any excuse to convince me to quit the FBI, and I wasn't sure my defenses were strong enough to withstand her arguments today.

She hovered in the doorway, her arms bunched over her chest against the cold winter air, or maybe against my rapidly cooling desire to be here.

Then the aroma of baking cookies wafted out the door and something inside me melted. Mom hadn't baked cookies in years, but instinctively she must've known I'd come home and need them. I tromped up the porch steps and threw my arms around her. "I'm fine." If I didn't count my queasy stomach or the double beat my heart made every other second or that I didn't want to go back to my apartment, especially now that it was getting dark. Other than that, I was peachy. "But I could really use some cookies and cocoa."

We weren't an overly affectionate family, and the hug threw Mom a tad off balance—psychologically, I mean. But that was okay, because I knew the cookies were her way of saying, "I love you even if you won't give up this job that will send me to an early grave with worry, or worse, without grandchildren."

Aunt Martha caught my hand and dragged me inside. "Was it one of Malgucci's guys in the truck?"

"Who?"

"Malgucci, the gentleman I asked about getting me a kidney when we went to Lou's Saturday night."

Mom's eyes bugged out. "You what?"

Aunt Martha waved off Mom's concern. "I was helping her with her case."

"I don't think so, Aunt Martha," I interjected before Mom could stop gaping. I'd been so sure the incident was connected to my undercover gig that it hadn't occurred to me that it might be related to my current case.

"Well, you must be close to a breakthrough if you've got the bad guys nervous enough to come after you."

Muttering a prayer, Mom locked the front door and pulled the drapes. "Come into the kitchen and have some cookies."

I dutifully obeyed, my spirits lifting at the mere thought of warm, gooey chocolate chips melting in my mouth and the prospect that Aunt Martha could be right about my current investigation. Maybe I was getting a little too close to the truth and black-pickup dude wasn't happy about that. Smiling, I shrugged out of my coat and helped myself to a cookie. "You might be right, Aunt Martha."

She pulled up a chair close to mine and whispered conspiratorially, "Is it the student you were looking for at Wash U?"

"How did you know about that?"

Mom set a mug of hot cocoa in front of me. "Your father mentioned running into you there."

"That lead turned out to be a dead end. The guy I was looking for was supposed to be studying in Paris at the time the Monet was sold to a dealer there. But according to customs, he never left the States."

"According to customs? So you haven't found him?" Mom asked, passing me a plate of cookies, seeming to have forgotten, for the moment at least, her mission to get me to quit.

"No, I don't have a current address for him."

"That sounds suspicious, don't you think? If I had the chance to go to Paris, I sure wouldn't give it up without a good reason."

"Me either," Aunt Martha chimed in. "Maybe one of his parents got sick and he didn't want to leave them."

"His father's dead and no one seems to know where his mom is."

Aunt Martha's mouth dropped open, and the cookie bite she'd taken tumbled back to her plate. "That'd make him the perfect pansy for a kidney donor." She scurried out of the kitchen and came back ten seconds later with her tablet. "When was this student last seen?"

Oh, boy. "No one knocked him off to harvest his kidney. There's a waiting list for those things, not to mention no way to guarantee the intended recipient would be a compatible match, let alone get it."

"Maybe he stole the painting in cahoots with someone else and his partner killed him," Mom offered.

Great, now Mom was sleuthing with Aunt Martha. I nodded, not bothering to mention that there was no record of Cody's death. I would've given Mom my don't-encourage-her look, but then she might remember that she didn't want me working these cases either.

"An unidentified male was killed in East St. Louis on New Year's Eve," Aunt Martha said, reading from an online news site.

"What?" I tilted the screen so I could read it too. "The victim was in his late teens to early twenties. Police believe he lost control of his bicycle and are asking anyone who may have witnessed the accident to come forward."

"In East St. Louis?" Mom dipped a cookie into her glass of milk. "That's not going to happen."

"You're a genius, Aunt Martha. I did an exhaustive internet search on Cody's name, but looking for something like this would never have occurred to me." I searched for more recent posts on the incident and found a follow-up. "The victim still remains unidentified. No one has reported any missing persons fitting his description."

"Well they wouldn't, would they?" Mom said. "If his mother's estranged and his friends all think he's in France."

A mixture of excitement and trepidation welled inside me. I didn't want this poor victim to be Cody. But if he was, Mom could be right about his cohorts in crime bumping him off. I sprang to my feet and grabbed my coat. "I've got to go. Thank you for your help."

Mom handed me a cookie tin. "These are for you to take home."

I kissed her cheek. "Thanks, Mom. You're the best."

"I'll keep searching," Aunt Martha called after me. "See if I can find you any more information."

As soon as I slid into my car, I called dispatch for the number for East St. Louis PD, then called their headquarters and asked to speak to Officer Davidson, since he was already up to speed on who I was looking for.

The operator took my phone number and said

Davidson would call me back at his first opportunity. Not wanting to wait, I maneuvered through rush hour traffic and hopped on I-64 to Illinois.

Davidson called me back as I reached the bridge. "I haven't had a chance to consult the yearbooks yet. I'm afraid last night turned out to be a long one and I got called out as soon as I arrived this afternoon."

"That's okay. I'm calling to find out what you know about the John Doe cyclist who died New Year's Eve."

"You think he might be your kid?"

"Maybe."

"I was one of the first officers on the scene. It wasn't pretty. The guy hit the pavement face first. No way we could make a visual ID. He had no tattoos, no piercings, short blond hair. I'd say he was probably close to six feet. The coroner's report would have the exact measurements, eye color, that kind of thing."

"Do you think it was an accident?"

"Could have been. He didn't have a wallet on him, which if he was only out for a ride makes sense. If it was a hit-and-run, it's doubtful the driver would stop to steal his wallet, but some other lowlife might've before we spotted him."

"Were there any witnesses?"

"You'd be better off talking to Detective Hanes. He drew the case." Davidson gave me the detective's number, then added, "Last I heard, all they had was that someone had seen a pickup truck in the vicinity."

I gulped. "A *black* pickup truck?"

"Not sure."

Great, and here I was back in East St. Louis, alone, after dark, when what I should be doing was having my head examined.

Except I'd already crossed the Mississippi by the time Davidson mentioned the *possible* pickup connection to Cody's *possible* murder, which might or might not be the same pickup that rammed my car. So choosing to ignore my fears, I drove to the police station to give Detective Hanes a rundown on my case in person.

Hanes sat behind an old metal desk from the days before computers. A computer screen and keyboard dominated two-thirds of the desktop. The half-chewed pens poking out of the pencil cup on the corner suggested Hanes was battling a smoking habit. That and his raspy voice and the telltale nicotine patch peeking out from his rolled-up sleeve.

"What happened to the victim's personal effects?" I asked after he filled me in on a few details Davidson had left out.

"Aside from his bike and the clothes on his back, there weren't any."

"He wasn't carrying a backpack?" The young woman at the museum, Cheryl, had mentioned seeing him with one when he left the museum.

"If he was, we didn't find it."

"Davidson said there was a witness?"

"Yeah, a dog walker on the next street said a dark pickup sped around the corner, tires squealing, and took off. But he never saw the truck actually hit anything."

"Make? Size?"

"Standard size. He didn't notice the make, although when he looked at photographs of different makes, he said it looked like a Ford."

A queasy feeling rippled through my stomach. "A black Ford pickup deliberately clipped the back of my car this morning on the highway."

"Before we jump to conclusions about this being the same truck, let's see if we can make a positive ID on the victim." Hanes asked his assistant to see if he could track down Cody's dental records. "Now, if Cody was here to visit a friend, you'd think the friend would've called the police when he didn't show up."

"Unless Cody was heading to a New Year's Eve party. It'd be easy for a host to lose track of who showed up and who didn't if the party was big enough."

"True." Hanes turned to the shelf behind him and pulled out a couple of high school year-books. "Let's see if we can find your student in one of these. If we do, and the coroner confirms a match on the dental records, I can call the kid's former classmates to find out who might've been expecting him at a party that night."

If Cody was our John Doe, what did that say about his involvement in the art heist? The whole reason he'd become my prime suspect was because the Monet had surfaced in Paris where he was supposed to be at university. The fact he never made it there totally unraveled the theory. Unless . . . like Mom had suggested, he'd been working with a partner who double-crossed him—killed him and took the painting.

The yearbook pictures all started to blur together.

If Cody's partner had been someone with no personal connection to the museum, with Cody gone, he had to figure there'd be little to link him to the theft. So maybe when Cody went unidentified after the hit-and-run, the killer deliberately sold the Monet in Paris precisely so we'd chase a ghost.

Then again, according to Cheryl, Cody and Burke had argued mere hours before Cody's death. But if they'd been partners, what possible motive would Burke have for running Cody down?

I nixed the morbid thought that a dead kid made a good kidney donor.

Burke couldn't have been in the truck that clipped me on the highway. He'd been at the hospital with his wife. Although if my theory was right that Burke saw Cody snatch the paintings and Cody bribed him to remain silent, Burke could've worried that once Cody left the country, his threats to snitch on him would lose their bite and gone after him to demand payment before he left.

I paused halfway through the yearbook. "Did the witness who saw the pickup get a look at the driver?"

Detective Hanes scanned his notes. "He said that the driver *might've* been blonde."

Like Linda Kempler. "Male or female?"

"Couldn't tell."

I didn't like it. Liked even less that my boss had tied my hands from investigating Linda. If only I'd gotten a look at the pickup driver that came after me, I might have some ammunition to fight him. But in both instances, the attacks had happened so fast that the only thing I remembered about the driver was that he or she wore dark sunglasses.

My cell phone rang and my heart jumped at the sight of my parents' home number on the screen. "What's wrong?"

"Serena!" Mom's frantic voice confirmed my intuition that something had to be seriously wrong for Mom to risk calling my cell phone when I might be working. "That mobster, Malgucci, just spirited away your Aunt Martha."

17

No, no. *No!* This couldn't be happening. "Excuse me," I said to Detective Hanes, then turned and spoke into my phone as quietly as my spiking blood pressure would let me. "Why did you let her leave with him?" Malgucci was a third cousin, twice removed, on his mother's side, to one of the most notorious crime bosses in the country, and although he'd never been indicted, every cop in St. Louis knew he had his fingers in the business.

"I didn't," Mom wailed. "It was your father. Said he didn't know he was a mobster. I was in the kitchen doing dishes when the doorbell rang. By the time I came out, Malgucci and Aunt Martha were out the door."

"Where were they going?"

"I don't know. A butcher shop, maybe. Malgucci said something about a kidney. But your father says Aunt Martha was as giddy as a schoolgirl, and she's never liked kidney, not even in steak and kidney pie."

My stomach heaved at the thought of the kind of kidney they would've really been talking about. Covering my mouth, I shot Detective Hanes an apologetic glance. "Have you tried calling her cell phone?"

"She left it behind. Your father says I'm getting

all worked up over nothing. But I've heard the rumors about those Malguccis, and your aunt hasn't dated much. If this is a date."

"Okay, Mom, I'll find her." I hung up and pulled on my coat. "I'm sorry, Detective. I need to go. Family emergency." As I hurried to the door, he promised to update me on what he came up with regarding his John Doe.

Outside, a mix of rain and ice pelted my face. *Perfect.* I wouldn't need a pickup's help spinning off the road in this. I jumped in my car, and as it crawled along the streets toward the bridge, I put the phone on the car's speaker and dialed Lou's restaurant. "Hey, Lou, my Aunt Martha wouldn't happen to be there by chance, would she?"

"Not tonight."

"Do you know where I might find Carmen Malgucci?"

"Try the bowling alley."

"Thanks." I disconnected and called Tanner next. "I need your help."

"What's up?"

I relayed the short version, and by the time I white-knuckled my car into the bowling alley parking lot, Tanner was sitting there in his SUV and motioned me to join him.

He didn't have to ask twice. I grabbed my keys and Mom's tin of cookies and dove in. Somewhere between the Mississippi River and The Hill, I finally admitted to myself that ten months as an FBI agent hadn't curbed my fear of danger one iota. Sure, I could do some fancy steering to get out of a tailspin and then pretend I wasn't scared the jerk would try again, but this was my aunt. What if I froze up at a critical moment, like I did the night that burglar murdered Granddad?

At least riding shotgun with Tanner relieved me of responsibility for calling the shots. I was clearly the underling of the two of us. In fact, I hadn't felt this green since my first day on the job. "Is Malgucci inside?"

"No." Tanner rammed his truck into Drive and peeled out of the parking lot. "Joe on the organized crime squad said Malgucci was seen entering Barnes Hospital half an hour ago."

"They have him under surveillance? Wait! That's where Burke's wife is." I squinted at every pickup we passed as I filled Tanner in on the John Doe that I suspected was Cody and on his accident that I suspected was no accident. At least my chest had stopped squeezing the air out of my lungs now that I was riding with Tanner. No one would dare run me off the road when I was with him.

Tanner banked the corner too fast for the road conditions.

I grabbed the armrest and braced my other hand on the dash. "Take it easy. I want to get to the hospital as a visitor, not a patient."

A few minutes later, Tanner turned into the hospital parking lot. "We're looking for a white Caddy."

"Stop! There she is."

Malgucci had Aunt Martha by the upper arm and looked as if he was muscling her toward a car, his other hand in his pocket.

Holding a gun? In my mind, I jumped from the SUV, my weapon drawn, and crouched behind the hood, shouting, "Hands in the air!"

In reality, I was paralyzed. Or . . . no, were those Tanner's fingers clamped around my arm? "What are you doing? They're going to get away."

"Your aunt doesn't look as if she's with him against her will. Look at her face."

Malgucci pulled his hand from his pocket, sporting a key, not a gun, and as he reached for the door handle, I could see Aunt Martha's face in the glow of the parking lot lights. She was smiling. Positively beaming.

Tanner's grip on my arm loosened. "How about you holster that gun and we go out and chat with them?"

"Right." I snapped my weapon back in place and shoved open the door. "Aunt Martha, you okay?" I stayed behind the cover of Tanner's hood while I gauged Malgucci's reaction.

"Serena? What are you doing here?"

"Looking for you." I glanced at Malgucci. "Mom was worried."

Aunt Martha weaved around the parked cars toward us, tugging him behind her. "This is Carmen and he's offered to be tested as a possible kidney donor for Mrs. Burke."

My attention snapped back to Malgucci. "Really?"

His gaze dove to the ground, his cheeks reddening.

"Ten years ago his wife needed a kidney and a perfect stranger came forward to help her," Aunt Martha explained. "After I talked to him Saturday night about Mrs. Burke, he couldn't stop thinking about her and wanted to see if he might be a match."

"Wow." I stepped around the hood of the SUV, joining Tanner. If this got out, it could do serious damage to his mobster reputation.

Aunt Martha moved closer and lowered her voice. "I think we put her poor husband in shock, though. He kept saying, 'I never thought she'd come through.'"

"I can relate," Carmen said somberly. "There were many times I thought my wife would never come through. When you have to wait so long for a donor, you start to lose hope. I was tested for my wife, and from those records, it looks like I might be compatible with Mrs. Burke, but we probably shouldn't have said anything before it's confirmed."

"You will be," Aunt Martha said positively. "I can feel it in my bones."

"Are you heading home now?" I asked, thinking about what Mom was probably feeling in her bones about now.

"I'll take her straight home," Carmen promised.

"Thank you." I mulled over what Aunt Martha had said about Burke's reaction as they headed back to Carmen's car. What if Burke hadn't been referring to his wife?

Aunt Martha's crazy theory flashed through my mind that the paintings had been stolen to pay for a kidney. I shook my head.

"What are you thinking?" Tanner asked me as Carmen and Aunt Martha drove away.

I muffled a groan. "If my face is that transparent, I need to seriously rethink going back undercover."

He laughed. "It's not to everybody. I just happen to know your tell."

"What? I don't have a tell."

He slanted me a look. "Mmm-hmm."

"I don't!"

Silence.

"Okay, what is it then? Tell me."

Tanner grinned. "Well, if I *tell* you, it wouldn't be a 'tell.' It'd be a . . . drumroll, please."

I rolled my eyes.

"A 'told.' "

"Tan-ner," I said, as menacingly as I could while stifling a laugh.

He finished chortling at his own joke, then relented.

"You nibble on your bottom lip when you're thinking about something that makes you uneasy."

"I do?" How could I not be aware of that?

"So . . . what were you thinking about just now?"

I sighed. "Aunt Martha's painting-for-a-kidney theory."

Tanner's head tilted. "You think Burke stole the painting? To pay for a kidney?"

I shook my head, already regretting even mentioning it. The last thing I wanted to do was arrest the husband of a critically ill woman. "I'd thought he might've seen who did and accepted a bribe to pay his wife's medical bills. But his 'I never thought she'd come through' made me think of Linda. Like what if the bribe wasn't money, but a promise to find him a donor?"

"We'd better talk to him," Tanner said. "Especially if you're right about that dead kid being one of your suspects."

We hurried up to Mrs. Burke's room, but her husband wasn't there.

"He was worried about the weather," she said. "Left about ten minutes ago."

The lights were off in Burke's house when we pulled up in front of it, and the driveway was empty.

"Doesn't look like he's home yet," Tanner said.

"Listen." I lowered the passenger window. "It's

a motor running, and it sounds like it's coming from the garage." I jumped out of the car, raced to the garage's side door, and peered through the tiny window. "His car's in there, but I can't see if he's inside!"

I rammed my shoulder against the garage door. Gave it a hard kick above the doorknob. "I've got a bad feeling about this," I said as Tanner ran up with a Maglite.

He shone the light through the window. "It looks like he's slumped over in the front seat. Call 911."

As I pulled out my phone, Tanner rammed his boot at the doorknob and the door splintered open.

"Show-off."

He pulled his jacket over his mouth and nose, jabbed on the lights and the remote that opened the bay door, then raced to the car and tugged on Burke's door. "This one's locked."

Following Tanner's example, I pulled my scarf over my mouth and nose and tried the passenger door. "This side too." Burke's face was ashen. "He doesn't look good." The garage reeked of engine exhaust, but carbon monoxide—odorless and deadly—was the real concern.

"Watch out!" Tanner snatched a hammer off the workbench and smashed the claw end through the passenger window.

It shattered into a thousand crumbly squares. I reached in and unlocked the door, then turned off the ignition and felt Burke's neck. "Got a pulse!"

Tanner raced to the driver's side. "Unlock this door so we can get him out without dragging him through the glass." He clamped his arms around Burke's chest and pulled.

I ran around and grabbed his legs. "Outside! He needs fresh air."

Sirens cut through the night as we carried him out. The icy rain had stopped, but the ground was still slick. Tanner backed his way toward the porch where it was drier.

My heart crunched at the sight of Burke's pasty complexion, and the memory of Granddad's lifeless face caught me by the throat.

Burke began to rouse.

"Mr. Burke, Mr. Burke, can you hear me?" We laid him on the porch and as I rubbed his hand, trying to get him to respond, Tanner balled up his jacket and tucked it under Burke's head.

"Why?" Burke whispered, a tortured expression twisting his face. "I told her I wouldn't tell."

I exchanged a glance with Tanner, not liking how this sounded. "Told who?" I patted his cheeks. "Mr. Burke, stay with me. What wouldn't you tell?"

Tanner caught me by the shoulders and pulled me away. "The paramedics are here."

I resisted letting him move me more than a few feet back. "Didn't you hear what Burke said?

Someone did this to him. A *her*. A *her* who was afraid he'd tell on her."

Tanner shook his head. "You're extrapolating. For all we know he could've been talking about something he told his wife."

"He has a contusion on the back of his head," one of the paramedics said. "Did you see how he got it?"

"No." We filled the paramedics in on how we found him slumped in the front seat of the running car, then repeated the story to the police officers who arrived shortly afterward. My friend Matt Speers was one of the responding officers. I told him what Burke said and about the contusion the paramedics found and that Burke was a witness in a federal case. "This wasn't a suicide attempt. You need to canvass the neighbors. Ask if anyone saw someone suspicious lurking around. A strange vehicle on the street. Anything out of the ordinary."

"We will," he assured.

Tanner gave Matt his card so he could keep us posted, and then we followed the ambulance to the hospital. The triage nurse relegated us to an empty waiting room.

Tanner motioned me to take a seat and pulled another chair up beside mine. "What do you think Burke knows?"

I reminded him of my theory that Cody had bribed Burke to keep quiet about something he saw, and my unconfirmed belief that Cody was killed in a hit-and-run by a driver of a black pickup.

"And now you think Cody's partner is tying up loose ends?"

"Yes."

"And I'm guessing you think the partner is Linda?"

"You heard Burke. He said *her*."

"Half the population is female."

"Yes, but Linda's the only one who's quit her job and skipped town since I started investigating this case. Not to mention convinced her powerful boyfriend to pull strings with Benton to get her off my suspect list."

"Benton wouldn't have done that unless he believed she was innocent."

"I have an informant who says a blonde tried to sell the Monet to a local pawnshop before Christmas."

"And what's that? Half the *female* population?"

"You got any better theories?"

"Nope. If he comes around enough for us to talk to him, let's run with that one and see where we go."

Matt Speers stepped into the small waiting room. "Doesn't look like any of us will get more information out of your witness tonight."

I sprang to my feet. "Did you talk to the doctor?"

"Yes, he says Burke hasn't regained consciousness, and if he does, the doctor doesn't want us disturbing him before morning."

"But he's going to make it, isn't he?" I asked.

Matt shrugged. "Apparently the CO levels in his blood are dangerously high."

I turned to Tanner. "We need to talk to his wife." I would have told him he could head home, but I needed him to take me to retrieve my car from the bowling alley's parking lot, and I didn't want to leave before I talked to Burke's wife.

Matt blocked our exit. "There's something else I need to tell you."

I didn't like the look of his jaw working back and forth or the shadow that crossed his eyes. "What?" My voice sounded unnaturally high.

"Two of Burke's neighbors noticed a black pickup parked on the street around the time he returned from the hospital."

I stared at him, feeling as if my mind were racing through the implications at the same time it was being sucked into quicksand.

"Did either of them get a license plate?" Tanner spoke up.

Matt searched my eyes before lifting his gaze to Tanner. "No."

I drew in a deep breath and sank into a chair. "But this is good, right? It means that everything's connected. Cody's death, if I'm right about that. The attempt on Burke's life. My"—I swallowed hard, searching for the right word—"excitement on the highway this morning."

Tanner hunkered down beside me and squeezed my hand.

Right, who was I kidding? A guy who'd run down a kid in cold blood and stuff an unconscious man in an exhaust-filled car didn't clip my car for the fun of it.

I slipped my hand from Tanner's clasp and lifted my chin. "The only thing Burke, Cody, and I have in common is my investigation into the art museum theft. The real culprit must've been afraid Burke was going to give him away. We need to post a guard on his room in case he tries again."

"Taken care of," Matt confirmed.

"Good, let's see what his wife can tell us."

The nurse intercepted us before we got to the room. "I'm afraid it's too late for visitors. Our patients need their rest."

I reached for my badge, but Matt was in uniform and said, "This is police business."

The nurse wavered a moment, then let us pass.

"You might want to post a guard outside her room tonight too," Tanner suggested to Matt before we went in.

Matt gently broke the news to Mrs. Burke about her husband's condition, sounding far more optimistic about his prospects for recovery than he had ten minutes ago. Not that I blamed him. Mrs. Burke looked so frail, lying in the hospital bed with oxygen under her nose and an IV taped to the back of her age-spotted hand. Matt motioned to Tanner and me. "These are the agents that saved your husband. They'd like to ask you a few questions."

Gratitude filled Mrs. Burke's eyes. "Oh, thank you so much for saving my Henry. I don't know what I'd do without him."

I pulled up a chair next to her bed as Tanner leaned against the wall beside Matt. "Mrs. Burke, your house wasn't burglarized, so it appears that your husband's assailant had been waiting for him. Do you know who would want to hurt your husband?"

She shook her head. "That can't be right. Everyone loves Henry. He must've surprised another prowler."

I recalled her mentioning hearing a prowler that first day I'd visited their house. "What was the prowler looking for?"

"I don't know. We don't have anything worth stealing."

"Your husband mentioned a woman, someone he'd made a promise to about not telling something. Do you know who that would be?"

The wrinkles on her forehead deepened. "No."

"Do you know what secret he'd promised to keep?"

Her eyes rounded. "You're wrong. We never kept secrets from each other."

"We think it might've been an employee at the museum," I pressed. "And he could still be in danger. If you know anything, anything at all, you need to tell us."

She gasped, panic lighting her eyes. "I don't! You have to be wrong. Henry is a good man."

Tanner pushed off the wall and whispered close to my ear. "Let's go. She doesn't know anything, and you've already got everything you need to know."

Yeah, that Burke was the kind of man who'd do *anything* for the woman he loved.

18

At the sound of a motor humming through my apartment door, I reached into my jacket pocket and palmed my small off-duty pistol. I didn't usually carry when out for a run, but with black-pickup dude playing pinball with my life, I wasn't taking any chances. On second listen, the motor sounded a lot like a vacuum.

What on earth? Hit men were cleaning up before their crimes these days?

I opened the door and followed the vacuum cord down the hall. I had a hard time believing Aunt Martha got bit by a cleaning bug, but she and Zoe were the only ones with keys to the place. Well, and Nate.

I hesitated halfway down the hall and nixed the homey image of Nate doing my chores. Nate wouldn't let himself in to vacuum, would he? That would cross waaaay too many boundaries.

I reached down and yanked the cord from the outlet.

"Lousy breakers," Mom muttered, shuffling out of the bedroom, blowing wayward hair out of her eyes.

"Mum? How did you get in here?"

"Oh, Serena, you're back. Good. I used the spare key Aunt Martha gave me when she lived here."

"Why?"

"Because she's gone out again with that Malgucci fellow and you need to do something."

I zipped the pocket hiding my pistol and dropped my jacket on my bed. "I have to have a shower and get to work. Besides, Carmen seems like a nice enough man." If you ignored his alleged profession. "And in case you haven't noticed, no one stops Aunt Martha from doing anything she sets her mind on."

Mom huffily wound up the vacuum cord as I grabbed my bathrobe and towel. Not that I was complaining. I'd rather her fuss about Aunt Martha's love life than mine, and if she wanted to go on a cleaning binge while she did it, bonus.

"What's with that orange smell?" Mom asked as she shoved the vacuum back in the closet. "The whole apartment smells like oranges."

"I was diffusing the essential oil. It's supposed to relieve stress."

"Stress? Ha! Wait until you have a daughter who wants to play cops and robbers instead of give you grandchildren, not to mention a crazy aunt who dates a mobster. Then we'll talk about stress."

"Mum, Aunt Martha is fine. She's not doing anything illegal."

"Where your aunt's concerned, I wouldn't be too sure. You never should've encouraged her sleuthing."

Okay, I would've conceded that point, but a call interrupted the discussion. Detective Hanes. I edged away from Mom as I answered. "Do you have news?"

"Yes, you were right. Cody's dental records confirmed he's our John Doe."

"I can't say I'm glad to hear it, but it's good to know. Thanks for calling." I clicked off the phone. "I'm sorry, Mum. There's been a new development in my case and I need to hurry." I didn't mention that the college kid I'd been looking for had been killed in a hit-and-run, possibly caused by the same jerk who'd tried to take me out on the highway. Wouldn't want to add to her stress.

Mom snatched her coat out from under the sleeping cat on the spare bed. "Okay, but if your aunt winds up in the slammer, you'll be the one we'll call to bail her out."

"Fair enough." And as much as I didn't think we needed to worry about her being out with Carmen Malgucci, I wouldn't be surprised if I got such a call. Aunt Martha was like one of those extreme sports nuts who didn't realize "safety harness" was a pseudonym for "hang on for dear life or you'll die harness."

I hurried through my shower and opted to stop by the museum before interrogating Burke, to gauge the reaction among the staff to news of Cody's death. I arrived half an hour before the museum opened and filled Zoe in on my plan.

She staggered at the news. "Didn't I tell you people were always getting killed in East St. Louis?" She shuddered. "And you really think it was the thief?"

"One too many black pickups causing havoc to be a coincidence, don't you think?"

She grabbed my arm. "You think it was the same guy who came after you?" She gasped, apparently only now making the connection. "And you think it's a staff member?"

"Since none of the staff members drive pickups, I suspect he's someone known to a current or former staff member."

"Known to someone besides Cody?"

"Yes."

Zoe immediately called an impromptu staff meeting and shared the sad news. Gasps went up all around the room. She held up her hand, asking for quiet. "Due to the suspicious nature of his tragic death in close proximity to the theft here, Special Agent Jones would like to speak to you about it."

I stepped to the front of the crowded conference room and scanned the faces of the group. "Have any of you ever seen Cody speaking to someone who drives a black pickup?"

Heads shook around the room.

"If any of you have observed someone driving a black pickup in the vicinity, please talk to me. The smallest detail might be helpful." I let my gaze travel around the room and rest momentarily on each face as Zoe dismissed them. Malcolm glanced from a frowning Irene to Petra, who was already heading out the door. *Curious.*

I hung back in the conference room in case any staff wished to talk to me.

None stuck around.

I walked over to the administrative area and cornered Irene. "What were you thinking back there? Do you know someone with a black pickup?"

She pressed her lips together, clearly reluctant to say.

"Irene, I know you wouldn't want to falsely accuse someone, but if there's the remotest chance he might be our driver, I need to know."

"Malcolm has a friend who drives a black pickup. I've seen them at the fast-food joint where my daughter works."

And presumably, Malcolm suspected Petra had seen his friend's truck too. Perhaps the night she joined them for drinks after work. Maybe he was wondering if she'd say anything.

Malcolm was waiting for me as I exited the administrative area. "Did Irene tell you?"

"Tell me what?"

Malcolm glanced over his shoulder and motioned me into an empty conference room. "That a guy in a black pickup picked Linda up a few times after work."

I tilted my head, wondering if this was a ploy to distract me from his friend.

"Linda Kempler?" I asked skeptically, even as my insides did a wild jig.

"I know what you're thinking. She was dating the senator, right? But there was this other guy too."

"Can you describe his truck?"

"Just a basic truck. Nothing fancy. No chrome or anything."

Okay, that fit the description. "Did you get a look at the guy? The license plate?"

"Nah. Sorry."

"And what about your friend's black truck?" I asked, because as eager as I was to get over to the hospital and press Burke on who the "her" was he'd been talking about, I couldn't ignore the fact that Malcolm had failed to mention his own friend's truck. "Could you describe it?"

Malcolm did a double take and glanced toward the admin office. "You mean Eric's? It's a short-box sidestep on monster wheels."

Okay, that didn't fit the description, but I'd run it by Irene to make sure it was the one she'd seen. "Thank you, I appreciate you coming forward."

I called Tanner, told him about Linda's purported friend with the black pickup, and asked him to meet me at the hospital to question Burke.

"Do you want to take the lead?" Tanner asked when we met outside Burke's room.

With a nod, I drew in a deep breath and told myself that no matter Burke's reasons, he'd brought this on himself.

Like I'd done with Mrs. Burke the night before, I pulled up a chair next to his bed and got straight to the point. "Did you see who hit you, Mr. Burke?"

"No, it happened too fast. He was wearing jeans and a ski mask. That's all I saw."

"It was a *he?* Last night you said you told *her* you wouldn't tell."

Burke's gaze jerked to mine, deep grooves furrowing his brow. He reached behind his head and massaged what I presumed was the goose egg his assailant had given him. "I . . . I don't know what I was saying."

"Do you have a suspicion of who attacked you?"

"No!"

"There was no sign your house was burglarized," Tanner cut in, "so it would seem your assailant was waiting for you. Why do you think that is?"

His breathing quickened. An alarm went off on the machine next to his bed.

A nurse rushed in and strained to calm him, found a detached wire, and reattached it, silencing the alarm. "Maybe it would be better if you come back later to finish your questions," she said to Tanner and me.

"This can't wait." Tanner crossed his arms over his chest, scrutinizing Burke.

The nurse wavered a moment, then left the room.

"I'm beginning to think you couldn't bear to see your wife waste away any longer," Tanner continued, "and decided to check out on your own terms."

I gasped at his callousness.

Burke fisted his hands, looking as if he wanted to rip him limb from limb, and I had to bite my lip to keep from saying, "Get in line." After months spent under Tanner's supervision, I was used to his out-of-left-field remarks. But this was a new low, even for him.

"Then when we foiled your suicide attempt," Tanner went on as if he hadn't noticed, or didn't care, "you made up the assailant story to cover up."

"You're wrong. I would do anything for my wife," Burke insisted through clenched teeth. "I'd never leave her to die alone. Never."

Tilting his head, Tanner met my gaze across Burke's bed and mouthed, "He'd do *anything*."

I felt as if I might lose my cookies. Tanner had an amazingly accurate intuition, but I didn't want to believe it was on the mark this time. Or that he was apparently leaving it to me to delve into what Burke meant by *anything*. Hating myself already, I returned my attention to Burke. "So if Cody had to die to conceal the secret you're keeping, that's okay, I suppose?"

Burke's face turned even whiter. "Cody's dead?"

Clearly, this was news to him, which made me feel a little better.

"I"—Burke's mouth bobbed open and shut like a gasping guppy's—"I didn't know."

Not surprising, if he didn't do it, considering that until two hours ago, the hit-and-run victim had still officially been a John Doe. "Well, my guess is that whoever silenced him got wind that I was close to figuring it out and was worried you'd crack once you heard."

His Adam's apple dipped. "I don't know what you're talking about."

Tanner moseyed to the door of Burke's hospital room and stuck out his head. "Hey, looks like we can pull the officer off guard duty. He doesn't think anyone is after him."

I gritted my teeth, hating how much Tanner was torturing the poor old man.

"No, please," Burke blurted.

Tanner's pinched mouth and the impatient glint in his eyes left no doubt he was waiting for an explanation.

"Okay, okay." Burke's gaze ricocheted off the walls like a trapped bird desperate to escape, then finally landed on me. "It was like you said." A muscle in his jaw twitched and his gaze shifted to my shoulder. "Cody stole the painting and bribed me to keep my mouth shut. I don't know who killed him. Maybe whoever he sold it to, but Cody never paid me."

"You better read him his rights," Tanner said.

Yeah, considering that in my mind, I'd probably already crossed the blurry line from victim to suspect when I brought up Cody's death.

Before I was halfway through reading the card, Burke started pleading, "Please, I can't go to jail. My wife needs me. I didn't take the paintings. I just . . . just . . . kept my mouth shut."

"Do you understand these rights?" I pressed on.

"Yes, but please, don't take me away from my wife." He closed his eyes and splayed his hand over his forehead. "What have I done? All I wanted to do was help her. If you arrest me, I'll lose my job, my medical benefits."

Tanner sighed. "It's too bad you don't know who Cody's partner was. We might've been able to offer you a proffer agreement."

Burke pulled his hand from his face, a hopeful light in his eyes. "What's that?"

A whisper of a smile rippled Tanner's lips as he and I exchanged glances once more.

Sometimes I wished I could climb into his head and figure out how he knew what a suspect's reaction would be three or four moves ahead. He must be a master chess player.

"A proffer agreement is when a suspect admits his guilt and agrees to tell us everything he knows or to act as an informant, in exchange for a reduced or suspended sentence," Tanner explained. "And since we don't want the bad guys to suspect our informant's a stool pigeon, his records are sealed."

"So . . . if I had information for an agreement like that, the museum wouldn't find out about my arrest? They wouldn't fire me?"

"That's right, but it's all academic, because you don't know anything that can help us."

"But I told you who stole the painting."

"You accused a dead man who can't defend himself," I ground out, irritated with myself for believing him two days ago when he'd sworn he didn't see Cody steal anything. Except I was still pretty sure he'd been telling the truth then . . . not now.

Burke grabbed his chest, and the bedside alarm blared.

The nurse rushed in and yanked me out of her way. "Out. Now!"

I stared at Burke's tortured expression. "Is he going to be okay?"

"Out!"

Tanner steered me to the door. "He'll be fine."

"He's having a heart attack," I squeaked, clutching my own chest and trying not to see my granddad's face in place of Burke's.

Tanner shook his head. "The nurse would've called a code blue. It looked to me like he pulled a wire from his chest again. Probably on purpose."

On purpose? My hand fisted of its own volition, and I forced it to my side. "Do you think he was lying about Cody stealing the painting?"

"Don't you? It sounded to me like he was parroting your theory. But this is good. It'll give him time to worry about what'll happen next if he doesn't come clean."

"Even if he gives me Linda on a silver platter, we can't offer him a proffer agreement."

"You don't think the prosecutor will go for it?"

"No, he probably would. No one wants to see a man go to jail for a desperate act to save his dying wife, but . . . how could we in good conscience allow the museum to unwittingly continue to employ him? Never mind that the head of security is my best friend!"

"Sometimes you got to do what you got to do."

I strode toward the stairwell. "What I'm going to do is canvass Cody's former classmates and professors. One of them must've seen him talking with the driver of a black pickup."

"Or with Linda?" Tanner arched an eyebrow.

I shrugged. "No matter what Burke's saying this morning, last night he seemed convinced that a woman was behind the attack. So he either doesn't think we can protect him if he spills, or—"

"He's in so deep, he's afraid we'll throw him in jail and his wife will be left alone."

I blew out a breath. "Yeah, or that."

• • •

Strolling the paths connecting the historic buildings on Wash U's Danforth Campus, west of Forest Park, felt like a stroll back in time. Well, if you ignored the latest fashion statements of passing students. I went to the registrar's office and hit Doreen up for a list of Cody's former professors and a class schedule of the classmates in the core classes he'd have been registered in if he were here.

I started with the professors, but not a single one recognized his name. A few recognized his picture. His art history professor studied the photograph for a full minute. "Yeah, he sat in the front row. Third seat from the left. Never said much. Took lots of notes."

"Do you recall who sat beside him?"

The professor squinted as if visualizing the room. "No one, most of the time. I had a lot of empty seats in that classroom. You might try talking to students at Etta's Café. That's where most of the art students eat."

Since it wasn't mealtime, I bypassed Etta's in favor of catching up to students outside of an international relations class that would soon be letting out. I figured hovering around outside the class seemed as good a plan as any for locating his friends. Unfortunately, *friends* seemed to be in short supply. By 4:30, I'd talked to more than two dozen classmates and professors and learned, one, that Cody was a loner, and two, that people don't pay much attention to what others are doing.

My phone chimed the *Murder, She Wrote* ringtone. It was too bad Cody hadn't had someone like Aunt Martha in his classes. I might have a lead on the pickup driver by now. I clicked on my phone.

"I found your missing painting," Aunt Martha squealed.

"My pai—what painting?"

"The Rijckaert."

"How did you know that was the second missing painting?"

She giggled. "I have better hearing than you think."

I closed my eyes, remembering our visit to the mall. Aunt Martha must've eavesdropped on my conversation with my informant after all. "Where are you?"

"Home. I bought it for a steal. Isn't it wonderful? You can come for dinner. Your mum is making toad in the hole."

"I'll be right there. Don't touch it . . . any more." Before I disconnected I could hear Aunt Martha call out to Mom, "I told you she loved toad in the hole." Toad in the hole is sausages cooked in Yorkshire pudding. Not one of my favorite meals since Mom had a tendency to overcook the sausages before adding them to the dough. But these days any meal I didn't have to cook suited me fine. I hurried across campus to where I'd parked my car and drove to my parents' place in record time.

Mom scurried into the front hall, drying her hands on a dish towel. "I don't know what Aunt Martha was thinking buying a hot painting."

"Where is it?" I dropped my coat on the hook by the door and followed Mom into the dining room where Aunt Martha was peering at the painting on the table through a magnifying glass like Sherlock Holmes himself.

"Is it the real thing?" Mom asked.

I pulled on latex gloves and turned the painting over to examine the markings on the back. They matched the stolen painting's perfectly. I turned it back over and held a hand toward my aunt's magnifying glass. "May I?"

"Well?" Mom and Aunt Martha prodded in unison.

"It looks like the missing Rijckaert. Good work, Aunt Martha." I pulled my notepad from my pocket and took a seat at the table. "Where did you find it?"

"Olsen's Antique Store in St. Charles."

"That Malgucci man took her," Mom hissed as if it was scandalous.

Aunt Martha blushed and self-consciously fiddled with the beads at her neck. "When Carmen heard that we were trying to find a stolen painting—"

We? I clearly had to be more careful about humoring Aunt Martha's interest in my cases.

"—he offered to take me around to all the places a thief, or their fence, might offload something like it. We visited art dealers, pawnshops, and antique stores all over the place. And thanks to his negotiating skills, the painting only cost me $2,000," she added proudly.

Mom shook her head. "The thief must've only got half of that for it. Makes no sense at all."

"The more valuable a painting, the harder it is to sell under the table," I explained. "Oftentimes a thief's happy to take what he can get to get it off his hands."

"But the feds will give me back my money when they take the painting, won't they?" Aunt Martha asked, suddenly sounding worried. "I borrowed the cash from Carmen. I have to pay him back."

Mom lifted her gaze to the ceiling and mumbled, "Lord, help us," then focused on Aunt Martha. "You knowingly bought a stolen painting. You should be glad Serena's not arresting *you*."

Aunt Martha's eyes rounded. "I could be arrested for that?"

"In theory," I said. "But since you clearly did it to restore it to its rightful owner, no, you have nothing to worry about."

"Except that you're in debt to a loan shark!" Mom added hysterically.

"It's not like that," Aunt Martha protested. "He's a friend."

"Don't worry, Aunt Martha. After I talk to the owners of Olsen's Antiques, they may be willing to return the money." I called Tanner and asked him if he wanted to accompany me for the interview. Since I had no idea what I'd be walking into, I was more than willing to wait until he was available. It wasn't as if the store owner was going anywhere, except laughing all the way to the bank over the easy money he'd made today. He probably had no idea what the painting was really worth.

"What happens to the painting now?" Aunt Martha asked as I disconnected.

"I'll send it to the lab for processing. We'll need to get your fingerprints, Malgucci's, if he handled the painting, and the store staff's for elimination purposes."

Aunt Martha picked up the magnifying glass I'd set on the table. "There are some fibers caught on the edge of the frame too. They look like they might be from a trunk carpet."

"Really?" I snatched the magnifying glass back. "They're not from Malgucci's because the store wrapped the painting in brown paper."

"This is good." Most thieves would've been smart enough to wear gloves, so as not to leave behind any fingerprints, but if we could match fibers from, say, Burke's trunk to those on the painting—I squinted at them for myself—it might be just the evidence I needed to convince him to talk.

By the time Tanner arrived, I had the painting wrapped back in the paper to transport and met him at the front door, coat on and ready to go.

"Mmm, smells good in here," he said, then held up a fingerprint kit. "We might as well collect your aunt's fingerprints before we go."

Aunt Martha clapped her hands like a giddy six-year-old who'd just learned she was going to Disneyland, a far cry from the reception she'd given him Friday night.

At Tanner's silly grin, I rolled my eyes and shrugged back out of my coat.

"By the way," Aunt Martha twittered, "those photos you doctored of Serena in Des Moines worked like a charm at convincing Mildred that Serena wasn't in Buffalo last week."

"Glad to hear it." He snuck a wink my way and whispered. "I think I won her over."

"You might as well both have supper with us before you go too," Mom chimed, in her there's-a-man-in-the-house-don't-let-him-get-away tone I'd come to recognize all too well. "It's ready, and your father should be home any minute."

"That'd be great, Mrs. Jones. Thanks," Tanner said without consulting me and proceeded to set out the fingerprinting materials.

"Anytime." Mom returned my perturbed glare

with one of her own, then bustled off to the kitchen, muttering that if she didn't take matters into her own hands, the only grandkids she'd ever get would be if she bought them from Auntie's mobster friend.

I stuck my head around the kitchen doorway. "Since Auntie's so tight with Carmen, maybe he'll give you a family discount."

Mom didn't laugh.

Dad walked through the door as Tanner was pressing Aunt Martha's inked thumb to the fingerprint card. "What has she done now?"

"I did good," Aunt Martha twittered. "I found the missing painting."

Mom rushed out of the kitchen. "And she owes a loan shark $2,000 for it. He probably charges interest by the hour."

"More like by the limb," I muttered morbidly, unable to help myself. Somehow I thought Aunt Martha was right about Malgucci, though. He didn't seem to be nearly as scary as the stories about him.

Dad plopped his briefcase on the coffee table and dug out his checkbook. "You can pay him off this minute."

"I was kidding, Dad."

"Don't worry, Mr. Jones," Tanner added. "I'll see Malgucci gets his money. The museum or their insurance company would probably be happy to pay it as a reward for the painting's recovery. If not, I suspect I could persuade Malgucci to consider it a donation to the museum."

Dad tore the check he'd written from his book and pressed it into Tanner's hand. "Well, if that doesn't work, give him this. I don't want Martha beholden to the likes of Malgucci."

"I didn't know you cared!" Aunt Martha threw her arms around Dad as Mom, Tanner, and I all yelled, "No!"

She hadn't wiped the fingerprint ink from her fingers, and Dad now had a perfect set of her prints polka-dotting the back of his blazer.

"Oh, no," Mom wailed. "That'll never come out."

Dad whipped off his blazer, frowned at the black ink, then snatched the check back from Tanner's hand. "On second thought, let Malgucci do what he likes with her."

Mom pried the check out of his hand. "No, dear, you don't mean that. I'm sure I can sponge it out with my spot remover." She returned the check to Tanner with a muttered "Somehow."

"I'm sure I can find something on the internet that will tell us how to get ink out," Aunt Martha interjected, wiping the ink from her fingers on a dishtowel as she sat in front of her tablet at the table.

Somehow we managed to get through dinner with no bloodshed, and Tanner and I made our escape with the hot painting in tow.

19

Olsen's Antique Store was on a quiet side street in the heart of the postcard town of St. Charles. It was the kind of town that in nicer weather tourists would stroll through to soak up the yesteryear ambience and hunt for unique bargains. The store was dark, but Tanner had done a quick search on its ownership before meeting me at my parents' place and learned that the owners lived above the store. We bypassed its front door in favor of the side one bearing a "Private Entrance" placard.

A white-haired man who appeared to be in his late sixties answered the bell. "May I help you?"

"Are you Mr. Olsen?" I asked.

"Yes?" A hint of trepidation tipped up his voice as I reached inside my coat.

"I'm Special Agent Serena Jones." I showed him my badge. "And this is Special Agent Tanner Calhoun. We need to ask you a few questions about the Rijckaert painting you sold this afternoon."

His face paled. "Yes, of course." He pulled the door open farther. "Come in." He motioned us up the stairs, but we waited for him to lead the way. The apartment was neat and tastefully decorated with an eclectic collection of antique furniture. Crocheted doilies graced the tops of the intricately carved end tables in the living area, showcasing Tiffany lamps and a collection of children's photographs, their smiles beaming from pearl-inlaid gold frames. "Can I get you any coffee? My wife's at her book club tonight, but I make a half-decent pot."

"We're fine, thank you." I perched on the edge of a Victorian chair and pulled out my notebook.

Mr. Olsen's gaze appeared transfixed by the notebook as he backed into a chair opposite me and plopped onto the seat. "How can I help you?"

"We need to know who you bought the Rijckaert from and when."

"My son Chad bought it. He scouts estate auctions and flea markets for me. We don't carry much art, but he has an eye for value."

"Where did your son pick up this particular piece?"

"I don't know, but I can call and ask him. He could come over. He lives around the corner."

"Thank you. That would be perfect."

His son arrived in under five minutes, looking frantic. "What's going on?"

Mr. Olsen hadn't asked us why we were inquiring about the painting, but he'd clearly gotten his son worked into a dither over our appearance. My gut told me that neither man was the type to knowingly buy stolen goods. I glanced at Tanner for his take, but he had his game face on. Great for fooling crooks. Not so great for me when I didn't know how to read it.

"We need to know where and when the Rijckaert painting was purchased," I repeated to Chad, after we made introductions.

"A guy brought it into the store. Said he was cleaning out his parents' place because they were moving into a nursing home."

"And you took him at his word?"

"Yeah." Chad nervously rubbed his palms down the tops of his legs. "He seemed honest. I'm guessing from your questions that he was really a thief."

"Or a fence," I confirmed. "Did you get a name?"

"No, he wanted cash. I offered him fifty bucks. He said it was worth at least a hundred. I figured he was probably right and paid him a hundred."

"You didn't think to check the Art Loss Register first?"

"What's that?"

"It's a service that catalogs stolen works of art so dealers won't give these thieves an honest market."

Chad shook his head. "I've never heard of it. I don't know much about art, but I figured the thing was old and would look good over someone's Victorian couch. From my quick web search, I figured we could get as much as five thousand for it."

"We'll give the woman her money back," his father cut in. "We don't want a reputation for selling stolen goods. We never would have if we'd known. I'll get my checkbook."

Tanner rose and followed him, no doubt to ensure that a check was all he was getting.

"Can you describe the seller to me?" I asked Chad.

"About my height. Long, sandy-colored hair, scraggly."

"How long?"

He pointed to a point an inch below his shoulder. "He was wearing a black leather jacket. I think he was wearing cowboy boots too. So he's probably shorter than six feet without them. And he drove a black pickup. I remember that because he parked in a no parking zone across the street and cursed when he saw the parking enforcement officer. Shot out of here like a fox with its tail on fire."

I did a mental fist pump. If he got a ticket, we'd be able to get his license plate number from the town, and then he'd be mine. "What day was this?"

"Monday morning. I remember that much, because I always bring in what I buy for the store at weekend events on Mondays, and then I man the cash register while dad sorts through everything in the back room."

"This past Monday?"

"Yes."

"You have security cameras in the store?"

"No."

"Would you be able to identify the man in a lineup?"

"Um, I'm not sure. I didn't pay a lot of attention to him. But yeah, maybe."

I took down his contact information and was thanking him for his time as Tanner returned with a check in hand. "I had him make it out to Malgucci," he said. "We can drop it off on our way."

"Oh, I almost forgot." I turned back to the Olsens. "We'll need your fingerprints for elimination purposes on the painting. Can we do that now?"

"Of course, whatever you need," the senior Mr. Olsen said for the both of them.

Tanner headed for the door. "I'll grab the kit."

The idea of driving to Malgucci's with a painting worth a lot more than Olsen had figured in the back of the SUV didn't appeal to me. Not to mention, the outside temperature was only a few degrees above freezing, and prolonged time in the cold wasn't good for it. We'd wrapped it in a comforter I borrowed from Mom's, but still. We needed to get the painting to headquarters ASAP. We made short work of getting the men's fingerprints and even shorter work of dropping off Malgucci's check at the address Aunt Martha relayed to us.

He lived in a surprisingly small bungalow on The Hill. If I'd had more time and been about a thousand percent braver, I might've asked Malgucci his intentions toward Aunt Martha. Instead, I let Tanner go to the door alone.

Yup, I was pusillanimous. And I really wished I'd tapped Mr. Sutton for a new word.

By 9:15 the next morning, the efficient staff at St. Charles' municipal offices had provided me with *nada*. It turned out their new parking enforcement officer, Grace, had a tendency to live up to her name and offer a tad *too* much grace to distracted drivers.

I called Olsen's Antiques next. "Do any nearby businesses have surveillance cameras monitoring the street outside your store?"

"Yeah, the jewelry store has a couple."

"Perfect."

By 10:15, thanks to Mr. Kaufman, the very cooperative jewelry store owner, I had a picture of my guy and a partial number on his plate.

"Yeah, that's the guy all right," Chad Olsen said, having joined me at the store soon after I arrived. Unfortunately, I hadn't gotten a good enough look at the driver who'd rammed my car to say for sure he was the same guy. I'd prepare a photo lineup for my aunt to see if she'd pick him out as the man who assaulted her outside my apartment.

Mr. Kaufman made a copy of the surveillance

footage for me, and I headed back to headquarters.

By 12:15 I'd matched the partial plate number to a black pickup owned by Asher Cook. I grinned at the driver's license picture that came up on my computer screen for him—a perfect match to the guy in the surveillance footage and, seeing him close up, I was pretty confident he was also Mr. Road Rage from in front of Wash U the other day. "Got you."

Tanner came around the corner of my cubicle. "Your pickup driver?"

"Yup, I'm running a background check now."

"I got a call from the St. Louis PD. They pulled an unidentified partial fingerprint off Burke's car key, so if your guy's got prints in the system, we might be able to clinch his tie-in to the attack."

"Unfortunately, aside from a couple of speeding tickets, it looks like he has a clean record. No known gang associations. No political associations. No online presence." Same as Cody. "Can you send a digital copy of the partial to the FBI lab? If it is Cook's, we should find a match on the painting we recovered. He wasn't wearing gloves when he handed it over to Olsen."

"Already on it." Tanner studied my computer screen over my shoulder. "Where's Cook work?"

"The loading dock at a big box store in the south end."

"So he's probably already finished his shift. Those guys start at 4:00 a.m. What are you thinking? You want to wait and watch? Try to find out who his associates are before you tip him off that you're on to him?"

"I'm afraid it's too late for that. I told the museum staff yesterday morning that I was looking for the driver of a black pickup."

Tanner pointed to the screen. "Cross-reference his school and occupation data with your other suspects."

I tried Linda's first, but nothing popped. Then I repeated the exercise with the info I had on Cody and then Burke, but there was nothing to link them either. I shoved away my keyboard. "This is getting me nowhere."

"You've got enough for an arrest warrant on trafficking stolen art, and once we verify his prints, the partial on the car key will connect him to the attack on Burke."

"But if he doesn't talk and the search warrant doesn't turn up any new evidence, I won't have enough to link him to Cody's death or to any partners in crime."

"So what do you want to do?"

I grabbed the photo lineup I'd prepared of ten blonde museum employees, in case he decided to be cooperative. "Let's go."

Tanner plucked the paper from my hand. "One of these Linda?"

I plucked the paper back and inserted it into a file folder. "What do you think?"

Tanner glanced in the direction of our supervisor's office. "You sure you want to do that?"

"Yes." Mr. Sutton's new word of the day was *doughty*—brave, courageous—and I liked the sound of it a whole lot better than *pusillanimous*.

We secured the arrest warrant and headed to Asher's address, a small apartment complex in a sketchy part of town. His black pickup was parked at the curb.

"Look at this," I said to Tanner, pointing to the lower lip of the truck's bumper. "That look like blood to you?"

Tanner scrutinized it more closely. "Could be." He tapped a number into his phone. "We'd better get an evidence team down here to process it before Cook figures out he didn't scrub his truck as clean as he thought."

We found his second-floor apartment and knocked on the door, identified ourselves. No one answered.

"Do you feel that?" Tanner held his palm at the door's edge. Cool air whisped past the frame.

"Great, he's pulling a Stan Johnson on me." I raced down the stairwell and around the building, expecting to find Tanner holding a man dangling from the window. Well, hoping anyway. Instead Tanner was leaning out the window empty-handed, only—I counted windows from him to the edge of the building—he wasn't in Cook's apartment.

"Any sign of him?" Tanner called down.

The street was empty, and a quick scan of the muddy ground below the open window, ten feet past Tanner's position, confirmed that no one had just dropped from it. "No. Doesn't look like he escaped this way."

"His neighbor says he went out on his motorcycle to take advantage of the warm afternoon. Come back up."

Warm? He called 48 degrees warm? I stomped back upstairs. After this, Cook's neighbor was bound to tip him off, and he'd keep right on riding. I found Tanner standing in the doorway of said neighbor—a long-legged woman who looked as if she might've just walked off a photo shoot—taking down her statement, or maybe her number.

"Do you know where Mr. Cook was headed?" I interrupted.

The woman tore her gaze from Tanner's. "His girlfriend's maybe."

My pulse quickened. "Do you know her name?"

"No, sorry."

I pulled the file folder with the photo lineup from my bag. "Would you recognize her picture?"

"I'm not sure. I only saw her once." The woman's gaze dropped to Tanner's notepad. "Is Asher in some kind of trouble?"

"We just want to talk to him," Tanner assured.

"And we'd appreciate any information that might help us locate him."

"Well, he usually didn't bring dates to his apartment, but I came home early a couple of days ago and saw a blonde leaving his place. Come to think about it, he acted kind of funny when I asked him about her, though. Like he didn't want to admit she was his girlfriend, so maybe he has more than one."

I opened my file folder and showed her the pictures I'd brought. "Was she one of these women?"

She ran her finger along the lines of photos and stopped at the photo of Linda. She tapped her perfectly manicured fingernail on Linda's face. "That's her."

"Thank you," I said, fighting to rein in my grin. "You've been a tremendous help."

Tanner gave her a business card. "If you see him come home, please don't mention our visit, but give me a call."

She gave him a coy smile. "I will."

Walking out with Tanner, I mimicked the woman's sultry tone. "I didn't bring you along to pick up dates, you know."

He shrugged nonchalantly. "Can I help it if women like me? That kind of thing just happens when you look like Gerard Butler."

"Ha. You haven't even got the same eye color as Butler."

He batted his lashes. "I hadn't thought you noticed."

Muffling a laugh, I shook my head. The man was incorrigible. He sure didn't need to know how much fun it was listening to him try to guess which movie star he reminded me of.

Not that I was sure he actually thought he looked like them or just enjoyed teasing me.

"So you're telling me a guy's eyes are the first thing you notice about him?" he needled.

Yanking open the car door, I tossed him a cheeky grin. "I'll plead the fifth."

Back at headquarters, I marched into Maxwell Benton's office. "We need to talk about Linda Kempler, aka Johnson, aka a known associate of Asher Cook." I slapped a picture of Asher on Benton's desk. "The man who sold the stolen Rijckaert to Olsen's Antiques. And the prime suspect in the attempted murder of Henry Burke and the murder of Cody Stafford, not to mention an assault on my aunt Martha and the bang-up job he did on my car."

Benton motioned to a chair. "Take a seat, Jones."

"I prefer to stand, sir." Only my legs started quaking, so I lowered myself into the chair.

Benton steepled his fingers on his desk, looking simultaneously contemplative and ticked. "Who is your source for this *known* association?"

"Cook's neighbor saw Miss Kempler leaving Cook's apartment."

"And how did this neighbor know Kempler's name?"

I caught myself squirming and lifted my chin. "She didn't, sir. I presented her with a photo lineup of blonde staff members of the art museum, and she picked out Linda's picture."

"I see."

"I have an informant who also saw a blonde attempt to sell the Monet to a pawn broker shortly before Christmas."

"And did this informant ID Miss Kemple too?"

"I haven't shown him the lineup yet, sir."

Benton leaned back in his chair, grilling me with his gaze.

"I'm not saying she stole the paintings, sir. But she knows this man and in all likelihood has information that could assist me in the investigation." I personally thought she was guilty as sin, but Benton clearly didn't appreciate his opinion of her being called into question.

"I'll take it under advisement."

I stared at him, not computing what he meant.

"You're dismissed," he growled.

My heart slammed my ribs at how much his "dismissed" sounded like *dismissed,* as in fired.

20

Less than twenty minutes after I'd left his office, I sucked in a breath as Maxwell Benton strode past Tanner's cubicle.

Spotting me there, he veered back around. "Jones, conference room four, now."

"Yes, sir." With fresh empathy for how Petra must've felt when Zoe escorted her in to be interviewed, I flashed Tanner a pray-for-me plea, then trailed Benton to the conference room at the far end of the hall. I missed a step when I reached the door and saw Linda watching me from the TV screen.

"Close the door," Benton ordered, and taking a seat, motioned me to do likewise.

In the video image, Linda was seated at an identical-looking table, a file folder open in front of her, and she was irritably flicking a pencil over it, tip to end, tip to end.

I lowered myself to the chair, almost missing it for staring at Linda. "What's going on?"

"This is Special Agent Linda Johnson with our Kansas office. She's been working here undercover."

"Undercover? Why didn't you just tell me that in the first place?"

"We couldn't risk jeopardizing my cover,"

Linda said. "Although thanks to my brother finding me, I couldn't openly play Linda Kempler anymore, which was why you found my apartment vacated. However, I hadn't counted on your tenacity, and at the time, it seemed unlikely there was any connection between our cases."

"And now?"

"We're not sure. Two months ago the senator received an ultimatum—vote against his bill to limit foreign adoptions or watch his daughter die."

I gasped.

"The next week, the senator requested a postponement of the vote until after the Christmas holidays. Two days later, the senator's daughter came into contact with peanuts while on a school trip to the art museum and went into anaphylactic shock."

"Is that so surprising? Lots of children eat peanut butter and jam on toast for breakfast or in their sandwiches for lunch. Anyone could have caused the exposure."

"That's true. And she always carries an EpiPen, which all her teachers know how to administer, so tragedy was averted."

"But you still think the exposure was deliberate."

"We know so. Or at least, the blackmailer took credit for it. He or she told the senator that if he played any more games the next time the vote came around, his daughter wouldn't be so lucky."

"You don't know if it was a man or woman."

"The voice was electronically altered."

"Maybe the blackmailer merely heard about the incident and decided to use it to his or her advantage to scare the senator."

"It's possible. However, the senator received the blackmailer's call within minutes of the call from his daughter's teacher."

"But what made you think the blackmailer is on the museum staff? I'm assuming that's why you took a job there."

"Yes."

"But anyone could've walked in and deliberately exposed the senator's daughter to peanut butter."

"There were no other visitors inside the museum, aside from parents helping with the field trip, at the time of the incident."

"But what would a staff member, or anyone for that matter, have to gain from blackmailing the senator?"

"That's not important."

"It is if your blackmailer is my art thief. Why did you pose as the senator's new girlfriend?"

"To bait the blackmailer. We hoped he or she might ply me for inside information to use against the senator."

"That's why you were so talkative with all the

employees, flaunting your relationships, asking about politics?"

"Yes, but the fact of the matter is, we never figured out who threatened him. He chose to vote against the bill rather than risk his daughter's life, and that was the end of the threats."

Or Cody's death was. "But the senator's vote didn't change the outcome of the bill one iota. What was the blackmailer's motive?"

"Apparently to prove that everyone has a price."

"One of the callers on a radio show after the vote said that same thing."

"Yes, that's where our two cases seem to intersect. The caller quoted almost verbatim what the blackmailer had said to the senator in a call after his vote, in addition to asking how it felt to be no better than any other sellout."

"A political opponent, do you think?"

Linda shrugged. "Not that we can prove. We traced the radio call to Asher Cook's cell phone. That's why his neighbor saw me leaving his apartment. I went there to question him."

"But you don't think he's the blackmailer?"

"We didn't think so. He was at work the day of the peanut butter scare. He claims that on the night in question, he was listening to the radio call-in show while filling up at a gas station, and a woman asked to borrow his phone."

"And you believed him?"

"Until Agent Benton informed me of Cook's connection to the stolen painting, we had nothing to link him to the museum. Now I'm wondering if he has a partner on staff."

"One employee mentioned seeing a male in a black pickup with you outside the museum. Is that true?"

She sighed heavily. "I hadn't realized I was being watched so closely. Yes, that was my handler."

Okay, so Malcolm hadn't been lying to deflect attention from his own friend with a pickup. "I thought the inside connection might've been my hit-and-run victim, Cody Stafford, and that Cook cut him out to have more for himself."

"Could be, although Cook doesn't seem like the brightest bulb in the house to take that kind of initiative. Which I guess was why I'd dismissed him as a suspect."

"He was bright enough to come into possession of a painting worth a quarter of a million dollars," I countered.

"But how much did he sell it for?"

"A hundred bucks."

"See, not too bright."

Okay, this wasn't getting me anywhere. "Have you had him under surveillance?"

She nodded. "For the first twenty-four hours after I talked to him, but he didn't go out, except to work."

"Wait." The black pickup rammed my car the morning after the radio show. That would mean . . . "When did you talk to Cook?"

"Wednesday evening."

Okay, that explained why the surveillance team didn't see him ram my car or attempt to murder Burke. "But the radio show was Tuesday night. Why so long after?"

"We heard about it after the fact, and the radio station received hundreds of calls that night. Now that we've connected him to the museum, we'll go back through their surveillance footage to see if we can spot him on the premises and reinstate surveillance, unless you're prepared to make an arrest immediately."

"He's not home at the—" I sprang to my feet. "Oh, no."

"What's wrong?" Benton and Linda asked as one.

"He could be going after Burke right now." I yanked open the conference room door and almost slammed into Tanner, who'd been about to knock.

He lowered his arm. "I just got a call from the lab. They pulled Burke's prints off the stolen painting."

"Burke's?" That didn't make sense.

"Yeah, he must've been Cook's inside guy."

Not Cody? "I must've had it backwards." I raced to my cubicle and grabbed my jacket.

"Cody must've been the one who threatened to go to the police, and Cook took him out before he could. Only Burke didn't know."

"So you think Asher Cook went after Burke, afraid he'd get all righteous once word of Cody's death got out?"

"Yeah, c'mon, we've got to get to the hospital."

Tanner drove as I filled him in on the senator connection and why Linda was off my suspect list.

"I remember that caller on the radio show. 'Everyone has a price,'" Tanner enunciated in a thick Eastern European accent. "She said it just like that too, as if she knew it for a fact."

A memory clicked in my brain. "Petra."

"Who?"

"One of the receptionists at the museum. I heard her say something like that."

"Does she have an accent?"

"No, but her parents were from Croatia, so I'm sure she'd have no trouble faking it."

Tanner swerved into the hospital parking lot and grabbed a parking ticket. "But what does she have to gain from the senator voting against the bill?"

"I don't know." Scanning the lot for motorcycles and remembering Irene's comment about Petra's old boyfriend riding a motorbike, I quickly texted Zoe to ask if Petra was working. Seeing no motorcycles and receiving a yes back from Zoe, I breathed a little easier. "Maybe Petra is allied with some lobby group, or maybe she just wanted to prove that everyone has a price."

"Or . . ." Tanner interjected, "maybe the incident with the daughter was a decoy to distract staff from the theft."

"Oh, that's brilliant. It would've been a perfect opportunity to sneak the painting out of the vault while everyone was distracted by the senator's daughter going into anaphylactic shock."

"But if Burke and Petra planned the robbery, why'd they let Cook sell the second painting for a hundred bucks?"

"I don't know." I rushed inside with Tanner. "Hopefully, now that we have fingerprint evidence tying Burke to the theft, we can convince him to talk."

"Whoa." A man in a gray suit halted our headlong rush into Burke's room with raised palms. "No one's talking to my client until his doctor says he's well enough."

I stretched to my full height. "Unless he starts talking, he might not live that long."

Apparently the senator wasn't the only person who'd sell out, given the right incentive, because an hour later, I'd left Tanner back at headquarters and was sitting in the prosecutor's office at the federal court building discussing terms for a proffer agreement with Burke. The truth was, I didn't want to see Burke do time. We didn't yet know the full details, but according to his lawyer, the mastermind behind the theft had preyed on Burke's desperation to find a kidney donor and had made the devoted husband an irresistible promise.

Zoe called as I was preparing to leave with the agreement in hand. "Petra went home sick."

"How long ago?" I hurried out to my car.

"About forty minutes ago. Irene said she'd complained of a migraine, but since you asked earlier if she was working, I thought you'd want to know."

"Yes, thank you." I turned my car toward Lindenwood Park, the neighborhood in the southwest end where Petra lived, and put a call in to Tanner.

"You ready to head back to the hospital?" he asked without preamble.

"First we need to go to Petra's. She left work early. I think Cook might've tipped her off that we're on to him. Can you meet me at her house?" I relayed the address.

"I can be there in twenty minutes. Wait outside until I get there."

I got to Petra's in eleven minutes. She lived in a small, two-bedroom bungalow, circa 1940s, on a deep, narrow lot, sporting a detached garage at the back. Her car sat in the driveway, the hatch-back up, the cargo area crammed with boxes. There was no sign of a motorcycle in the vicinity.

I parked close enough to head her off if she tried to leave but far enough back that she wouldn't notice me.

Two minutes later, Petra stepped out of the house, wearing an unzipped winter jacket, carrying a purple suitcase and a grocery bag, but no purse—a good sign that she wasn't quite ready to take off. Except after she stuffed the suitcase and bag in the cargo area, she shut the hatchback. I waited until she slipped back inside and then, inching my car closer, gave Tanner another call. "Looks like she's getting ready to run. How far out are you?"

Sirens blared to life on Tanner's end of the phone. "ETA six minutes."

Petra appeared at the side door, carrying her purse this time.

"I need to move in. Hurry." I pulled my car in the driveway behind Petra's just as she stepped out of her house, keys in her hand. I turned off my engine and jumped out. "Hey, where are you off to?"

"Oh, hi, Miss Jones. I'm going to visit friends for the weekend."

"The museum said you came home sick."

She ducked her head. "You won't tell them, will you? I was going to finish my shift and drive up tonight, but they're calling for freezing rain later."

I squinted at the clear sky. "Really?"

"Was there something you wanted to ask me?"

"Yes, I have a few questions."

"Come inside then." She opened the door and waved me in.

The door opened to a landing. To the right, stairs went down to a second landing, then turned into the basement. Straight ahead, four steps led up to the kitchen. I glanced downstairs and listened but didn't sense anyone was lurking down there. I climbed up the stairs into the kitchen, rounded the square wooden table that dominated the center of the room, and peeked into the adjoining living area. A sofa, two chairs, a lamp and table, and a small TV were the extent of the furnishings. A hallway extended the opposite direction with four doors, all closed. "You live alone?"

"Yes. Can I get you a glass of water? Make you a cup of tea?"

In the face of her unexpected cooperation, doubts crept in. "No, thank you."

"Do you mind if I finish putting away groceries while we talk?" She scooped a bag from the floor. "I didn't realize that I missed this bag."

"Go ahead." I pulled out my notebook and pen and decided to go for broke. "What can you tell me about Asher Cook?"

"Asher?" Petra had been clunking cans of peas and corn onto her cupboard shelf and paused mid clunk. "He's a sweet guy."

So she didn't deny knowing him as he'd denied

knowing the woman who'd borrowed his phone. "We've recovered one of the museum's missing paintings from Olsen's antiques. The owner ID'd Cook as the man who sold him the painting."

"No way," Petra exclaimed, betraying no hint of anxiety. Except her pallor didn't match her conviction. "He's got to be mistaken. You know how people are. They think every long-haired, thirty-something-year-old looks the same."

"Then comparing his fingerprints to those found on the painting should clear up the confusion."

"I'm relieved to hear it," she said, with only the scarcest wobble in her voice.

"Do you know where I might find him?" I asked, hearing the crunch of Tanner's footfalls approaching the door.

Petra glanced at the clock above her stove. "I think he said something about seeing a hockey game tonight."

Her gaze shifted past my shoulder, and an unfamiliar men's cologne slammed my senses. I pivoted on my heel a nanosecond before Asher lunged for my neck with both hands.

Ducking, I sprang past him and caught him in the lower back with my elbow.

"Asher, what are you doing?" Petra cried out as I drew my gun and yelled "Freeze!"

"Saving you." Asher snatched up a kitchen chair and swung, knocking the gun from my hand and sending me reeling into the counter.

"No!" Petra screamed as he roared toward me like a rampaging bull.

I grabbed a can of peas from the counter behind me and smashed it over his head.

Asher dropped to his knees, and I scrambled for my gun.

Petra backed away, her arms raised in surrender. "I don't know what's gotten into him. I've never seen him like this."

Was she feigning innocence because she knew I was onto her? Or was she the victim of his misguided compulsion to protect her?

"What are you saying? Isn't she your stalker?" He looked at her, sounding genuinely hurt and confused. "I came here to save you."

"Is that why you went after Cody and Burke?" I asked as he too raised his hands. "To protect her?"

"They would've hurt—"

"Shut up, Asher." Petra's voice turned steely hard. "Don't you see what she's doing? She's trying to turn you against me."

Right. And from the sounds of the stalker story she'd fed him, she'd be the expert at how to do that. Clearly Petra was the one calling the shots. I reached for my handcuffs.

"No one's taking you away from me," he shouted and sprang up so fast I didn't see his can-filled fist coming until pain exploded in my head.

21

I staggered out of Petra's house as a car swerved to a stop in the middle of the street.

Tanner.

The hand I was raising dropped to my side as he jumped out and sprinted toward a car backed into a telephone pole.

I blinked. "Hey, that's my car," I said to the empty porch. I pressed my hand to my pounding head. How long had I blacked out? My hand came away sticky. Staring at it, I took a couple of seconds to register that it had blood on it. My blood.

"You're hurt." Tanner stood in front of me, his face dark.

Huh. How'd he move that fast?

"I'm . . ." The frown on Tanner's face made his deep brown eyes appear almost black. "Are you mad at me?" I tried to frown myself, but it kind of hurt.

"Of course not." He reached out and grasped my upper arms in a surprisingly gentle grip. "Serena, can you tell me what—"

"Oh, no! She's getting away!" I tried to jerk out of his hold, but his grip tightened. "Tanner! We have to go after her."

Why was he just standing there, letting our suspect get away?

"Serena," he said.

My gaze raked the empty street as I pried at his fingers, but he only released one arm, then reached into his coat pocket with his free hand.

"*Serene*-uh," he said, and the softness of his tone penetrated my panic.

"What?"

He held up a clean white tissue. "Hold still."

"Oh." Mesmerized by the gentleness in his eyes, my hands dropped to my sides as he pressed the tissue carefully to the side of my head.

"Didn't your airbag go off?"

"My—?" I pulled my eyes from his and focused over his shoulder, on my smucked car.

"Oh." I took over pressing the tissue to my head and backed up a step. "I wasn't in the car. I was in the house talking to Petra when Asher showed up and jumped me. They raced off in her car and must've rammed mine to get it out of their way."

Two police cruisers careened to a stop on the street, corralling our vehicles between theirs. Thanks to Petra's fevered escape, in addition to being a suspect in my initial investigation, she was now facing charges for aiding and abetting an assault, reckless driving, and leaving the scene of an accident. But by the time Tanner and I fielded the officers' questions, and convinced them to freeze and seize her house so we could get the paperwork started on a search warrant, not to mention issue a BOLO for Petra's car, I was desperate for a pain pill.

"You got any ibuprofen or acetaminophen on you?"

Tanner finished issuing directions to the tow truck driver for my car, then guided me to his SUV. "You can ask them that at the hospital. I think we'd better let the doctor look at you before you start popping pills."

"I don't have time to sit in the ER. We still need to get a judge to sign the search warrant, talk to Burke." The ground seemed to undulate under my feet, and Tanner tightened his grip on my arm.

"Tell you what. I'll take you to the hospital Burke is in. Okay? Petra's house can wait."

I suddenly felt so woozy that Tanner practically had to hoist me onto the seat. "Yeah, okay."

He fastened my seatbelt for me, as if I were a helpless three-year-old, and I didn't even protest. In truth, the feel of his warm arms reaching across my middle and the closeness of his body felt incredibly comforting, and I had to resist the urge to reach out and snuggle into him.

Serena Jones, kick-butt FBI agent.

Straightening, he adjusted the belt at my shoulder. "You okay?"

"You smell good," I said.

Tanner looked startled.

Oops, did I say that aloud?

His eyes smiled for just a second, then he gave

me a sharp look. "Ooh-kay, definitely getting that head injury checked."

"I'm fine," I mumbled, sinking into my seat. *Too-ootally fine.*

He grinned and patted my knee. "Good, 'cause I don't want you throwing up in here."

Ha. Such a nice guy. I was tempted to toss my lunch just to spite him.

The SUV hit a bump and I winced. "What are you doing? Aiming for the potholes?"

"Sorry." He slowed right down, slanting anxious glances my way every time we hit the slightest bump. Then when we reached the hospital, he insisted I wait for him to bring a wheelchair out for me.

"I can walk," I insisted, although as I leaned on Tanner's arm, I wasn't so sure he could. He seemed to walk on a tilt.

The ER doors slid open and Tanner stiffened as a familiar male voice said, "Whoa, what happened to you?"

"Nate!" My happy tone earned me a sharp look from Tanner. "What are you doing here?"

"Theresa accidentally jabbed her husband's eye with a knitting needle." Nate grabbed a wheelchair and positioned it beside me. "Here, sit, before you fall over." He reached for my free arm.

"Do I look that bad?"

"Yes," Nate and Tanner said in unison as they had a tug of war over helping me into the chair.

I grabbed the armrests and lowered myself under my own steam. "I had a run-in with a suspect."

Nate looked me up and down. "Do you ever have a normal day?"

"Sure. Once. It was a Tuesday, I think."

He smiled. "At least you've still got your sense of humor."

Tanner grabbed my wheelchair's handles. "Hey, thanks for helping out, Nate. We really appreciate it."

Nate's smile dimmed.

Tanner's grew cocky. "Don't want to keep you. Sounds like someone better go referee that knitting needle altercation."

Nate nodded, stepping out of the way, but he shot me a wink. "Let me know if you need help with anything. Okay? You want me to look in on Harold?"

"Yes, thank you. That would be good."

"Happy to help."

"Regular Mother Teresa, that guy," Tanner muttered under his breath as he steered the wheelchair toward the triage nurse. Amazingly, he sweet-talked her into fast-tracking me straight into an examining room, then slipped away and soon returned with Burke in a wheelchair, and his lawyer. And . . . the signed search warrant.

"How on earth did you manage to get this so fast?" I asked.

"Guess the judge likes your smile." He winked.

"The judge was in the room next to my client's, visiting his mother," Burke's lawyer interjected.

Tanner shrugged. "That too."

Burke looked much better than he had yesterday, not counting the pasty color his skin turned when he caught sight of my gash.

"I'm so sorry," Burke said. "I never would've taken Petra's offer if I thought people were going to get hurt. I just . . ." He shook his head. "The paintings were sitting there in storage doing nobody any good, and I thought if a couple could save my dear Ella's life, what was the harm? It could be decades before anyone went looking for them."

I sympathized. I really did.

"I never imagined they'd kill Cody to ensure his silence or"—his voice cracked—"go after you."

"Hey, don't worry about me." I strained not to wince as the doctor slathered my stitches with another douse of antiseptic. "I've got a hard head."

Tanner grinned. "Yeah, she's the hardest-headed agent I've ever trained."

I shot him the evil eye, and our bantering seemed to put Burke at ease.

The doctor wrote me a prescription for pain meds and handed me a list of symptoms to watch out for. "You're good to go."

Tanner walked him to the door. "Thank you,

Doctor. We'll just use this room for a few moments longer."

"Okay, how about you walk us through the whole story?" I said to Burke as Tanner pulled out a notebook.

Burke's gaze dropped to his hands twisting in his lap. "Petra said that for $20,000, she could find someone willing to donate a kidney to my wife. I figured she meant someone from a poor country, like where she came from, you know? So I believed her. But I told her I didn't have any money."

"What did she say to that?"

"She suggested stealing a couple of paintings from storage. She said she knew a guy who could sell them under the table and no one would find out."

"When did you steal them?" Tanner cut in, probably testing his decoy theory.

"Just before Christmas. When everyone was fussing over that girl that went into anaphylactic shock."

"Did Petra plan the diversion?" I clarified.

Burke frowned. "Not that she told me. But that morning, she did say to be ready."

I sighed. It was enough to cast suspicion but not to nail her. "Okay, continue."

"Since I didn't know if she'd really come through with a donor, I only gave her one of the paintings and told her she'd get the second when my wife got her kidney. Every week since, she's given me an update on the donor search, so I really thought she was on the up and up. But then after the museum called you in, someone broke into my house and stole the second painting. That's the real reason I rushed home that day you were at the museum doing interviews. But I couldn't report the theft and she knew it."

"A fool and his Monet are soon parted," Tanner quipped.

I rolled my eyes. "It was a Rijckaert." I returned my attention to Burke. "You think Petra stole the painting?"

"Well, someone she sent, since she was working. No one else knew about it. And it was the only thing that was taken."

"What about Cody? Didn't he know about it?"

"Yeah." Burke stroked shaky fingers over his forehead. "He confronted me the day after I took the paintings. Said he knew what I did. He figured I was desperate to pay my wife's medical bills, but he said that wasn't the way. He said he didn't want to report me, but he would if I didn't return them." Burke's eyes squeezed shut. "I told Petra about his threats and she said she'd take care of it. I figured she'd make a deal with him. I never thought for a second she'd kill him."

"Did you confront her about the theft from your home?"

"Yeah, she denied it and asked me how I was

going to finish paying for my wife's kidney. Intimated that if I couldn't pay, she wouldn't be able to deliver. I was furious and threatened to go to the police, tell them everything. But she warned me that I was the one who'd go to jail, since I did the stealing."

I nodded. Petra had no doubt chosen Burke as her thief for exactly that reason.

Tanner showed him a photo lineup that included Asher Cook, and Burke picked Cook out, without a moment's hesitation, as the man who'd attacked him, despite his earlier claim that he hadn't seen his attacker. Amazing how a little immunity could loosen the tongue.

We were just wrapping up our questions when Aunt Martha called.

The baby shower! I glanced at my watch. Whew. I wasn't late yet. "Hi, Aunt Martha, what's up?" I asked cheerfully.

"Thank goodness you answered the phone," Mom, not Aunt Martha, exclaimed in my ear. "We heard a report of a federal officer being assaulted and the car in the video looked like yours, and then you didn't show up to ride with us to the shower. You haven't forgotten the shower, have you?"

"No, I haven't forgotten. But I might be a little late."

"Were you even going to call?" Her pitch rose exponentially, and I had to pull the phone away from my ear. "Didn't you know we'd be worried? And you know how nervous I am about calling when you're working. I've been so scared you were wounded, I could kill you myself!"

Tanner laughed out loud.

"Is that Tanner? This isn't funny!"

Tanner took the phone from me. "I'm sorry, Mrs. Jones. I'll make sure Serena gets to the party ASAP." Then he clicked off before I could say anything more.

"Tanner, I have a splitting headache. I don't think I'm up to making googly eyes over baby blankets."

He helped me up from the examining table. "You have to. I promised I'd deliver you." He plucked the paper the doctor had given me from my hand. "We'll fill your prescription on the way and get you good and doped up," he added with a wink.

My cousin's house was decked out in streamers and bows and, from the look of the cars lining the driveway and street, stuffed to capacity with giddy women from fourteen to ninety-four. All of my mom's four sisters lived within a four-hour drive and guaranteed every last aunt and girl cousin would've made the trek. I flipped down the visor mirror and adjusted the funky beret Tanner had scooped up for me at the pharmacy.

"It looks good," he said. "No one will know."

I touched up my makeup. "Sure, if they're polite enough not to question why I have a black eye."

He grinned. "Just tell them you lost a sparring match with your partner."

"Ha! They'd never believe it."

"True," he said with a wee Irish lilt. "A guy who looks like Pierce Brosnan would never hit a woman."

I giggled, then immediately grabbed my head. "Oh, please, don't make me laugh. It makes my brain hurt."

He handed me the gift bag we'd retrieved from my apartment. "Get out of here. And have fun. I'll call if we locate Petra and Asher."

"And supervise the search of the house?"

"Yes."

"Thanks." I let myself inside to avoid drawing attention to my late arrival and slipped my gift onto the stack in the center of the living room, then made the rounds. "Suzie, look at you," I exclaimed when I reached my cousin from Kansas. "I didn't know you were expecting too."

A sweet blush swept across her beaming face. "I'm due in June."

"Congratulations!" I hugged my way around the rest of the circle, and after I'd congratulated Janessa, the mother-to-be, a cousin two years my junior, my mother caught my hand.

"Doesn't she look happy?"

"Yes, Mom, she looks very happy." Of course,

what Mom was really saying was, "Wouldn't you like to be that happy?"

Just as Mom did a double take on my own looks, Zoe waved her arm from across the room and pointed to the empty seat beside her.

I pried my hand from Mom's. "We'd better grab our seats so they can get started." I sprinted to Zoe's side and plopped myself down. "Thanks for the save."

"Are you talking about my saving you the chair, or saving you from your mother?"

"Both!"

"You know she only wants you to be happy."

"And she wants grandchildren."

Zoe chuckled. "Right."

"And she wants me to quit my job."

Zoe scrutinized my face, then peeked under my beret, as if she'd guessed exactly why I'd worn it. "Would quitting be such a bad thing?"

My Aunt Tina passed by with a tray of punch, sparing me from responding to Zoe. We both helped ourselves to a glass, then leaned back and listened to Suzie explain the game we'd be playing.

Three games later, the mommy-to-be started unwrapping gifts, and conversations around the room turned to plans for Valentine's Day.

Zoe squealed and grabbed my arm. "I forgot to tell you that your lawyer friend, Jax, invited me to go skating with him tomorrow afternoon."

"That's great," I said, happy she had someone to spend Valentine's with.

My aunt Karen, sitting on my other side, nudged me with her elbow. "What are your Valentine's plans?"

"Uh." I glanced at my mom across the room and nixed the impulse to say I'd be tracking down fugitives. Instead, I grinned at Zoe. "We on for the 15th?"

"Raiding all the stores for half-price chocolate? You better believe it."

"Mmm, good idea," Suzie piped up from across the room. She rubbed her bulging belly. "Can never start them too young on chocolate."

Aunt Karen tsked. "When I was your age, men used to bring chocolate and flowers and treat their sweethearts to a night on the town."

"Sounds nice," I said. And it did. I glanced around the room at all my smiling aunts and their giggling girls. Maybe Mom and Zoe were right. Maybe I should get another job or find a man and get married and have kids like my cousins. Spend my days taking them to the zoo and the science center and Turtle Park. I always loved climbing around on the giant stone turtles in Turtle Park. I could take them skating and to the history museum and the art museum. I'd have more time to paint. "I could finger paint with the kids too. That would be fun."

"What are you talking about?" Zoe asked.

Oops, I guess I did the talking-my-thoughts-aloud thing again. I pressed my fingertips to my temple to ease the pounding that seemed to be short-circuiting my brain. It was on the tip of my tongue to make up a story about a new art class at the drop-in center that Nana—my dad's mom—sponsored, but I was already feeling guilty about how easy it had become to color the truth to do my job, without letting the habit lap over to my personal life. I crossed my arms to stifle a shiver and, leaning toward her, lowered my voice. "I was thinking about having kids."

"Without a husband?" Shock pitched her voice high enough to attract a few glances.

"No, of course not," I whispered. "I'd get married first."

"You actually have to date for that to work, you know."

Uh-oh. Mom must've heard the *m* word. She was hurdling baby blankets and teddy bears to get to me. "You want to get married?" she exclaimed, nearly tumbling into my lap.

The buzz of conversations around the room came to an abrupt stop and *ev-er-y-one* gaped at me.

I laughed. Except it sounded a tad maniacal, so I pressed my lips together and looked pleadingly to Zoe.

"Of course, she wants to get married someday," Zoe, my dearest, true-blue friend jumped in.

"She's just waiting for the right guy. Although," she added under her breath for my ears only, "I don't see what's wrong with the ones you keep turning away."

Mom squeezed my arm and let out the most contented sigh. "I'm so happy to hear this."

Uh-oh. She had that look. The one she got whenever she thought she'd found the perfect young woman for my brother. The sudden bursts of "Oh, I know just the young man for Serena" from my aunts scattered about the room confirmed it.

"I don't need any help finding the right guy," I said. "Okay? Please."

Mom patted my arm and nodded. "We understand," she said in that mother-knows-best voice that sounded as if she was already making plans.

22

"Owwwww!" I reached over my pillow and grabbed whatever had landed on my wounded head and flung it off.

A banshee-sounding "yeeee-oooow" followed by a thud in the vicinity of the bedroom floor jolted me fully awake.

I jackknifed out of bed and could just make out the silhouette of a cat in the faint morning light slanting through the blinds. "Harold? What is wrong with you?" I clutched my now pounding head. "I'm sorry. I'm sure you didn't mean"— I cocked my ear toward the bedroom door. The pounding wasn't in my head. It was in my apartment.

I sucked in a breath. *Asher?*

"You're supposed to attack the intruder, not me," I hissed at Harold as I snatched my gun from my night table drawer. Only . . . an intruder wouldn't knock.

I grabbed my bathrobe and hurried to the kitchen to find Tanner rapping on the outside door. "What are you doing here?"

"You didn't answer your phone."

"Oh. I guess those pain pills must've really knocked me out. I probably wouldn't have heard you knocking if the cat hadn't pounced on my head." I picked Harold up and gave him a nuzzle. "I'm sorry, boy. You were just trying to get my attention, weren't you? And I go and throw you across the room."

Tanner's eyebrow arched. "You threw your cat across the room?"

"Don't worry. He landed on his feet. Now, what was so important that it couldn't wait"—I peered at the clock on the stove—"another two hours?" He'd already called me last night to let me know the house search hadn't produced anything helpful to the art theft investigation. Then my brain suddenly came online. "Oh! Did they find Petra and Asher?"

"Not exactly. They found her car. In the river. No bodies inside."

"What? What river?"

"The Mississippi."

"Does it look as if they were in the car when it went in?"

"We won't know until they haul it out. They're working on it now and searching the shoreline for any sign the pair came ashore. How's the head?"

"Feels like a marching band's stomping around inside it, but I'll survive. Give me fifteen minutes."

By the time I returned to the kitchen, Tanner had poured us two steaming mugs of coffee. He held one out to me. "Happy Valentine's Day."

"Oh, I love you," I said, snatching it up.

His dimples winked at me.

"Uh, I mean . . ."

"I know. I know. You just said that because I look so much like Cary Grant."

Coffee spurted from my mouth.

"Oh, Serena, Serena, Serena," he said, doing a pretty fair imitation of Grant's famous "Judy, Judy, Judy" line, and handed me a paper towel.

I shook my head. "You do realize Grant died before I was born."

"But I notice you're not denying the resemblance." Tanner grinned. "Anyway, back to business, I thought you might want to question Asher's colleagues before we go to the river."

"Mmm, yes, good idea." I swigged down what was left of my coffee. "Thank you for picking up the slack for me last night."

"No problem. The assault and collision investigations were the PD's domain anyway."

"You've got to understand that Asher has some kind of mental challenge," one of his female co-workers at the big box store where Asher worked informed us a half hour later. "He's the sweetest guy you'd want to know. He'd give you the shirt off his back and protect you with no thought to his own welfare. But he's gullible."

"Have you seen people take advantage of that?"

"A few of his co-workers have. From what he's

said about his new girlfriend, I kind of think she's the type who might."

"Do you know her name?"

"He calls her Pet."

Tanner chuckled.

"It's kind of weird, hey?" the girl went on. "When he isn't around, the guys sometimes joke that he must be dating a real dog. They'd never say it to him though, because they know he'd probably punch their lights out."

"He's hit colleagues before?"

"No, none of us, but there was an incident last summer at the company picnic. A guy threatened one of us girls and Asher went after him like a madman."

I stiffened, mentally replaying my personal experience with the madman routine. But Asher didn't have a record. "The police weren't called?"

"No, we broke the fight up pretty quick. We found out afterward that his sister used to get bullied and got really hurt one time. I guess it made him kind of obsessive about needing to protect any woman he sees in trouble."

A trait that would've played nicely into Petra's hands.

"Did he work Wednesday?" Tanner asked, throwing me a sidelong glance that reminded me of my excitement with the black pickup late Wednesday morning, *not* afternoon.

"No, that's his day off."

Perfect. No alibi. "Thank you for your time," I said, ending the interview.

Next, Tanner and I drove to the river to check on the extraction of Petra's car. "What do you make of Asher now?" he asked.

"He thought I was stalking Petra, so chances are high that Petra told him as much, hoping he'd try to scare me away. But his moral fiber would've had to have been pretty elastic to be persuaded to take out Burke and Cody for her."

"Unless Asher testifies against her, all you've got is circumstantial evidence to connect her to the attacks on Cody and Burke. Burke assumes she ordered them, but he doesn't know if it's true any more than we do."

"Yeah, and I wouldn't blame the jury for not believing it. She seems like a nice person. Even I let my guard down when she was being so cooperative. I suspect the defense would have no trouble bringing in a parade of character witnesses to raise the jury's doubts about the allegations."

At the sight of a familiar car by the river, I grabbed the dash. "Is that my aunt?" I jumped out the second Tanner pulled to a stop. "What are you doing here?"

"Oh, there you are," Aunt Martha said. "I heard on the news that a museum employee's car was found in the river and dashed straight over." She reached up and brushed the hair from my face. "Is that what she did to you?"

I fingered my bangs back over my stitches. "No."

"Oh, come on. Nate asked me how you were recovering when I showed up at the apartment this morning. That tells me you were the federal officer who got assaulted, and I assume that the driver of this car was the perp?"

Perp? Tanner mouthed at me, amusement dancing in his eyes. Admittedly, the TV-version cop talk did sound funny coming from Aunt Martha, but I wasn't in a laughing mood.

"No, Aunt Martha, she wasn't the person who gave me the cut. You need to go home and let me do my job." I'd take care of strangling Nate later.

"They said she wasn't in the car. Have you put a watch on her bank account and credit cards? She's going to need money to get out of town."

I sent Tanner a pleading look.

"Yes, we're on it," he reassured her. "Tracking down addresses of all the friends and relatives who might take her in too."

Oh, whoa, yeah, I should've been doing that last night. That whack on the head really messed me up.

"Of course," Aunt Martha said in a conspiratorial whisper, drawing closer, "if she sold that other painting for a lot of cash, she could be on a plane to anywhere by now. It's not that hard to get fake ID if you know the right people. Carmen says—"

"Yes, Aunt Martha," I interjected, not up to

handling the deep dark secrets she'd gleaned from her mobster boyfriend.

"He would've come with me, but he was afraid people would get the wrong impression if they saw him here. You know? Think it was a mob hit."

"He said that?"

She laughed. "No. The mob would've had her swimming with the fishes a long time ago, if you know what I mean. Go on with you. I'll get out of your hair."

"I like her," Tanner said as Aunt Martha trundled off. "I can see where you get your spunky sense of humor."

Great. Let's hope spinsterhood wasn't also hereditary.

"Scratches on the inside of the car doors and the broken rear window suggest that the vehicle may have been occupied when it hit the water," the officer in charge of the excavation reported to us. "But divers haven't found anyone."

"They couldn't have gotten far if they went in the icy water."

"My officers haven't found any sign along shore that they dragged themselves out."

"I think she's playing us," I said to Tanner. "She wants us to think she died so she can start a new life somewhere else without looking over her shoulder."

Tanner's mouth twisted sideways. "They found

a blonde wig and voice-altering equipment in the car. The wig could incriminate her as the one who tried to sell the Monet to the pawnshop and the sound equipment as the one blackmailing the senator. If she set this up, don't you think she would've destroyed any incriminating evidence?"

"Unless that's what she expected us to think and figured we'd be more likely to assume she's dead if we found the evidence."

"You think she's that conniving?"

"Yeah. No. I don't know, but I know one man who'll likely give us the unvarnished truth."

"Who's that?"

"Her ex-husband."

"Tell her I'm not in," Petra's ex's oh-so-very-*in* voice floated from his receptionist's intercom.

She yanked up the handset and scrambled to silence the speaker mode.

I reached across the desk and did the give-it-to-me finger flutter until she shakily handed over the handset. "Mr. Horvak, this is Special Agent Serena Jones. We seem to be starting off on the wrong foot here."

I'm pretty sure I heard a gulp.

"I'd like to believe you're merely a busy man—being tax season and all—and didn't realize you just asked your receptionist to commit a felony."

The poor woman's face blanched.

Liam Horvak owned his own accounting firm,

and by the looks of the limited edition prints gracing the walls of the reception area and the plush leather armchairs for waiting clients, he was successful. But from his stonewalling, I had to wonder if some of the success might be thanks to creative bookkeeping.

"I won't keep you long, but I do need you to answer a few questions. Now."

A door down the hallway to my right opened and a dark-haired, thirty-something man in an expensive suit stepped out. "This way, Special Agent."

I handed the phone back to his receptionist, then accepted his offered hand. His handshake was firm, although a tad moist. Not surprising since I'd already used the word *felony* and we hadn't even been properly introduced yet.

He motioned me toward a chair and took a seat behind his expansive mahogany desk. "I apologize for the misunderstanding. How may I help you?" he said, closing files and stacking them on the side of his desk.

"I'm trying to locate your ex-wife. When was the last time you heard from her?"

The abrupt intake of breath, sudden twitch in his left eye, and clenched jaw buoyed my hopes. I glanced around the office, half-expecting to find a closet door she might tumble out of.

"I haven't seen her since our divorce was finalized eighteen months ago."

Not exactly what I'd asked. I rested my forearm

on my crossed leg and leaned toward him, lowering my voice. "You do know it's a felony to lie to a federal agent, right?"

Sweat beaded his upper lip. "I haven't heard from her either. Unless letters count. She sometimes sends me letters. But I don't pay any attention to them. She's certifiable. And it's been months since she's sent any."

Okay, rule number one about exes, they tend to exaggerate. But there's usually a grain of truth to what they're saying, and given the innocent act Petra had put on for me versus the tortured look in Burke's eyes when he'd made his statement, I was inclined to believe the ex wasn't far off on the "certifiable" part. "What do you mean by certifiable?"

"The letters are nothing but newspaper clippings with 'See?' written across the top."

"Do you have them?"

"No, I threw them out."

"What were the articles about?"

He raked his fingers through his hair, leaving it thoroughly mussed, not at all like the put-together executive he'd appeared when I first arrived. "There was one about a guy who'd torched his business for the insurance money, and another about a single pastor who ran off with his married secretary."

"And what did she expect you to 'see' in them?"

"I have no idea."

I suspected she might've been taunting him about clients, but I wasn't here to investigate his business practices. "Do you know where I might find her?"

He shook his head. "No idea."

"Can you give me the names and addresses of friends or relatives she might visit?"

His fingers fiddled with the edges of a couple of pages poking out of his stack of files. "Neither of us have any living relatives. I wouldn't know who her friends are now."

"How about here in town?" I wasn't buying that he didn't know where she'd be, not given his lack of curiosity about why I was inquiring. "You moved here together several months before the separation, correct?"

"Yes, but she didn't socialize much."

"How about where you previously lived?"

His fingers stilled and his breathing shallowed.

Ah, I was onto something. Restraining a smile, I flipped back in my notebook to the page I'd recorded the address on. "At 35 Appleton Drive in Winchester. Who were her friends?"

His Adam's apple bobbed. "I was busy getting my career off the ground. I didn't pay much attention to who she spent time with when I wasn't around."

"Mutual friends then?"

"Didn't really have any. When I wasn't working, we wanted the time for ourselves."

"Neighbors?"

He shrugged. "Didn't know them." His fingers started their fiddling again.

Thinking of Petra's alleged threats to the senator, I asked, "Does Petra have strong political views?"

He laughed. "She doesn't know the difference between a Democrat and a Republican." His phone buzzed and he pushed the intercom button. "Yes, Tracey?"

"Your 11:00 appointment is here," his receptionist said.

"I'll be a few more minutes." He released the button and lifted his gaze to mine. "Was there anything else?"

Tilting my head, I held his gaze. "Aren't you curious why a federal agent is asking about your ex-wife?"

He looked away. "The last thing I want to know about is my ex-wife's troubles."

I flipped my notebook closed. "Okay, I won't take up any more of your time. However, if you hear from Petra, hear where she is, or receive another one of those letters from her, please call me immediately." I handed him my business card.

"Will do."

I walked back out to the reception area, where no 11:00 appointment was waiting. The receptionist averted her gaze, clearly realizing I'd seen through the subterfuge.

"When was the last time you saw Petra Horvak?" I asked.

"Me?" The receptionist looked like a scared rabbit.

"Yes, you."

"I've never met her. Mr. and Mrs. Horvak had separated before I was hired."

"When was the last time she called the office?"

"Oh." Her gaze shifted sideways. "I don't recall that she ever has, not since I've been here, anyway."

Okay, that was slightly more believable than the politicians' favorite "I don't recall" line. Hopefully, the Horvaks' former neighbors on Appleton Drive would be more forthcoming.

I put a call in to headquarters as I drove and asked for an analyst to look into the two news articles Horvak had mentioned to see if they were connected to his business or Petra somehow.

The small town was a pleasant twenty-five-minute drive from Horvak's current location and from its size, seemed like a place where neighbors might know more about their neighbors' business than Horvak would like. Appleton Drive was part of a typical suburban development of single-family homes. Large treed lots, at least one car or minivan in the driveways, suggesting a mix of young families and retired folks.

I knocked on number 37's door to the right of the Horvak's former place. No answer. Next, I tried 33's.

A curly-haired senior opened the door. "Yes?"

I introduced myself. "I'm trying to locate Petra Horvak who used to live next door."

"Oh, such a sweet girl. It hasn't been the same around here since she moved away. Come in. Come in." Mrs. Landers poured me a cup of tea and was soon regaling me with stories about the Horvaks. "Oh, my," she said, "I'd never seen Petra so happy as the day she brought home that baby."

I almost fumbled my teacup.

Not seeming to notice my stunned reaction, Mrs. Landers added, "I was so sad to see them move soon after. Nothing would've made me happier than to be little Liam's adopted grandmother. I'd hoped she'd keep in touch, come back to visit now and again." Her eyes glistened with moisture. "But I haven't seen her since."

I set down my teacup and struggled to make sense of this new information. "I didn't realize Petra had a baby."

"They adopted."

Adopted. Was that the connection to the senator and his bill?

"An adorable wee boy he was." Mrs. Landers's eyes shadowed. "Petra's husband didn't seem to take to him, though. They fought a lot after the baby came. And it wasn't more than a month before they moved. Petra was in tears. She didn't want to go. That's why I was so surprised when she didn't come back to visit, but a baby keeps you busy, I know."

I nodded, my mind still scrambling to put the pieces together. Petra had said they'd divorced because her husband didn't want a baby. But had *she* given up the child too? Was he taken away from her? "Do you happen to recall the name of the adoption agency they used?"

"No, sorry."

"No need to apologize." I handed her my business card. "You've been very helpful. If you happen to hear from Petra, please call me, okay?"

"Of course. She isn't in any kind of trouble, is she?"

"I'm afraid she might be, yes, which is why I'm so anxious to speak with her. Is there anyone else in town that she might've contacted? A close friend?"

"I don't know. I never saw her have friends over." Mrs. Landers's eyes widened. "Her husband wasn't abusive, was he? I never thought of it before, but I've heard abused women will cut themselves off from friends to hide what their husbands are doing."

I patted Mrs. Landers's hands. "No, it's nothing like that." She didn't act like an abuse survivor, but I wasn't discounting any possibility for what drove the pair apart eighteen months ago. My stomach dipped at another possibility—they'd moved to cover up the baby's death.

23

"There are no birth, death, or adoption records for a Liam Horvak in the state of Missouri," the analyst at headquarters reported back to me as I once again parked outside Horvak's accounting firm.

His BMW was still in the lot, despite it being Saturday, so nothing was going to keep me out of his office until I got some real answers.

"It might've been a foreign adoption," I said.

"I'm way ahead of you," the analyst responded. "I checked with customs. But the Horvaks haven't left the country in the past five years. Do you want me to check immigration records for a Liam Horvak?"

"Sure, it's worth a shot, thanks." I strode through the front doors of Horvak's firm and waved off the secretary's attempt to stall me. "I'll see myself in." As I reached Horvak's door, I could hear the receptionist's voice in stereo, from down the hall and coming from his intercom, warning him I was back.

This was probably a waste of both of our time, but a niggling voice in the back of my mind said that what happened to their baby two years ago was somehow connected. Not to mention that I was sure Horvak was hiding something. Maybe Petra's whereabouts.

Horvak sprang to his feet as I darkened his doorway. "Special Agent, what brings you back?"

I reclaimed my previous chair. "I had a nice long chat with your former neighbor Mrs. Landers."

"Oh?" His voice cracked.

"Where's Liam?" I said in my best you-better-come-clean-now-or-you'll-be-sorry tone.

"Uh." To his credit, Horvak didn't try to deny the boy's existence. "The adoption didn't work out. We returned him to the agency."

"Which agency would that be?"

His ears reddened and he tugged at one nervously. "I don't recall the name."

Spying a yellow pages directory on his side bar, I flipped it open to Adoption Agencies and slapped it onto his desk. "Which one?" I wasn't sure why it mattered, but my gut told me it did. Big time.

His gaze traveled down the list. "It isn't in here. It must've shut down."

"Was it in another county?"

"Uh." He fidgeted guiltily. "Yeah, maybe. Do I need a lawyer?"

"Why would you ask that? We're just talking."

"Oh." His gaze dropped to his desk.

"Whose idea was it to return the baby to the adoption agency?"

"That was over two years ago. How's it going to help you find Petra?"

"Is there a reason you don't want to answer the question, Mr. Horvak?"

He did the hair raking routine again, this time accompanied by some serious sighing. "Because giving up that baby shattered her. She was inconsolable for weeks afterward. But it had to be done."

"Why?"

He clasped his hands together on his desk, wringing them so tightly they turned white. "Because it was wrong. And she knew it. Of course, she accused me of not wanting a baby as much as she did."

"Wrong how?"

Horvak's hands fisted. "Why are you doing this to me? Look, I didn't know it was a black market adoption agency until after she brought the baby home."

Whoa, Mom's jest about needing to buy grandkids from a mobster suddenly seemed uncomfortably *not* far-fetched.

"As soon as I found out, I insisted we give him back. Yeah, I probably should've reported them to the police, but you know what the mob does to people who snitch on them. You can't blame me. And you didn't read me my rights, so you can't use what I said against me, right?"

Oh boy.

"And I won't testify against them. Did Petra say I would? Is that why you came? She sure wouldn't. She'd adopt again in a heartbeat if she was given half the chance. That's why I insisted on a clause in the alimony agreement that would terminate payments if she pursued another adoption."

Okay, this conversation was veering into a whole other investigation. "I'm not investigating the adoption agency, Mr. Horvak. I need to find Petra. Where is she?"

"I already told you. I don't know."

Now that I understood the misapprehension he'd been under earlier, his shifty responses made perfect sense. Unfortunately, that also meant that I'd just wasted half the day tracking down dead ends.

The receptionist knocked on his door.

"Not now," he shouted at her. "Can't you see we're busy?"

"But"—she held a small envelope in her hand and fluttered it in my direction—"a letter from Petra came in today's mail. I—" She swallowed, looking as if she was seriously doubting her decision. "I thought it might help."

Horvak rounded his desk and snatched it from her hands. "Yes, thank you, Tracey." He returned to his desk chair, muttering once more about Petra being certifiable. "I didn't say it when I mentioned the articles before, but I know why she sends them. They always come with a letter. After the divorce, she became obsessed with proving to me that buying a black market baby was brave, not unethical. She claimed that anyone with a backbone would skirt the law if something was truly important to them."

I thought of my hesitation to manipulate a teller into giving me Linda's banking information. Maybe it hadn't been so cowardly. "Everyone has their price," I mumbled in Petra's own words.

"Yeah, pretty much."

Okay, if Petra had orchestrated the kidney donor scheme and threatened the senator to somehow prove her "thesis," she might be certifiable after all.

Horvak reached inside his desk drawer.

I drew my gun. "Freeze." I don't know what I expected him to pull. Well, yeah, clearly I'd assumed he was going for a gun. Why on earth I thought he'd suddenly turn on me, I don't know. Maybe some remnant effect from the head bonk Cook gave me.

Horvak's hands shot into the air. "I was just getting my letter opener."

"Sorry." I kept my gun trained on him as I eyeballed inside the drawer. "You wouldn't be the first interviewee who pulled a gun on me." Yeah, it was bravado to cover my paranoia, but I don't think he could tell. I returned my weapon to its holster. "Okay, go ahead."

He slit open the envelope and spread the newest clipping on his desk. "It seemed that whenever she found an article about a guy who'd done something she figured *I'd* deem wrong—self-righteous so-and-so that I was . . . her words—she clipped it out and mailed it to me. I'm not sure if she was trying to appease her own conscience for the baby-buying attempt or if she figured this stuff proved *I* was the one with the problem. Maybe a little of both."

The article was about the senator's vote.

A chill ran down my spine. If she orchestrated the senator's about-face on his proposed bill, did she induce the actions reported in the other clippings as well?

"The other articles you received, were they also from a St. Louis paper?" I asked.

"No, from different newspapers around the state."

Papers from towns where she'd been living at the time? According to her file she'd lived in four locations in the past eighteen months. I scanned the letter that accompanied the clipping. She claimed the near death of the senator's daughter just before Christmas had been a scare tactic to induce the senator to vote against his bill. Something only the perpetrator or those closest to the senator would know. "In the other letters you mentioned, did Petra give you the impression that she was somehow connected to the events?"

Horvak frowned. "Now that you mention it, she did seem to know a lot more details about what happened than what the newspapers reported. Although she probably just made the stuff up to prove her point."

"Hmmm. Have you received any letters about a theft from the museum where she works?"

"No, but I'm sure it won't be long before she weaves that into some fantastical underdog-defying-the-government-to-feed-his-family story."

Except it wasn't a story that would make the papers.

As I headed back to the city, Tanner called. "We've got a dead body in a dive motel three quarters of a mile from where we fished Petra's car out of the river."

"Is it Petra?" I changed course to that direction.

"No. A male. No ID. Paid cash for the room. But he fits Cook's description. I'm on my way there now."

"Do you have any other details?"

"Just that the maid found him when she went to clean his room. The coroner is on his way."

"Okay, I'll be there in about twenty minutes," I said and prayed it didn't make the 6:00 news. Reports I'd had to deal with a dead body, on Valentine's Day no less, would send my mother into heart failure.

When I arrived at the motel, the kind of place that people usually paid for by the hour, Tanner was talking to an oily-haired male clerk at the front desk. "Did the deceased check in alone?"

"Yeah, although I'm sure he had company for

part of the night." The guy winked at me. "Our clients usually do."

"Was he wet?" I interjected.

The clerk blinked. "What?"

"Were his clothes wet? When he checked in."

"I don't know. Not that I noticed."

If Cook had just hauled himself out of freezing cold river water and hiked almost a mile to find a place to warm up, surely the clerk would've noticed. Then again, he didn't look like the type that noticed much, certainly not the grime caking his lobby. "Did the deceased drive here?"

"I wasn't paying attention. He didn't have his own car, but he might've come in a cab or hitchhiked."

"Okay, thank you for your time." Tanner steered me back outside and around the corner of the building. Two cruisers, an ambulance, the coroner's car, and the evidence response team's van dominated the side lot, centered around a room halfway down.

The coroner was finishing up his initial assessment by the time we reached the room.

"Cause of death?" I asked after introducing myself and explaining my interest in the victim.

"Looks like a heroin overdose."

Tanner directed my attention to a sopping pile of clothes in the bathtub. "Looks like he went in the river with the car, shed his wet clothes after he checked in, and soothed his grief over losing Petra by shooting up."

I scrutinized the carpet just inside the door. It was dry, as were his boots sitting by the door. I picked one up and examined the tread. "Be sure to check whether this tread matches the print left outside my apartment last Saturday." Next, I edged back the blanket concealing Cook's naked body and checked his arms and between his toes. There were no tracks from habitual drug use that I could tell. "Doctor, did you find any evidence of previous drug use?"

"No."

I turned to Tanner. "If he wasn't a user, he wouldn't have been carrying heroin, so where did he get it? How did he pay for it? There was no wallet in the room"—I turned to the police officer finishing up processing the scene—"was there?"

"No."

I met Tanner's gaze. "So we're supposed to believe he went into the river with the car, somehow survived with money to pay for his room and drugs, even though he's not carrying a wallet, and then in his grief, accidentally OD'd?" I pitched my voice skeptically to ensure Tanner got how unbelievable I thought it sounded. "And he just happened to know where to buy heroin around here? A guy who rarely ventured out of St. Louis's south end."

"Okay, what's your theory?"

"Petra wanted to make his death look like an accidental overdose, only she failed to account for the things that didn't fit, such as where'd he get the drugs? Why are his boots dry if he went in the river?" I picked up the shirt from the tub and sniffed it. "Why do his clothes smell like chlorinated water instead of river water?"

"Maybe he took them off to rinse them so they'd be clean in the morning," a police officer offered.

"Then why leave them in a pile in the tub? Wouldn't he hang them to dry?"

"Good point," Tanner conceded, although I doubt he'd really bought in to the theory he'd been fielding anyway. "So you think Petra masterminded this elaborate plan to sink her car and then off Cook—why?"

"To make it look like she's dead and he's guilty, so we'll stop looking for her."

"You really think she's that calculating?"

"Yes. But I doubt she'd be careless enough to leave her fingerprints in the room. We'll need to canvass the other occupants and residents between the river and the motel. Hopefully someone saw her."

A call came in from Petra's ex. "Yes?"

"You said you wanted me to call if I heard from Petra?"

"Did you?"

"You know I don't have anything to do with whatever trouble she's caught up in, right?"

"Is she there?"

"No! *No.* She phoned. And that's another thing. She's never called me before today. Not since the divorce. Well, other than a couple of times in the first few months. That's the truth."

It was pretty clear he didn't want to go to jail for his wife's crimes. Not two years ago. And not now. "What did she want?"

"She's talking crazy."

"What did she say, Mr. Horvak?"

"She's delusional."

"Mr. Horvak," I growled impatiently.

"Okay, okay, she brought up that art theft you asked about."

"What did she say about it?" I held the phone so Tanner could hear the response too.

"That one of the security guards stole a painting to bribe a down-and-outer into donating a kidney for his wife."

Tanner met my gaze. "If she wanted us to believe she died in the river, why'd she call her ex? She had to know we'd question him. And that her knowledge of Burke's motives would corroborate his claims."

Yeah. With every new piece of information Petra's motives were looking more and more like an untangleable web. I covered my phone with my palm. "When I interviewed her ex, he said she was obsessed with proving everyone has a price. Or, as in her baby buying attempt, anyone would do something wrong for the right payoff."

Tanner's gaze darkened. "Then if the payoff has become silencing anyone who could testify against her, she might take out her ex next."

My heart jumped and I snapped the phone to my ear. "Mr. Horvak, where are you?"

"Did you hear what I said? She's crazy if she thinks this would win me back."

Whoa, back up the train. I clearly missed something. "Can you repeat exactly what she said?"

"She said she was doing it for us. So I'd see she was right. So things could go back to the way they were . . . when she was happy, with the baby."

"Did she say she was coming to see you?"

"No, do you think she will? I told her she was crazy."

Okay, not a smart thing to tell a delusional woman. "Listen, Mr. Horvak, Petra has shared information with you that incriminates her. If she thinks you're not on her side, she might feel compelled to silence you so that you can't testify against her."

"What?" His voice pitched up a thousand decibels.

"If you see her, call the police. If you receive a suspicious package or see anyone acting suspicious around you, your office, your car, your home, call the police."

"Did your wife call you on her cell phone?" Tanner interjected.

We'd tried to trace its location last night but hadn't been able to.

"I don't know. It came up on call display as a private number."

I took down the number on which he'd received the call so I could try to locate where the incoming call originated. "Okay, thank you, Mr. Horvak. We're doing everything we can to track her down. In the meantime, please be careful." I quickly phoned the sheriff's office in Horvak's town and alerted them to the potential situation and gave them my contact information as Tanner attempted to have the number run down.

"Maybe I should go back there and wait and watch," I said to Tanner. "Catch her red-handed. What do you think?"

His phone rang.

Tanner held up a finger to signal me to hold on. A few seconds later, he said, "Come on. We've got to go," and raced out of the room.

"What's going on?" I shouted, sprinting after him.

"Petra's call to her ex came from a pay phone at the hospital."

"What hospital?"

Tanner yanked open the door of his SUV and shot me an urgent look. "Burke's."

24

"What do you mean he was released this morning?" I practically screamed at the nurse outside the room that used to be Burke's and now housed a Big Bad Wolf lookalike who looked as if he might've swallowed Burke *and* Little Red Riding Hood. "Why weren't we told?"

The nurse gave us a helpless look. "You'll probably find him visiting his wife upstairs."

Right. Of course. I raced for the stairs with Tanner on my heels.

He caught me by the arm, yanked me into an elevator, and jabbed 14.

"Wait, no." I blindly jabbed the button with the double arrows pointing toward each other. *No!* "I didn't mean that button!" I jabbed the one with the arrows pointing away from each other, but I was too late. The elevator jerked into motion.

I stiffened, stared at the numbers above the door. Eleven floors to go. What could that take? Ten, fifteen seconds, tops. I gulped. Could feel the sweat beading on my forehead.

"Breathe," Tanner whispered in my ear.

What was he talking about? I was pretty sure I

was hyperventilating. If the doors didn't open soon, I might actually pass out. I would've flashed him an annoyed scowl for yanking me into the moving metal trap, but it was taking all my energy to hold myself together. Yeah, I know it's a crazy phobia. The elevator safely deposited people on their desired floors a gazillion times a day. But . . . but . . .

The doors opened and I sprang out. "Do you remember her room number?"

"Room 16."

I scanned the door numbers like a madwoman and skidded to a stop in her doorway. The bed was empty. So was the bathroom. I commandeered the first nurse I caught sight of. "Mrs. Burke in 16, where is she?"

"Treatment room 3."

I raced back down the hall and a sergeant-major wannabe halted my headlong sprint two strides from the door. A split second after my annoyance passed, I conceded that the nurse had done me a favor. I was *not* acting like a professional. If Petra was already on the floor, what did I think I'd accomplish by barreling into the room? That elevator ride had seriously messed with my brain, which was still reeling from the number Cook did on it yesterday.

I needed to be paying closer attention to the orderlies, the visitors, whoever Petra might be pretending to be to get close to Burke.

Tanner showed the nurse his badge. "We need o speak to Mr. and Mrs. Burke."

"Ella is in the bed on the end, but her husband left a few moments ago with his daughter."

Daughter? I mentally hopscotched over the family photos adorning the walls of the Burke's home. They had sons. "Do you mean daughter-in-law?" I asked as Tanner slipped into Mrs. Burke's room.

"Oh, maybe."

I whipped out my phone and scrolled to Petra's photo. "Is this her?"

The nurse squinted at the picture. "Could be. I didn't pay close attention."

Tanner emerged from the room. "Mrs. Burke says her daughters-in-law don't live nearby. Carmen Malgucci stopped by to visit after his tests, so her husband headed to the cafeteria for a late lunch."

"Oh," the nurse said, "I guess I'm mixing up the patients' spouses. Sorry about that."

Tanner headed for the elevator.

"I'm taking the stairs," I called after him.

"The cafeteria is twelve floors down."

I spun on my heel and called over my shoulder, "Still taking the stairs." More times than not, I could beat the elevator, since it inevitably got stopped on other floors, and this way we'd cover all our bases. At least that's what I told myself as I raced down the hall.

By the time I reached the cafeteria, Tanner had

already whisked around it in search of Burke. "He's not here."

We walked up the steps to check the coffee shop. Nothing. "What next?" I bobbed my chin toward the bridge that led to the parking garage. "Go across here and check out the parking garage? Or go out at street level?"

A teen girl walking across the bridge paused at the window and, pointing to the street below, screamed back to a security guard in the garage. "There's a woman out there with a gun."

Pandemonium broke loose.

Drawing our weapons, Tanner and I raced down the escalators and out the street level exit.

My racing heart jumped to my throat as I skidded to a stop. "Aunt Martha?"

"She's trying to kidnap Henry," she said, both hands clamped on a tiny silver pistol, her purse hanging from the crook of one of her arms.

"Get her to cover," Tanner ordered, maneuvering closer to Petra, who had a gun pressed into Burke's ribs.

As I moved to disarm my aunt before the approaching security guards took her out, Tanner ordered Petra to drop her weapon.

Taking a backward step, Petra used Burke as a shield.

Jabbing Aunt Martha's gun into the back of my waistband, I flashed my badge to the stampeding security officers. "FBI. We got this."

They came to a halt, their gazes bobbing from Tanner and Petra to Aunt Martha and me.

"Drop the weapon," Tanner repeated uselessly as I edged toward Petra's flank.

Burke clutched his chest, not looking good.

"Shoot her," Aunt Martha shouted. "She looks like she'd make a good kidney donor."

"Get her inside," I hissed at a security guard taking cover behind a nearby car.

"How can you live with yourself?" Aunt Martha continued ranting at Petra as the guard bodily escorted her toward the hospital entrance.

But to Aunt Martha's credit, she'd distracted Petra long enough for me to get in position so that she couldn't shield herself from me and remain unexposed to Tanner.

Cruisers swerved into the parking lot.

"Drop the gun, Petra. You're out of options."

Petra didn't try to guard her flank from me. Instead she turned a spine-chilling grin in my direction. "You couldn't leave it alone, could you? This is your fault. If you hadn't gone digging around in East St. Louis, I wouldn't have had to worry about Burke losing his nerve."

"It's over, Petra. We've already got his testimony. Drop the gun."

"Or what? You'll shoot me? Because you always get your man?" she taunted.

Burke's hand splayed over his chest. He didn't look like he'd hold out much longer.

"But you don't always get him, do you? You haven't figured out who killed your grandfather yet."

How did she know about my grandfather? I tightened my grip on my gun, fighting to not let her rattle me.

She cackled. "No, I didn't think so. See, that's why you won't shoot me, because *I* know who killed him."

My breath stalled in my throat as my peripheral vision caught sight of a sniper taking up a position behind her and dozens of other officers crouched behind their cruisers, their guns aimed at her too.

Suddenly Burke buckled over.

Gunfire exploded from every direction.

"No!"

25

I fought to wrestle free of Tanner's hold on my arms as hospital staff whisked Burke and Petra inside on gurneys. "I need to talk to her."

Tanner's grip tightened. "She's not talking to anyone right now."

"She can't die. She knows who killed my grandfather."

"Or she knew which buttons to push, like she did with Burke and with the senator."

I stilled. "But how?"

Tanner's expression softened. "She could've researched your family history. Eavesdropped. Made good deductions."

I recalled Billy's similar deduction as we'd chatted about my job while he changed my tire. But he'd known me all my life.

"You need to let it go." Tanner's hold on my arms loosened. "We've got a crime scene to help process."

I nodded, and he turned to the officer waiting to question us. I spotted Aunt Martha answering another officer's questions, Carmen at her side. Gritting my teeth, I resisted the urge to stomp over and read him the riot act for giving her a gun. Except Mom was going to kill me if they arrested Aunt Martha for a weapons violation.

Blast. I headed toward them. My legs felt as if they were encased in cement, growing heavier by the second when Aunt Martha plunged into a visual demonstration of how she'd tried to stop Petra.

A few steps closer, I realized the officer questioning her was my childhood friend Matt Speers.

He turned to me, smiling, as I joined them. "Sounds like your aunt saved the day."

"Uh, yeah. Petra might've gotten away if Aunt Martha hadn't confronted her." My fears for her lightened. It was the truth, after all.

"Carmen and I went up to see the Burkes. Did I tell you the tests confirmed he's a match?"

"No! That's great news."

Carmen ducked his head as Aunt Martha beamed.

Matt cleared his throat.

"Oh," Aunt Martha continued. "On our way to the room, I saw another friend I knew and stopped to talk to her, while Carmen went on. That's when I saw that woman walking unusually close to Burke. I thought she might be his daughter, so I tried to catch up to them to introduce myself and saw she had a gun pressed into his side." Aunt Martha shifted her gaze from Matt to me. "If I'd known you were here, I would've called you. Anyway, I managed to jump into the same elevator as them, so I pretended I didn't know anything was going on and hoped a security guard would be close by when we stepped out."

Carmen shook his head. "Security's never around when you need them."

"I didn't want to risk losing them by going off looking for one," Aunt Martha went on. "So I made a show of holding the gun on them"—she demonstrated once more—"figuring that would get the 911 calls going."

"You're lucky Tanner and I were the first on the scene or the police might've prioritized taking you out."

Aunt Martha's gaze dropped to the blood staining the parking lot where Petra went down. *"Oh."*

Carmen tucked her arm through the crook of his. "But everything worked out. That's the important thing."

Not everything. Petra might not survive.

"Was she the art thief?" Aunt Martha asked.

"I can't discuss the case."

Aunt Martha visibly deflated. "It was just I heard Burke tell hospital staff that her name was Petra Horvak."

"That's right," I confirmed, since that much would soon be on the news anyway.

"It's not that common a name and yet it seems so familiar."

Because of someone connected to Granddad? My heart did a crazy jog. "Familiar how?" I blurted, unable to keep the hope from my voice.

Aunt Martha couldn't have heard Petra's claim. She'd already been escorted inside the hospital by then.

Aunt Martha squinted as if it would help her wrack her brain more easily. "It's no good, I can't place it."

"If she works at the art museum, you probably saw the name on her name tag," Carmen said.

"Hmm, you're probably right."

But what if that wasn't the reason? What if—?

Tanner tapped my shoulder. "We need you over here." Only instead of leading me to the officers he'd been talking to, he ushered me to a quiet corner behind the mobile command post.

"What's going on?" I asked.

The compassion in his eyes knifed through my heart. "Petra didn't make it."

My knees buckled, but Tanner held me steady.

"I'm sorry. I know you were hoping she had information about your grandfather, but I think it was a ploy."

"No, Aunt Martha recognized her name."

"But Petra was your age, which means she would've only been ten or eleven when your grandfather was murdered."

My shoulders sagged, defeat washing over me.

"And her name wouldn't have been Horvak back then," Tanner added softly.

My gaze snapped to his. "That's it."

"What's it?"

"The name. If the name's familiar to Aunt Martha, it could be because someone in Petra's husband's family was connected to my grandfather."

Tanner hesitantly nodded. "It's something you can look into," he said, not sounding all that assured the inquiry would go anywhere.

But my hope resurged. It was a start. "Burke might know something too. When he started getting antsy about my investigation, Petra might've confided that she had information I wanted, in hopes of bolstering his confidence."

Tanner still didn't look convinced. "For now, you need to concentrate on wrapping up this case."

"Right."

Zoe rushed toward me, clasping Jax's hand, just as we were finishing up in the hospital's parking lot.

"It's okay, let them through," I called to the officer manning the crime scene perimeter.

"Is it true?" Zoe asked breathlessly. "Did Petra try to kidnap Burke? Is he okay?"

"He had an angina attack, but it sounds as if he'll be fine. You didn't have to interrupt your skating date to come down here. You could've just called."

"We were heading out for dinner when we heard the report on the radio. So what does this mean? Is Petra the thief?"

"Let's talk over here." I steered her away from the milling officers, and she reluctantly released Jax's hand. "How's the date going, by the way?"

She blushed. "Pretty wonderful."

"I'm glad to hear it." I gave her a brief summary of the suspicions I was at liberty to share, which didn't include why Petra kidnapped Burke, but Zoe was so relieved to know that I solved the case, the omission didn't seem to register. It was kind of unsettling to realize that even I'd had a price—hesitating to shoot her because of her granddad comment.

"I guess she didn't tell you where the Monet is now?"

"I doubt she knew." My voice hitched at the finality of how that sounded. "The painting has changed hands at least twice since she sold it. But my counterpart in France will continue to try to track it down. We might find it yet."

"I can't thank you enough."

"Just doing my job. Now go back to enjoying your date!"

She grinned. "Thanks for that too."

Tanner joined me as Zoe and Jax walked away hand in hand. "Another matchmaking accomplishment?"

I shrugged.

"You did good. Made a lot of people happy today. I suspect your mom might even bake you another cake."

I slugged his arm, knowing he was probably right. "She'll be expecting me for Sunday dinner. You want to come? After all, it was a team effort."

"Sorry, I got me a pair of Blues tickets for tomorrow night." He winked.

Ah, yes, the bribe that had gotten him to the last family dinner.

I sloughed off the rejection with a carefree wave of my hand. "Your loss."

Standing on my parents' front porch Sunday evening, I inhaled a deep breath. I should be happy. The case was solved, I'd alerted the feds to a black market baby scheme operating in the state, one of the two paintings had been recovered, and Mr. Burke would escape jail time. But even after grilling Petra's ex-husband about family connections to the art world or my grandfather and coming up empty-handed, I couldn't escape the stomach-churning feeling I'd let the one chance to identify my grandfather's killer slip through my fingers.

The door burst open. "What are you doing just standing there?" Mom exclaimed, dragging me inside. "Dinner's almost ready."

The aroma of something baking—spice cake, if I wasn't mistaken—tugged a smile from my lips. No matter how much Mom would rather see me in a safer job, I could always count on her to celebrate my successes.

Dad padded in from the living room and pressed a kiss to my cheek. "Aunt Martha told us you solved another case. We're so proud of you."

"Thank you." I swallowed the lump edging into my throat at the thought of the lives lost in the process. "We haven't recovered the second painting."

He patted my shoulder. "The difference between what you get and what you could've gotten is greed," he expounded in his usual investment-based words of wisdom. "I was just telling Nate that investors always regret selling too soon, or not soon enough, and if they don't learn to let go of the regrets, they'll fret themselves into an early grave."

Yeah, I knew all about regrets. I'd been second-guessing my reaction to Petra ever since the shootout. I unzipped my coat. *Wait. What?* "Nate's here?"

Dad helped me untangle my arms from my coat sleeves. "Your aunt invited him for the celebration. After all, he did save her from one of the bad guys outside your apartment last week, right?"

Nate appeared at the corner, sporting an amused grin. "It was more like I kept her from running after the guy and getting into worse trouble."

Aunt Martha swatted his arm. "Watch it or I'll uninvite you." As Dad wandered back to the living room and Mom bustled off to the kitchen,

Aunt Martha hooked her arm through mine and drew me deeper into the entranceway. "Did you bring me back my gun?"

"*Your* gun? Carmen didn't give it to you?"

"No, it's mine."

"Do you have a permit to carry concealed? Never mind. I don't want to know." Oh, man, Mom would have a bird if she knew. "But you know it's illegal to carry a gun into a hospital, right? You're lucky Officer Speers didn't charge you."

"I didn't draw it until I was outside," she said calmly, as if that mattered, which it didn't.

"And she has a permit to carry concealed," Nate interjected, as if that made a difference too. "She got it while you were at Quantico."

Seriously? Why was I the only one left in the dark here?

Aunt Martha beamed up at him. "He drove me to the firearms safety class they made me take."

"Oh, and how are *your* secret agent classes going?" I asked Nate. What had he been thinking, encouraging Aunt Martha to start carrying a gun at her age? "Aunt Martha, you know that pulling out a gun only makes the other guy more likely to shoot. You're not invincible, you know."

"Oh, you'd be surprised," she said cheerily, tossing Nate a wink.

Mom whirled out of the kitchen carrying a

platter of meat and set it on the dining room table. "Supper's ready."

"I can't believe you encouraged her," I whispered to Nate as we walked to the dining room.

"Oh, Nate's always encouraging people," Mom said. "He's the one that got that retired professor started on sharing a word of the day. What was his name?"

"Mr. Sutton."

"Yes, Mr. Sutton. Cheered him right up after he got so depressed after retiring. Isn't that what you said, Aunt Martha?"

"Yes, cheered him right up."

"A regular Little Miss Sunshine, aren't you?" I said to Nate.

Nate laughed.

We joined hands around the table to say grace. Nate's grip was warm and firm, and after Dad's "amen," Nate gave my hand a quick squeeze before releasing it. "You don't have to worry about your aunt. She knows how to handle herself. Just look at what she pulled off yesterday."

"So it's true?" Mom spooned a two-man pile of potatoes on her plate in her excitement. "Aunt Martha really did thwart a kidnapping?"

"Absolutely," I said. Never mind that she'd scared me half to death. "Of all the people they passed leaving the hospital, Aunt Martha was the only one who noticed the gun. Without her keen eye and quick action, the kidnapper might've gotten away."

And I wouldn't be potentially one clue closer to finding Granddad's murderer.

"Oh, pfft." Aunt Martha waved off the praise. "You young people have better things to think about than an old lady's shenanigans."

"I don't see any old ladies here," Nate said, making a show of looking around.

"Don't encourage her," I whispered.

He grinned, unrepentant.

"Oh, that reminds me, speaking of old," Aunt Martha went on. "Since you both like old movies, I brought you something to watch tonight after you get home."

Aunt Martha said "home" like we lived together. Not just in the same apartment building. Separately.

"Cool," Nate said, clearly unfazed by Martha's not-so-subtle matchmaking efforts. "Which one?"

Aunt Martha smiled serenely. *How to Marry a Millionaire.*

Nate choked on his water.

Frowning at Aunt Martha, I reached out and patted Nate's back. I'm sure she hadn't meant for it to sound so insensitive, even though she had to know Nate wouldn't make a ton of money as an apartment superintendent. Who cared? He was a nice guy. That's what really mattered.

Not that I was looking. In the relationship sense.

Nate recovered and smiled at Aunt Martha. "Great choice. That was . . . thoughtful of you. And don't think we aren't onto you, trying to deflect from your accomplishment." He raised his water glass in salute. "I propose a toast. Degas once said, 'Art is not what you see, but what you make others see.' Here's to Martha for spotting the evil artist."

"Here, here," Mom and Dad joined in, raising their glasses.

My hand halted with my glass at half-mast. Petra had been good at making people see what she wanted. Which meant Tanner had probably been right about her saying all that about Granddad just to push my buttons.

I muffled a sigh, trying not to lose hope that Burke might know something or that a connection between Petra and my grandfather might still turn up. But whether one did or not, I wouldn't have been any closer to finding Granddad's murderer if I'd quit after last week's undercover scare. If nothing else, I'd proved to myself that I could rise to what needed to be done. And that I could count on the support of my family and friends. Mom even seemed to have scaled back her one-woman campaign to convince me to quit.

And Petra's seeming motive for her crimes had given me something else to consider. If everyone had a price, then, given strong enough motivation, even the most unlikely suspect in Granddad's murder might've been capable of pulling the trigger. I'd always assumed the thief's motive was that he didn't want to be caught, but what if the theft was a cover-up for the murder instead of the other way around?

My ringing phone jolted me from my thoughts. I glanced at the screen—Matt Speers. "Sorry. I need to take this."

"We just got a call about an art theft in Westmoreland. The victim's claiming the stolen piece is worth over six figures."

That was the magic number for the feds to get involved in a residential art burglary. I took down the address. "Okay, I'll be right there." Hanging up, I turned to my family. "Sorry, gotta go. Duty calls."

Mom's lips tightened as she rose abruptly and went into the kitchen.

Dad beamed proudly. "Go get 'em, Sweetheart."

Nate walked me to the door. "Be careful out there, huh?" He smiled, and ridiculously, my heart skipped a beat.

Mom bustled toward us holding a care package. "Your cake." She kissed my cheek. "I am proud of you. Grab one of our umbrellas. The weatherman said it's supposed to rain tonight."

"Thanks, Mom, I'll be fine."

Twelve minutes later, I parked behind Matt's

cruiser, a fine rain misting the windshield. I pushed open my car door and the sky let loose a torrent of gumball-sized raindrops. Hiking the back of my coat up over my head, I raced through the downpour to the victim's front porch.

I should've listened to my mother.

Sandra Orchard is the award-winning author of many inspirational romantic suspense and mysteries, including *Deadly Devotion*, *Blind Trust*, and *Desperate Measures*. Her writing has garnered several Canadian Christian Writing Awards, a *Romantic Times* Reviewers' Choice Award, a National Readers' Choice Award, a HOLT Medallion Award of Merit, and a Daphne du Maurier Award for Excellence in Mystery/ Suspense.

In addition to her busy writing schedule, Sandra enjoys speaking at events and teaching writing workshops. She especially enjoys brainstorming suspense plots with fellow writers, which has garnered more than a few odd looks when standing in the grocery checkout debating what poison to use.

Sandra lives with her husband of more than twenty-five years in Ontario, Canada, where their favorite pastime is exploring the world with their young grandchildren. Learn more about Sandra's books and check out special bonus features, such as deleted scenes and location pictures, at www.sandraorchard.com. While there, subscribe to her newsletter to receive subscriber-exclusive short stories. You can also connect with Sandra at www.facebook.com/sandraorchard.

Center Point Large Print
600 Brooks Road / PO Box 1
Thorndike, ME 04986-0001 USA

(207) 568-3717

US & Canada:
1 800 929-9108
www.centerpointlargeprint.com